RANDOM ACTS OF LUST

RANDOM ACTS OF LUST

Primula Bond

Published by Accent Press Ltd – 2010

ISBN 9781907016356

Printed and bound in the UK

Cover design by
Red Dot Design

Shadows

THE PHONE RANG AND I dropped the casserole.

All over the floor. All over John's cracked terracotta. Brown cubes of lamb, button mushrooms, half-baked dumplings, green spits of coriander, twigs of rosemary, diced orange carrots, the rest of the Rioja. The *bouquet garni* made it as far as my new boots, spattering mottled gobs over the dagger-sharp toes.

'That was Suki. They're on their way. About twenty minutes now.' John came into the kitchen and tried twice to shove the phone back into its stained plastic wall mount.

'It doesn't go there. That's the hall phone.' The oven door gaped beside me, belching out heat. Inside, drenched in olive oil, my root vegetables were crisping black. I leaned against the huge old fridge and frowned at the way he was fumbling. 'Not nervous, are you?'

The door hummed against my spine. I wished I could just stay there all day, stuck like a novelty magnet. I stared at the star-shaped splatter all over the floor. All over the cracked terracotta. The heavy central mess. Stripes of sauce elongating like limbs making a bid for freedom. How stupid was that, trying to cook *boeuf bourguignon* for an awarding-winning chef?

The dish itself was intact apart from a heart shaped crack in its side. The lid was in smithereens.

1

'What do you mean?' He looked vaguely round at me. 'About this visit?'

'About seeing him. It's been six years –'

'Darling, he's been busy on the other side of the world, that's all. We're not estranged. Not any more. He's got used to the idea of my marrying again. So it's time he met you. Time he met my bride.' John rubbed the palms of his hands together and swivelled the top half of his body in a stiff, military movement. 'So what happened here?'

I held the oven gloves out, still linking my wrists like handcuffs. 'There's a hole in these. I was checking the casserole and the phone rang and the fingers burnt right through.'

'I'm sorry. Should have got new stuff sorted out. We never used to bother. This was only ever meant to be our holiday home.' John took a couple of j-cloths off the sink and flapped them at me. 'Don't worry. It wasn't our best china. And don't be pissed off just because of a flawed oven glove?'

The cloths dangled uselessly between us. His dead wife's j-cloths. I crossed my arms. My breasts enveloped them, warm and heavy. My pale green sweater felt tight. It was probably way too tight for this grand introduction, but sod that. I liked the way my breasts jutted out in that Hollywood starlet way, expensively upholstered and impossible to ignore. They might be lifted by satin-covered whalebone and kissed by cashmere, but my breasts were still my best friends. They'd earned me a fortune over the years, even when my face didn't fit. And I was only a handful of years older than my scary stepchildren, for God's sake. Why should I shroud myself in some shapeless blouse and mash myself into another woman's peeling wallpaper?

'I'll have to go to the village and get something else to

eat. They must do some sort of ready meal. Takeaway. Anything.'

'I doubt there's anywhere open on a Sunday in these 'ere parts.' John's mouth twitched at his evil attempt at a Devon accent. 'Bread and cheese will do. Soup. I don't know why you went to so much trouble in the first place, Flo. They're not royalty. And Suki knows you hate cooking.'

'I can't have your son coming all the way from Sydney for a lump of Stilton. What would Gordon Ramsay's mini-me make of that?'

'They're not coming for the food, for God's sake.'

John wrapped his arm round me. It's why I married him, despite all the clicking tongues. Because when he wasn't covered in paint and dust he wore mossy tweed jackets like a proper gentleman and the moment those arms were round me I calmed down. On our wedding day three months before I shook like a leaf. He wrapped his arm round me on the steps of the registry office while the smattering of guests took pictures. *Relax, darling. They're not the paparazzi,* he whispered, *more's the pity.* He made me laugh. So I never told him why I was shaking.

'Those are cool boots,' he said now, and we both bent to look. 'Not what I'd call suitable for trudging along a rough old beach, but cool nevertheless.' Normally it would have been exactly the right thing to say. He knelt down with the j-cloth and wiped the droplets off the ox-blood red leather. Then he kissed my foot. 'A sex kitten like you needs a good seeing to, preferably twice a day, so what's the matter with me?' He ran his hand up my leg, tweaked the top of my stockings. 'Christ! Getting a hard-on these days is like getting blood out of a stone!'

My chest tightened. My new husband's fine head of hair was thinning on top.

'Get up, Johnny, please.' I tugged at his shoulders. 'I hate you grovelling about on the floor. It doesn't suit you. And nor does the stud talk.'

He was unable to hide the wince as his knees straightened. The hand holding the dirty cloth smoothed feebly at his hair as if he knew what I'd been thinking. But how could he know that the sight of him looking suddenly old was making me panic?

'Just making you even more gorgeous for our guests.' He tipped my chin up. 'My beautiful wife. You're like a pure-bred Arab mare, you know that? Always jittery.'

I let him admire me for a moment longer. His long fingers traced the faint scarred hollow of my cheekbone, pressed my lips into a sexy pout. Some red lipstick smeared onto his fingers. A year ago he traced my cheekbones for the first time, when my agent commissioned him to sculpt a bust of me. That's how we met. John carved me out of stone, like Pygmalion.

And though he was only supposed to be sculpting my head and shoulders that day he went on moulding the rest of my body and I couldn't stop him. I was cold all over, we both were. It was mid winter, like now, and he was a widower. I was the scarred survivor of a stupid accident, and when he touched me I started shivering. His fingers were so warm, and strong. He was used to wrestling shapes out of blocks of wood or stone and he was just as rough with me. And it was exactly what I wanted. He pummelled my arms and legs and neck and spine, twisted me about, his hair white and wild, so different from any other lover, like a sexy muscular wizard.

And after he had recreated my head and shoulders, my bust, and stuck it on a plinth ready for casting and paced round it a few times, he came back to me and ran his hands all over me, feeling me, cupped my breasts, then

4

my buttocks, slid his fingers into the warm crack there, trailing them through the dark cleft splitting under me and up to where it opened up, pink like blossom. My knees shook as he stood behind me, measuring every secret inch. Gradually my thighs opened wider for those rough, roaming fingers until he reached my pussy and peeled me open like a fruit.

Then he calmly took the robe loosely covering me and ripped it right away, leaving me naked, white and trembling, freezing on that pedestal thing, my skin pricking up in tight goose bumps. My breasts, usually photographed tickled by exotic lingerie, juddered with each heartbeat and rose upwards as if fighting the cold air. My nipples stood stiff and red like sore berries in the harsh winter light flooding his glass studio.

That day, barely a year ago, he was still strong enough to lift me and throw me down on some lumpy old sacking in the corner where he reared over me, pinching my nipples until they burned with the desire rocketing through me. He opened my arms and legs like a sacrifice, then pulled his cock out of a gap in his overalls. I bit my lip, squealing with shock and tasting blood, as he knelt on my legs and held my arms above my head to keep me still. All the time his blue eyes were on me. His big fingers closed round his cock and he pummelled himself rapidly, just there above my splayed, bare pussy, and I squirmed with frustration, trying to lift my pussy, thinking he was going to come all over me, but then I could see his cock was huge and hard and ready and he let go of it, let it spring free from his fist but it was so hard it barely moved. He took his weight on his hands and with one fierce jab of his hips he stuck it into me, pushed it right up and in, and fucked me because our lives depended on it.

5

His eyes fluttered closed now for a kiss. A shadow of that first, fast, furious fucking. This was what made me shake on our wedding day. I was afraid that soon it would all be shadows.

I darted forwards to peck him first, on the mouth. It felt hard, and bristly. Odd. Normally he was scrupulous about shaving. I reached round him for the car keys. His shoulder felt bony as I brushed against it. 'Nevertheless, this won't do. I'm going out to find something proper to eat.'

'You're the one who's nervous. You've already met Suki, so that's ticked off.' John dabbed the end of my nose with the cloth. 'And Stuart will love you, because I do.'

I opened the back door and the world rushed in. It was like switching on a soundtrack. Sea gulls, the slow drag of pebbles followed by the muffled crash of waves. You had to scramble down a little path to get to the beach. But you could still hear it.

'I wish we could just have Christmas here on our own. Me and you.'

A breeze batted past my ears, flipping the pages of my recipe book. I tied a scarf round my head like a fishwife.

'Don't rush off, Flo. You're acting like a teenager, not a siren of the glossies –'

'*Ex* siren of the glossies –' I fingered my scar.

'*My* siren.' He held up his hand. Yes, it was still shaking, but now he looked like a stern headmaster, just the way I liked it. 'I want you here with me, Mrs Floyd, gliding about with champagne.'

Dead grass scraped against the half-open gate behind me. I backed out of the kitchen door, sensing freedom and wondering why I wanted, so badly, to escape.

'Well, don't be long, will you?' John was bending

down again, laboriously mopping at the congealing lunch. He looked up. There was a very slight film across one of those cobalt blue eyes. 'I need you.'

The village store was open, and stocked with tons of food. Into the boot went wine, more milk and cheese, cream, chocolate, the last remaining organic chicken. Surely even I could manage that? Smear it with lemon juice and thyme like they do on the TV, use the roasting time to sink the last of the Dom Perignon John had saved from his farewell exhibition?

The French patisserie next door was open, too. It was so warm in there. I couldn't decide, just stood and breathed the aroma of fresh bread, buttery croissants, custard doughnuts, apple pies, bulging, shiny pasties.

'Made your choice?'

'I'd like to stay in here all day.' I smiled at the bun-faced lady behind the counter. 'Bit of a gathering back at home.'

'John OK? He's not been down here, since – for years,' she said as she took my money. Or rather, John's money. She tapped the side of her head. 'And I heard he'd gone downhill?'

I let the coins rest on the palm of my hand, quelling the anger. 'I'm the new Mrs Floyd, actually. And he's fine. Stopped working, because of the arthritis, but he's fine.'

'Well, he must be fighting fit, a glamorous young wife like you to keep happy. I'm afraid we're closing now, dear. Nearly Christmas. All got homes to go to.'

The bags of unnecessary food rattled and bumped about in the boot where John's easels and chisels and drums of plaster used to go. I drove as slowly as I could out of the car park. I couldn't put it off for ever. They'd be there any minute now. My new stepson, the conquering hero, crowding into that cluttered kitchen. His small, restless sister scrutinising her mother's empty cupboards, shrouded as always in expensive black. I'd never seen Suki wear anything colourful or clinging, had no idea if she possessed womanly breasts or the narrow hips of a boy. She would turn about slowly, silently arch her thick eyebrows.

Get a grip. I was the mistress of the house. Yeah. Mistress was the word. My shag-me boots and the short, flirty skirt made me feel like some tart their old dad had picked up in a bar.

A broad shaft of sunshine suddenly swept a path of gold across the grey beach. I jumped out of the car to follow it, all the way to the silvery water's edge, running awkwardly in my high heels over the uneven sand. *Not suitable for trudging along a rough old beach.*

'Lick my boots!' I yelled at the waves. 'I dare you!'

My voice was catching in the wind. All I could see then was my husband, crouched at my feet on the kitchen floor, amongst the stew I'd just trashed, trying to clean my boots. I tried to see the sexy side of it, but my stomach clenched with nausea. My champion. Everyone said he'd rescued me, breathed life back into me, immortalised me too. And he had. But while my youth was set in stone for the moment, he was withering before my eyes.

The water was reaching to grab at me again, straining but not quite reaching me. Every so often a wave rolled over, offered me a reluctant flash of sky blue.

Up on the cliff John must be been puffing life into the logs, because smoke was threading out of the chimney.

I could smell the wine and the log fire and a dazzling, nostril-pricking cologne as soon as I stepped in from the cold. I entered through the back door, bustling with provisions, the lady bountiful, but no one saw me.

'Not stone. She was like alabaster. Her skin glows, you know.'

'Like a weeping angel?'

'Och, no, Stuart.' Since when had John acquired a Scottish accent? My Flo's no angel!'

They had their backs to me, but that was OK. It meant I could hover in front of the hall mirror, tug my hair across my uneven cheek, smooth on a little more lipstick.

They were arranged in front of the bay window. There was John on the right, Suki on the left, in something black, kneeling on the wide sill. A stranger in the middle. It was like the captain's window, curved round the bow of the ship to survey the ocean.

'And that's just the way I like her.' John's chuckle was deep in his chest. But as he lifted his glass I noticed him press the flat of his other hand against the panelled wall.

'I'm sure you do, Dad. Because in fairy stories,' the third person, speaking in John's deep voice, half turned so that the harsh light etched out his profile, a long sharp nose, the full curve of a lower lip, 'the wicked stepmother is always the sexiest.'

His eyes caught mine on the word 'sexiest' and pinned me back. I'd taken a step towards my husband but the man in the middle stopped me. He caught me hovering on the edge of the room like a moth and pinned me right there so I couldn't move. Shadows flitted between the two men, the younger face stitched briefly onto my husband's to show me how he used to look.

No sick thumping of the heart now. It stopped beating completely.

I could even hear the waves on the beach below. My senses were pricked up like antennae. I could hear John swallowing, the creak of the windowsill as Suki stood up. The hiccup of the fridge in the kitchen. All I could see in the flickering fire light was the stranger's cobalt blue eyes and the way his hands fell down to his sides as if he'd been shot.

'Here she is. The hunter and gatherer returns.' John cleared his throat. 'Darling. Come and have a drink.'

'Hello, Flo. Meet my brother Stuart.'

I nodded in Suki's direction, but I still couldn't drag my eyes away. The air around him and me crystallised, locking us inside.

'Florence. How do you do?'

When I didn't move he walked over the old carpet and took my hand. I started to jerk it up and down like a robot, tilting my scarred cheek automatically away.

'Stuart. You're here at last.'

My voice rushed in my ears like the last thing you hear before you faint. He was lifting my hand towards his mouth. He had dark curly hair and was unshaven like a rock star and like all rock stars he seemed terribly young. So young. His curved lips parted slightly and I wanted him to lick my fingers. I wanted to stuff my fingers between his teeth so that he had to eat them.

But he kissed the back of my hand. His lips were warm and damp and, Christ, was that the tip of his tongue brushing across the skin? My pussy twitched, sucking the flimsy silk of my knickers up between my lips and releasing the sharp scent of my own arousal. He closed his eyes briefly, his nose still pressed against my knuckles, and that's when I knew it for sure. The stark difference between despair and desire.

'You old charmer! Where did you learn to do that?'

Suki pushed him jokily aside. Her arm hooked round my neck. I gave a silly, fluttering laugh and scrunched my shoulders like a child aping pleasure. Suki's jaw bumped against my ear, moving my hair.

'You must be starving, driving all that way?'

I was talking to Stuart but Suki dragged him away to the old sofa and sat against him, her hand on his thigh. I rested my elbow on the mantelpiece, acutely aware of the way my breasts seemed to swell up and out with the movement. My back was to the mirror, the heat of the flames licking my legs, pricking my nipples into life, sending sweat trickling down my spine. And then at last I looked at John.

His face was a mask, like one of his own sculptures. Only for a second. His eyes had dropped backwards into his skull as if they were looking along a tunnel. His eyes weren't on me, they were on the tableau of us all, but he pushed himself off the panelled wall and came towards me.

'That's my position, surely?' He copied my stance by the mantelpiece, elbow crooked, legs crossed nonchalantly at the ankle. 'The head of hearth and home?'

I laughed again, but this time my laugh was low and perfectly calm. I turned my body towards my husband and laid my hand over his. But every part of me sang as if I'd been stung by nettles, because Stuart was here now, on the other side of the room. Suki started to chat, her voice a little higher than usual, and the cobalt blue eyes of her brother roamed the room so subtly that no one else would know it, fell on his father, his sister, the furniture, and at last on me, each part of me in turn, savouring toe, wrist, hip, mouth, oh God, and breasts. I was being surreptitiously stripped.

I smiled widely at John while his son looked at my breasts and my nipples stiffened and pushed at the soft cashmere, so wicked to be so turned on in that room, with those particular people, at that significant moment, nipples shooting the message through my body that I desired my stepson.

'Dad said you were worried about the lunch,' Suki said, taking the champagne out of the bucket. 'You dashed out into the cold to feed us.'

'Yes.'

'No need.' She nudged her father's arm, making him spill a little of his drink. 'Stuart can do it.'

John slid his fingers out from my hand and tapped them restlessly. 'Stuart? Would that not be a bit of a busman's holiday?'

I noticed a cleft in Stuart's chin. John has one just the same.

'No more than you coming home to sculpt your beautiful wife every night.'

There was another hush, like the pause before a wave turns. He made the word 'sculpt' sound filthy.

'I don't work any more. Didn't Suki tell you?' John held his hands up like surgeons do once they've scrubbed in. 'These are useless now.'

'Not useless, Johnny,' I tried to say, but I was studying Stuart's shoulder, where the yarn of his fisherman's sweater was unravelling.

Suki wagged her finger. 'You look like a Victorian patriarch, Dad, glowering from the fireplace like that. You know, asking if Stuart's intentions are honourable.'

I glanced at Stuart and he at me, tiny unknowable glances already perfected.

'I should have been here this summer to ask *you*. I heard you married Florence virtually the moment you met!' Stuart's eyes snapped towards his father. 'Who knows? Perhaps I might have stopped you.'

'But can you blame me for wanting her? Look at her.'

And all three Floyds looked at me.

'But you also had a deadline, didn't you, Dad?' Suki broke the silence, holding her glass tightly in front of her mouth. 'To finish the sculpture for that facial scarring exhibition –'

I let my breath out sharply, blowing my hair from my face. 'Thanks for that, Suki.'

'I don't blame you at all, Dad.' Stuart stared frankly at my face, my cheek carved with the pattern of a shattered windscreen. 'You were lucky to get there first.'

'Ours was the star exhibit,' John replied quietly. 'And once I'd tasted her body there seemed no point in waiting.'

I blushed hot. Maybe we all did. I don't know if he looked at me then because Stuart and I were staring at each other again as if staring might go some way to satisfying the gnawing hunger.

'No, Dad,' Stuart said quietly, 'no point at all.'

'And so now,' I said, turning to leave the room again, 'we are going to have a bloody good weekend. That right, Stuart?'

'Absolutely right. But only if I can help with the lunch.'

'Us youngsters have to be off in the morning. Big reunion. I've organised a parade of old flames for Stuart to re-ignite.' Suki perched forwards on the sofa as if she'd been trying to grab him, but already Stuart was following me out of the door. 'So there's not much time for catching up.'

'Well if my son's busy getting to know his stepmother,' my husband said, rousing himself, 'Suki and I had better take a walk together.'

'Is Stuart what you expected, Flo? Or should I say Florence.' Suki flung her scarf round her neck. A tassel

13

caught me in the eye. She came closer. 'He's gorgeous, isn't he? I'm so proud of him.'

'Yes. He's gorgeous. Exactly like your father.'

'Here that, Dad? You've got competition.'

A blush scorched the edges of my scalp. 'Competition?'

'Well, Dad got the trophy wife, but Stuart's the rising star. Everyone in Scotland's talking about him.'

'Scotland?' John and I spoke in unison.

'Didn't we tell you? He's not going back to Australia. He's staying in Edinburgh with me.'

In the kitchen, Stuart was sharpening a knife.

'His *tiramisu* is wicked.' Suki giggled. 'So who's king of the heap now?'

'Don't be silly, Suki!' John opened the front door and the wind barged in. 'No one can hold a candle to my wife. And what's the point of *tiramisu*? This is Britain, not Sicily.'

'*More's the pity,*' I said, laughing into his cheek.

John rested against me briefly, then he was gone.

'He's worried that you and Stuart won't get on. So make it work, Flo. OK?' Suki leaned into the kitchen, one leg up behind her in a coquettish ballerina pose. 'Sure you want to be stuck in here, honey?'

Stuart didn't answer. I banged the door shut, and somehow my hand landed on his chest.

'What's your scent?'

There was no need to keep staring at him. Those cobalt eyes. Those curved lips. He was John, thirty years younger. A great wave of regret washed over me. But here was his son, real, warm, and drawing me like a magnet. I could feel his heart racing.

'Something citrus I picked up in Morocco.'

'It's like the bouquet in a Benedictine. Makes my nose

14

prickle.'

He laughed, a deep reverberation under my hand. Then he swung the rucksack. 'I'm afraid I'm very sad. I bring my own herbs. Do you mind?'

I shook my head, letting him go. I swung one leg across the breakfast stool. 'So chicken OK?'

'No time. We'll have smoked salmon for lunch. And my gift to you and Dad. Figs.' Out of a brown paper bag rolled green and purple ovals. He picked one up, made a cross over one end, then squeezed the other end. The green skin of the fruit puckered and ripped slightly, and there was the moist redness of the innards, studded with tiny seeds. 'These Greek ones are in season now.'

My whole body felt loose, as if I could fall off that stool any moment. My armpits were damp, my breasts were tingling. Up between my fidgety legs, my pussy was getting wet.

'I lace the figs with honey, mascarpone, if there is any. Some liqueur. So sweet,' he said, scooping out the flesh and letting it ooze between his fingers. 'Try it.'

I smiled as juice dribbled over my bottom lip and on to his finger. He wiped the finger across my mouth again so that my lips yielded and opened. He pushed his finger in between my teeth. I tasted the mixture of clean skin and moist fig. My heart was racing. I whimpered as I sucked his finger right in to my mouth. His mouth parted, lips glistening as he smiled and pushed it in further. The rush of desire knocked the breath out of me.

Then he pulled his finger out with a sticky sound. I sat up, crossed my legs primly. Cleared my throat as if everything was just dandy. Slowly, nonchalantly, he put the same finger to his own lips and licked it. My pussy clenched tight. Moisture seeped into my knickers.

'And what will you do with the poor chicken?' My

15

voice was husky as he backed away to the table.

He bent to chop the green herbs, coiled in that way chefs have, feet dancing impatiently. Dark strands of hair fell over his eyebrows. He wiped at his forehead with his arm.

'Marinade until this evening.' He made incisions in the plump flesh, and started to rub a butter and herb mixture all over the chicken. Into the cavity between the bird's legs. His fingers were long. 'It has to go in deep. It'll taste orgasmic, you'll see. Push gently like you're making love to the bird. Never fuck it.'

I closed my eyes as the word drove in to me. I tipped my head back on my neck, ran my tongue over my lips. It's how I used to pose when I was modelling lingerie. But that was simulating excitement in a studio full of cameras. There was no simulation here. I was ready to come right there on the stool.

He washed his hands. My whole body tightened as he moved back across the floor in slow motion, hands still wet, so close I could see the boyish flush streaking his face.

'They'll be back soon.'

He nodded, looking up my body. That's how young men look. Like boys, like it's still so new. The present before it's unwrapped. He pulled me close. Closer. I was grasping for breath.

'Dad was right. You are pure alabaster,' he said, lifting a strand of my hair away from my face. Away from the scar. He looked at it without flinching. 'I can see why he fell for you.'

But the shadow of his father didn't stop the next thing happening. I lifted my face and he smothered my mouth with his, all hot wet lips and teeth and tongue.

'Oh Christ, Stuart, we can't, we –' I tried to stop,

honestly I did, but all I could see were those eyes and that face, so beautiful and familiar yet so bloody *young*. He pulled away, and that sweet, genuine effort clinched it for me. I needed that cold space between us, that empty space between my legs, I needed it filled, and so then we were tangled in the kind of violent, greedy, blood-letting kiss that makes you go deaf and blind.

'Not enough time, oh God, no time.' He slammed me back against the ancient, sturdy fridge and inside it wine bottles rattled. But we went on kissing, his tongue ramming into my mouth, me unable to breathe, my pussy throbbing and aching for him now that it was grinding against the rough fabric of his jeans, grating the tender lips so that they eased open to rub the sore clit inside. He ran his hands under my sweater, squeezing my breasts, making my skin shiver, but that wasn't enough, he unhooked my bra expertly and why oh why did an image flash up of him undressing younger women before I had the chance to find him, his first girl, first love, first fuck – but then he was kneading my breasts, flesh yielding like dough under his hands and I moaned as he lifted my breasts like two warm cakes and kissed them, running his tongue over the pale skin, then circling each raspberry nipple, tasting everything like food, and he moaned, too, sucking one dark nipple into a point, shocks of pleasure streaking through me, then sucking the other, two tight beacons burning hot, showing the world how bad we were being.

'Did he touch you like this the very first time?' He squeezed my cheeks between his hands. 'When he was sculpting your lovely face? Did you fuck the first time?'

'Yes,' I said brutally.

'Christ, how am I going to bear it?'

The wildness and fury was just like John that first time

17

we fucked in his cold studio. Desperate laughter coiled in my chest.

I gasped, pushing his mouth back onto my nipples. 'What can't you bear?'

He bit me, hard, then still sucking he flipped my skirt up round my waist, then sank his fingers into the soft flesh of my butt cheeks to lift me so that I was forced to wrap my legs round him. God, he was strong. My pussy slicked open against his stomach, moistening the lacy knickers as my skirt drifted round my waist.

'The jealousy, Florence. You, in his bed, night after night. The fucking jealousy!'

I kissed him, tangling my fingers in his hair. I wanted to hear more.

'That he got here first, met and married you before I got the chance –'

'You're not making sense,' I laughed softly. His words were shadows of my own. We were rocking together against the fridge, his cock hard in his jeans. 'You've met me now!'

'Yes, but it's too late! He's got you. He's got you to touch, to fuck, whenever he wants, and I –'

I tightened my thighs round his hips and reached between them to unbutton his flies.

'And you, my darling, are fucking me right now!'

He groaned and dug his fingers into my butt cheeks, easing them apart, and then his fingers were in the damp crack between them, searching and sliding over my tender flesh, slipping easily in and out of my wet cunt. I was seething with excitement now, opening myself wider to swallow his fingers, to grip him, grinding my cunt against his sweater, smearing it with my pussy juices as I wound my fingers in his hair to smother him between my damp breasts.

18

He groaned unevenly as his fingers slid in and out of me, releasing more of my strong, musky scent, driving me wild with wanting. I slid my hand into his jeans and found his cock, hot and hard. We were both gasping and grunting like animals, slamming and banging against the fridge. His teeth nipped again and again at my nipples.

Suddenly we could hear, far below on the cliff path, the murmur of voices and my heart plummeted.

Stuart lifted his head, lips wet with sucking, and we stared at each other, eyes glittering in the fading afternoon light. I was quivering violently now, with the effort of gripping him and with the ferocious desire to have him, right there in his mother's kitchen.

'Christ, Florence, what are we going to do?' His gorgeous face was so close to mine. 'I have to stop –'

'No, you can't. Be quick.' I kissed him hard. He paused, then his tongue pushed hungrily around mine and I let my feet drop to the floor and we staggered backwards to the table.

I barely felt the scratch of rough wood against my back as we fell and he reared over me on his hands and knees. I unzipped his trousers and there was his cock standing hard and straight and there were my legs, hooking him into me.

He shoved me hurriedly across the table. Something else made of china toppled off and smashed. Above us as my head jammed over the edge I could see elongated splashes of *boeuf bourguignon,* all across the ceiling. Our bodies were stuck together now and we both breathed in and held it as his cock slid into me. I was so wet, but my body gripped him, held him tight inside, my arms and legs were wound round him as if welded to his bones and his hands were still squeezing my breasts, pinching my nipples as he bit and licked at my neck, pausing to listen,

19

and then we were rocking wildly together, his cock thrusting up and through me and filling me totally.

Outside the voices were closer but we still had time and though it was wrong it felt right. No way could we stop. My body sucked in my stepson's cock, scraping across the table as he fucked me. I squeezed him harder until he groaned and shuddered and then I was too excited to hold back and I ground myself against him, coming and coming, scratching his lovely back to give him something to remember, as every bit of me would remember him, and then even as we leapt apart and got shakily back on our feet the ecstasy, in me at least, kept coming in waves until we could breathe again.

John and Suki were climbing slowly up the cliff path. My mouth was bruised. We stood inches apart, upright like soldiers.

Suki looked up to open the gate. Saw us side by side in the bright room against the darkening world outside. John waved but the vigorous gesture took his balance. As if he'd got older in the tiny hour that he had walked with Suki along the beach, now he sketched an old man's dither in the lane, his feet treading water to turn him, his hand gripping out for Suki. Or for me.

He saw us framed in the kitchen. Maybe he could see how our lips were wet. And his face froze.

'He's old, and he's ill,' I told Stuart as Suki opened the door and let in the chill. 'And I love him.'

'I love him, but I love you too,' Stuart said, peeling away a sliver of smoked salmon. 'So I'll wait.'

The Glass-blower

JENNIFER DIDN'T KNOW WHAT the hell she was doing on a singles holiday, let alone in Venice of all places. Everyone on the trip denied they were looking for love, or even sex. Just enjoying the view with like-minded people. But why else had they paid through the nose to join a dating agency? Why else were they spending a long weekend traipsing round the most romantic city on earth?

And what a motley crew they were. At least Jennifer had a couple of broken engagements under her belt, and could prove, if necessary, that she'd lost her virginity. This lot were like some kind of sociological experiment deposited from outer space. The men were like defrocked priests, blinking dazedly in the cold light of real life. And the women were like kids playing dress-up in their too tight clothes and too bright lipstick.

And yet. Like the animals in the Ark they were, stealthily, pairing up. Keith and Vince, the accountants, had been seen slurping oysters in a dingy waterside bar with Serena and Alissia, the highlight-flicking chalet girls. And Michael, the psychotherapist, had definitely copped off with Jane the violin teacher. You could tell by the love bite.

'I'm not sure I can stand it another day. Don't know why I signed up for this in the first place,' muttered Jennifer to Hazel, the pale gardening columnist, as they

21

sat on the windblown *Zattere* fulfilling the pizza-eating section of the itinerary. 'Ain't never going to have sex again at this rate, let alone find the man of my dreams.'

'Forget romance, then,' replied Hazel, licking olive oil off her lower lip. They both stared through the steamed-up window at a huge cruise ship plying down the Giudecca canal, dwarfing the city.

'Concentrate on finding pure sex, do you mean? Because I'm frustrated as hell! It's been *months –*'

'Me too!' Hazel blushed, then laughed. 'But what I meant was, we're all desperate now we're forty, but that's no reason to be a quitter.'

Jennifer hadn't realised how husky Hazel's voice was. In fact, she'd never heard her speak before. The heat in the restaurant had made her cheeks glow, and the oil had made her normally chapped lips glisten.

'But they've marched us round all the sights, haven't they? Rialto Bridge, the Jewish quarter, coffee at Florians – what else is there?' Jennifer swallowed her cold beer. 'It's all very lovely here, but I ought to get home before the credit crunch closes me down completely –'

'But what's waiting for you in London, apart from your shrinking property company?' asked Hazel, curling her tongue round a long strand of melted mozzarella. 'The singles scene there is shit.'

'Too true, sister.' Jennifer dabbed a blob of melted cheese off Hazel's chin and then they clinked their thick beer glasses, blushing.

'Anyway, there's one thing we haven't seen yet,' Hazel winked. She had very long eyelashes and zero make-up. 'Tacky and touristy it may be, but you can't leave Venice without seeing them blowing glass.'

*   *   *

Which is how they came to be standing round a kind of freezing warehouse on the island of Murano. In front of them, blazing heat like a scene from Dante's *Inferno,* complete with doomed souls. Behind, a vicious breeze cutting straight off the iron grey water separating them from the domes and spires of the city, rising like a herbaceous border on the horizon.

Then this guy sauntered out from a back room, unbuttoning a loose white shirt. No fanfare, except some sort of greeting and a long hard stare straight into Jennifer's eyes. The tour leaders clapped, but Jennifer was rigid with excitement. The shirt came off, and as he took up a long metal pipe and plunged it into a bubbling furnace the back of his head, spine and legs were splashed with darkness, his face, chest and arms thrown into relief by the roaring light.

'Caravaggio, wasn't it?' Frederick the ex-police officer remarked from the back of the watching group. 'Didn't he paint Bacchus and all those tortured saints in exactly this half-light?'

'I think the tourist board makes them do this deliberately,' Hazel giggled softly. 'You know, look all virile and sweaty.'

'Sexy as,' breathed Serena.

'Open fire, bare hands, unprotected face. Obviously have no truck with health and safety,' added Keith.

Everyone spluttered like school kids trying to be good in church.

The muscles in his shoulders and arms flexed as the glass-blower grasped the pipe. His ribs jabbed through his skin, the heat must knock the breath out of you, and running down his stomach – the jeans low-slung, hanging off his hips – a thin line of dark hair ran from his navel down, down into his jeans. Into his boxers where the hair would fan out round his big, sleeping cock.

Jennifer's pussy twitched. *Sod this bunch,* she thought, tracing hearts in the dusty floor with the pointed toe of her boot. *I'll have this one washed and brought to my tent.*

Now a wedge of muscle thickened down each side of his back as he manipulated his iron pipe, dipping it into the furnace again. Jennifer's stomach swallow-dived.

'Apparently that's called the glory hole!' Hazel whispered. Her blonde hair tickled Jennifer's face like wisps of silk. 'How naughty is that?'

Jennifer squealed with laughter. 'He can plunge his pipe into my glory hole any time!'

The glass-blower scoped out a sort of jelly and skipped like Nureyev across to a slab of marble where he rolled and flipped it, constantly lifting and twisting and swinging his pipe. Then he lowered his mouth and his cheeks pulled in as he started to suck. Jennifer gasped. She put her hand into her coat, down between her legs. Her pussy felt hot and damp under her jeans. The glass-blower rotated and twisted his pipe as his cheeks blew life into the red-hot globule gathered at the end and coaxed it into shape.

'*Magnifico,*' sighed Hazel.

The glass elongated at the end of the pipe and, as it swelled and grew, yes, just like a hard-on, a frantic desire gripped Jennifer. Her pussy felt really wet now. She wanted something, the pipe, the guy's cock, whatever, hot and hard, filling her. He sketched another *pas de deux* with his instrument, loving it, his fingers coaxing the elegant line of metal as he breathed air down the tube, and look how the globular mass responded, fading from garish tangerine to a rosy hue and conformed into a lovely oval.

'That's the sexiest thing ever.' It came out as a growl. She could hardly breathe. She wanted those hands running over her, coaxing her into amazing shapes and then a mind-blowing climax. 'I'm going to follow him home. I'll go mad if I don't have him.'

'Christ, you really are horny, aren't you?' Hazel was still very close. She slid her arm briefly round Jennifer's waist. Jennifer liked the feel of it there, and it was cold when Hazel moved away. 'But you're crazy! You'll get lost.'

'I want an adventure, Hazel.'

The ballet slowed as the glass-blower, still swinging his pipe to keep the momentum, rolled the dark pink mass onto another slab and then suddenly, with his free hand, took pincers to the neck of the glass, which had stretched into a column. Jennifer expected it to screech out for mercy as he tightened his grip and decapitated it. Then it was over. The glass had turned into a beautiful vase and the glass-blower wandered out of sight.

Jennifer clutched at some nearby display shelving. There was a frantic rattling of fragile glassware as she rapidly, and silently, came.

Magnifico was the word.

Hazel was right. Jennifer did get lost. At first the solitude was blissful. The strain of being nice to all these earnest strangers was getting to her. She wriggled away from the others and followed the glass-blower on to the *vaporetto,* back into the city. The alleyways cobwebbed like veins as she tried to keep up with him. Then he ducked through a green stained arch into a tiny dove-grey- and honey-coloured *campo.* No one passed her. There was the odd tinkle of music through a half-open window, the clatter of cutlery, the snap of a bed sheet, but only brief snatches, as if voices or music or footsteps were an interruption to some other, deeper, process flowing through the water beneath.

She had only paused for a second. But the glass-blower had vanished.

She panicked, then, heart thumping. Glanced around wildly. It was dark, and she had no idea how to get back to the hotel. Suddenly she missed the others and their inane laughter. Hazel with her map.

Then someone sighed, across the square, quietly, definitely female, and answered by a rough male sigh. No words. So quiet they were just like breaths, in and out. Surely it was him. The glass-blower. She looked around. A curtain curled like a red tongue out of a window in the corner, but nothing else moved. Somewhere a bell tolled.

The private sighs stretched into elongated moans. The hairs on her arms started to prickle. She walked towards the house, stopped by the door. There was a creaking of bed springs which sang slowly, in a rhythm. The ragged moans rose into wordless gasping, so close to fear or pain, now panting in time to the creaking. Jennifer's nipples stiffened, her silk underwear clinging to the hard points, and once again she felt moisture seeping into her knickers. It was like she was in there with them, whispering, kissing, touching, arousing each other in their secret room. The square reverberated with the rhythmic sounds, their animal groaning as the man's cock thrust into the woman. The bed was banging and they were groaning, the moans rising to that uninhibited pitch where pleasure meets pain. Jennifer was rocking, too, on the doorstep, cold hands rubbing at herself under her coat, one finger matching the heady rhythm echoing from the window, finger running up, down her crack, making it wet, making her so jealous, she could picture the sex-soaked scene through that shuttered window, the wrinkled sheets, the bed thumping against the wall, a man's muscular buttocks slamming between a woman's wide-open thighs.

Like a wildlife film when you see lions humping. They were hard at it up there, and her fingers rubbed faster across her crotch and then the woman was straining for breath, hissing 'yes, yes', though surely it should be '*si, si*', maybe she was riding him, breasts bouncing, hard nipples catching between his teeth, his fingers digging into her haunches to keep her rammed onto his big cock. Jennifer moaned as her pussy clutched frantically at nothing real and then she subsided on to the step, cold and exhausted.

'Jennifer!'

'Sssh, don't disturb me – them.' She pointed to the window. The lovers were done.

'The glass-blower wasn't the answer, sweetie. Come on. Let's get you back!'

'How did you know I was here?' she asked, letting Hazel lead her through another archway, down another silent alleyway.

'Followed you, silly. Look, here we are already!'

Hazel pushed her into a little yard studded with lemon trees and up a stone staircase. Ripples of watery light slipped through lamplight. Somewhere out there gondolas and *vaporetti* plied the khaki water, carrying tourists, barge-loads of food, works of art.

'And here's my little room.'

It was enormous, like a palace. Arched doors looked over the Grand Canal. Acres of marble floor stretched from the door to a four-poster bed at the far end. Hazel lit some red candles round the bed and waved a big bottle of Chianti.

'How the hell did you score this?'

Jennifer sank into mounds of duvet and pillow, kicking

27

off her tight boots and taking a big swig of Hazel's wine.

'Persuaded the manager on the first night, of course. I sucked his cock.' Hazel sat down beside Jennifer and pulled off her coat. 'I'm sick of hotels taking the piss out of us singletons and putting us in broom cupboards with a supplement. This is the honeymoon suite.'

'I don't believe you, Hazel. Seducing that great lummox? You're just a wee mouse!' Jennifer took another swig of wine and lay back. 'And anyway, what about the honeymooners?'

Hazel pulled her woolly jumper over her head, kicked off her jeans. 'Who honeymoons in December?'

'Always moving, always busy, Hazel.' The wine had gone straight to Jennifer's head. Warmth was seeping through her, loosening her limbs. 'What are you doing now?'

'Need a shower. Cocktails at the Danieli, remember?'

Jennifer closed her eyes. 'Too tired to get ready.'

'Just watch me, then.'

Something in Hazel's voice pricked at Jennifer. She opened her eyes. Hazel was by the bed, wrapping a towel round her naked body. Her skin was translucent white and with her pale blonde hair she looked like an angel in the candlelight.

Jennifer gasped.

'Christ, you look amazing, Hazel. Almost as if clothes get in the way! If you *did* seduce Signor Whatsit that first day he'd have died and gone to heaven.'

'Not just the first day.' Hazel shrugged. She opened the towel briefly, showing her milk white body, then tucked it in again. 'He sound happy to you just now?'

Jennifer blinked.

'In the square? You had no idea that's the back of our hotel? The couple you were listening to just now was him and me.' She took Jennifer's jumper and pulled it over her head. 'I pleasure him every evening, before he opens the bar.'

'Pleasure him?' Jennifer shivered as the cooler air crept over her arms. 'Oh, darling Hazel, I love the quaint way you talk –'

Hazel lifted one long pale leg and sat astride Jennifer, her towel falling open over her thighs, slipping down over her breasts.

'But at least I'm having sex, Jenni.'

'OK, OK, don't rub it in.' Jennifer slapped at Hazel angrily. 'So everyone's at it except me!'

Hazel caught Jennifer's arm and held it down. 'You don't have to be left out, not now you're with me. I really fancy you, Jenni,' she said quietly. She leaned over and brushed her lips across Jennifer's mouth. 'You see, I know I've been fucking the manager, but actually it's women I'm really into.'

Jennifer was too stunned to stop her. The other woman's lips felt so soft compared with a man's. Like pillows. And wet.

'You're in the wrong place,' Jennifer muttered, when Hazel pulled away. 'I'm not a lesbian, you know.'

'Oh fuck it, who needs labels?' Hazel's face was close. She smelt of warm skin and sweet custard. 'It's sex you're after, isn't it, Jenni? Well, I can give it to you, right here on a plate.'

'Not what I want.' Jennifer tried to slide backwards off the bed. 'I mean, that doesn't really count as sex, does it?'

'You do talk bollocks.' Still pinning Jennifer down with her legs, Hazel unbuttoned her shirt and opened it. Jennifer's breasts rose up, shocked at their exposure. 'So if you haven't been touched by a woman before, I want to be the first.'

Jennifer turned her head, tried to move away, but the bed was so comfortable. The sounds outside so foreign. The candlelight so hypnotic. And Hazel's hands, sliding down Jennifer's ribcage, over her hips, pulling off her jeans, were so soft and gentle that Jennifer was powerless.

Suddenly Hazel reached round and unclipped Jennifer's bra. The breath rasped in her throat as Hazel took Jennifer's breasts in her hands. At the touch of her fingers Jennifer pushed herself towards Hazel, she couldn't help it, her nipples shrinking into points as the air met them. Her insides started swirling as Hazel sat across her legs, fondled her breasts, biting her lip with apparent pleasure, squeezing and pressing them together as each forefinger circled each hard raspberry nipple, flicking at them until they were sore and tingling with shocked desire.

And then Hazel leaned down and took one nipple into her mouth and started to suck it. Jennifer's pussy went tight as she watched Hazel's lips pucker and suck, lick and kiss, and the nipple growing hard and wet with Hazel's saliva. Then Hazel pinched that nipple and started to suck the other one. Jennifer fell back on her elbows and realised that she was spreading open her legs under the weight of Hazel's bare bottom, and grinding up against her automatically, her frustrated, empty, hot cunt aching for something to fill it.

Hazel felt her move, and lifted her face.

'This girl stuff not right for you?' she asked in her customary whisper. Her mouth, wet from all that licking, slid over Jennifer's face. She flicked her tongue across Jennifer's lips, coaxing her mouth open. 'Want me to stop?'

'God, no don't stop. I want you to keep doing it!'

Jennifer's head felt as if it was going to fly open. She

30

started to suck on Hazel's tongue, circling it in and out of her mouth, then probing in, hard, like a penis, and then she realised that this must be how men felt. Because suddenly she wanted to dominate little Hazel, take her over, touch her, feel her. All over. She reached up to pull the towel off, running her hands over Hazel's cool white shoulders and spine and then brought them round to the front and nearly screamed as Hazel's soft white breasts bounced heavily into her hands, big and warm, similar yet so different from her own, and anyway she had never really fondled her own, just let others do it, but now she relished the sexy softness of another woman's tits.

She pulled away from the wet kiss and watched her fingers pinching and teasing, arousing Hazel, watched the pale nipples filling with colour, growing long and tight, demanding to be suckled and there, that was the entire point of them. To be suckled.

Electrical charges sizzled through Jennifer. She fell onto her back and shifted Hazel slightly up so that the nipples were dangling above her like ripening berries and Hazel hung there, smiling down, as her breasts crushed into Jennifer's nose and cheeks, warm skin and a musky perfume as everything pressed into her face and she took one hard nipple into her mouth, feeling it grate against her teeth, slide onto her tongue, and then she sucked, hard, stroking the soft flesh of Hazel's breasts pressing into her face, biting first one nipple then the other, feeling her own nipples burning in response.

'That's it, Jenni, suck me.' Hazel's voice was a whisper as she pushed her nipples into Jennifer's mouth and now she was pulling at Jennifer's hips, lifting them so she could slide her knickers off, and then her pussy was rubbing against Jennifer's, neatly at first and then spreading open the wet lips to expose all the tender bits.

Then she was touching herself in little darting movements, grinding cunt on cunt, how about that, wet clit bumping over wet clit.

'And look, Jenni. See? Watch us in that amazing mirror.'

Hazel pulled her nipple out of Jennifer's mouth and turned her face on the pillow. The wall beside the bed was hung with an enormous Venetian mirror, reflecting not only the bed but also the windows and the lights of the city, that strange watery light ripping across the mottled walls of the bedroom.

'How kinky is that?'

In the mirror a blonde woman sat astride a redhead, her sweet breasts wobbling, her nipples jutting like nuts. The redhead was grasping the blonde's buttocks, her long fingers digging hard into the plump flesh there, and their legs were twined round each other. The two women were joined, glued together, at their pussies, and that sight made them both, still watching in the mirror, move, rock together, Hazel lifting her hands to fondle her own nipples, Jennifer staring at that magical reflection as her cunt heated up under Hazel's hot pussy, her sex lips grating against the other woman's, opening her right up, desire shafting through her as they rocked faster, Hazel tossing her silky hair, totally abandoned now, grinding furiously against Jennifer, staring at the mirror then down at Jennifer as Jennifer's fingers dug deep between Hazel's buttocks, found the warm crack there, probed greedily to find the little arse hole hidden, never even thought of that before, but Hazel's eyes went wider and she bit her lip hard when she felt Jennifer's finger pushing up, forcing open that cute butt hole, forcing it to suck her finger right in to the tight slippery warmth.

'Oh, fuck me Jenni, now fuck me baby!'

'Christ, you're sexy when you talk dirty,' Jennifer groaned, fucking Hazel's arse with her finger, loving the way the tight tunnel sucked her finger in and up, and feeling the wild bundle of excitement start to unravel as Hazel's head fell back and she went limp, jerking uncontrollably, her sweet lips flashing red and swollen as her pussy tilted towards Jennifer and she came, almost singing with ecstasy.

Jennifer kept her impaled on her finger because that was driving her wild, too, and then she took Hazel's fingers and shoved them up inside her own convulsing pussy and then Hazel, still gasping from her own climax, fucked Jennifer with her long white fingers, pushing them up into her hot tight cunt. Tongues of ecstasy started lapping at her, shafting out of Hazel's clever fingers, which pumped rapidly in and out while Jennifer's wet pussy sucked at them with its spasms. Her fingers and thumb played Jennifer like a rasping violin and then juices dripped down her trembling legs and the climax came, hot and quick, and shook her until at last she came, gasping with surprise and shuddering with pleasure.

Hazel laughed softly then fell down on top of Jennifer, breasts squashed against breasts and hearts banging together.

'If only I'd known about you from the beginning.' Jennifer murmured after a while, tangling her fingers in Hazel's hair.

'There's plenty more where that came from.' Hazel rolled off and wandered across the room, bare bottom gleaming in the candlelight. She leaned down to pick up a petticoat. 'Unless you want to go looking for the glass-blower again?'

'Yeah, how about that? We know where he lives. A threesome, maybe?' Jennifer jumped off the bed and

33

grabbed Hazel from behind, running her hands over her bottom again. Already her stomach was twisting with fresh excitement. 'But it's our last night. We've no more time.'

Hazel wriggled against Jennifer.

'Oh, haven't you heard? Those floods in Piazza San Marco? The manager tells me the *aqua alta* is the highest it's been for 20 years. Hotels are closed. Ferries cancelled.' Hazel turned round slowly and pulled Jennifer towards her, sliding her fingers between her legs again, tickling her open. 'Honey, we're stranded.'

Mademoiselle

'CHRIST, SLUT REALLY IS a dirty word to you, isn't it?' Poppy marched into my pristine kitchen and started messing about with my corkscrew. 'And not in a good way.'

'The youngsters come with you this year?' I glanced outside, armpits prickling with anxiety. My sisters' cars were already parked up. They were marching up my little drive, laden with goodies. 'All the neighbours are invited. Hilde from next door's bringing over some German cookies.'

'All got thumping hangovers, but yes, they're here. Trust you to insist on this bloody tradition of lunch on New Year's Day.'

Trust me, indeed. The annual invasion. Something to be endured before I could go back into hibernation. I left the front door ajar and tried to ignore the red wine Poppy was about to spill all over my quartz-effect work surface. I gripped my knife. 'Anyway, how can anything be dirty in a *good* way?'

'Because sex goes with slut! But you can't even say the word without spraying it with Pledge!' There it was. Nearly half a glass of Merlot. All over my chrome hob. She glared at me through her long red fringe. Too much henna to enhance the natural auburn. She looked like a slightly ageing Red Setter. 'And you've obviously forgotten what that means.'

'What what means?' I caught the red drips with a j-cloth. 'Pledge?'

'Slut!' She was screaming it now. The hotter and redder she got, the colder I became. On the surface at least. My skin, my hair, my demeanour. Inside, my heart was juddering with fury. 'This kitchen, this house, it's so sterile it's like a Swiss clinic or something! And you, Mary. Behind all this Stepford wife thing going on you're still beautiful. In a Meryl Streep kind of way. Those cheekbones! But what's happened to you? You barely even drink any more! You're like the living dead –'

'I just like everything tidy –' I picked up my knife and went on peeling satsumas for the punch. Very sharp, that little knife. 'I haven't seen the youngsters for years. Just want everything to go well.'

'You used to be slut of the century! The decadent auntie! Life and soul! Men positively spinning round the revolving door to get at you!'

'Watch it, lady.' I peeled the pitted skin away from the fruit. The citrus aroma made my nostrils prickle. 'Anyone else I'd kill for insulting me like that.'

'Whatever! Someone's got to say it!' She gulped noisily and wiped her mouth with the back of her hand. 'The simple problem is you've been on your own for too long. All dried up! You make Anne Robinson look like Pamela Anderson!'

'In a good way!' The gaggle of nephews and nieces and hangers-on crowded into the doorway, laden with nothing more than youth, beauty and packets of fags. 'We're liking Auntie Mary's new dominatrix look!'

'Behave, you lot!' I tapped the wrist of the nearest one with a wooden spoon. 'You may be a foot taller than me now, but you don't scare me. Don't forget I used to give

36

you your bubble bath when you were babies!'

They all snorted. 'But isn't this spooky,' said my niece Chloe dreamily, twiddling long blonde hair round her finger. 'I thought Mum and Mary were chalk and cheese, but if you take away the outfits –'

'– and the hair dye!' someone else piped up.

'– you sisters are quite alike.'

Poppy was close beside me. For every stone I'd lost, she'd put on two. She'd become all bohemian and eccentric – just like I used to be – all velvet and scarves and beads. Well, in a quiet moment I would get my own back and tell her to take a good look. For God's sake. Being lectured by someone who looked like Beth Ditto's mother.

My style these days was all primly tailored silk and tweed. I wanted to look simple. I'd stopped all that preening you need around a man. Just liked the sharp, tight whisk of a zip closing me in.

'I'm just saying, loosen up, Mary. You should never have stopped work. And a bit of heartbreak can't turn you into a block of ice for ever. You could lick this floor, it's so spotless,' Poppy said, pouring herself another glass of smoky red wine and pushing past me. 'Sad thing is, you wouldn't see the fun in that!'

A motorbike choked round the corner, and accelerated towards my end of the cul de sac. My party guests, swigging punch in the sitting room, reared their heads like wildebeest at the watering hole. The men herded out into the road to take a look.

'It's Charlie from next door! I recognise the Harley!' someone yelled, letting cold air into the house. 'Over here, mate!'

'Fuck, what a sex dog! That really little Charlie? What happened to the buck teeth and nerdy glasses?' Chloe was wriggling wildly on her stilettos as if she needed a pee, twisting her hair up into a fetching knot. 'Ooh! Now he's taking his helmet off –'

Everyone spluttered. My stomach twisted in my own kind of secret laughter as I watched the newcomer raking oily, sun tanned fingers through matted dark hair as his mother Hilde kissed him and the men trooped back into the house. They all glanced at me as I brought the *vol au vents* through on a silver tray. 'You wipe his bottom too, Auntie Mary?'

'I wish!' The laughter gasped out of me. 'Gave him extra French lessons, actually!'

'And Christ, wasn't Mademoiselle Mary every schoolboy's dream!'

Charlie stamped into the hallway, brushing frost and pine needles onto my cream carpet. I stared at the dirty specks he was dropping on the floor, at his steel-capped boots, up the long legs encased in black dusty leather. Further up to the crotch, I couldn't help it, leather trousers do that, don't they? Lead the eyes. Up to where the leather was worn round the crotch as if tired from straining round some massive, permanently stiff cock. Heat rose through me. Those tanned fingers, unzipping the leather jacket, reaching into the adoring audience for a drink.

'You don't mind if he gatecrashes, do you love?' Hilde bustled in with her plate of gingerbread. 'He's just turned up out of the blue! I thought he was visiting the German relatives somewhere in Arizona! Turns out he's on his way to France –'

'I'm amazed Hilde trusted you giving private lessons to that one. You were the local *femme fatale*!' Poppy whispered, coming up behind me to untie my apron strings.

'He was a shy skinny kid then, Poppy. Not some hunk straight out of *Grease* –'

'Well, he's hot now. A bit young. But I can tell you're turned on.' She breathed into my ear as she pulled the apron over my head. 'Your eyelids are drooping like Marilyn Monroe's. See? Still time for you to thaw out, Mare. You're still human, after all. And once a hussy, always a hussy –'

'For God's sake, I was, still am, twenty years older than him! An old bag forcing *la plume de ma tante* past his Adam's apple!'

'Yes. But he's just said you were his wet dream! And he's still got a lot to learn. I bet he wouldn't mind shoving his plume up your *tante* given half the chance!' She nudged me in the ribs and this time I giggled with her. The others started to move back into the sitting room. Chloe had her fingers round Charlie's wrist, dragging him with them. But he was staring at me, a slow smile creasing his mouth. Those blue eyes, *sans* glasses. White, straight teeth. Amazing, these orthodontists. Amazing, that mouth. Never noticed how full his bottom lip was. Was that the tip of his tongue flicking out? I couldn't find the gawky teenager anywhere in that strong-jawed face.

My knees felt weak. I knelt down on the carpet and started picking up flakes of drying mud from Charlie's boots with my fingernails.

And he sure as hell wouldn't find his vibrant, crazy old French mistress anywhere in me, this uptight, cold-looking spinster –

'Well, if I can't sink my teeth into that particular morsel, I'll make do with one of your sensational salmon blinis, sis.' Poppy kicked me lightly on the bottom. 'Take five. You looked stressed out. Stop scrubbing for five minutes and get yourself dressed!'

She was right, damn her. Even my party clothes, laid out on my bed, looked like surgical instruments. Pussy-bow blouse, tight pencil skirt. String of pearls. Scent. Stockings. Somehow, lying wrinkled and lifeless on my duvet, even they looked more industrial tool than seductive apparel.

'Something's burning, Mary! Think it's the cheese straws!'

Someone was screeching up the stairs.

'Leave her be. She's getting gorgeous.'

Heels clattered on the white kitchen tiling. Voices laughed, doors slammed. Wine and food smells seeped through the air. Music started playing.

I tugged off my shirt and slacks and stepped into the skirt, zipping it smartly as I stood in front of the long mirror by the window. Lit by the cold winter light I stared at the flat stomach I yearned for when I was younger. The slim thighs I'd only recently acquired. I turned sideways, breathed in, and was suddenly aware that my window looked straight on to Hilde's house. But there was no one there, stupid. I smiled. They were all over here, having fun.

God, the winter light was brutal. But it was forcing me to look. After losing all that weight my waist was tiny now but my breasts were still big. Well, they were huge before. Impossible to ignore. My pride and joy. My hippy, floaty dresses and jewelled tee shirts were always low cut, even at work. People glared, gaped, grinned, groped. My lovers would be in such a rush to see them, get their hands on the heavy, warm flesh, their eager lips and teeth nuzzling round my instantly hard nipples, that they would strip away my easily slipped off tops, leaving the rest of me often hidden, their greedy cocks fucking me under my clothes as an inevitable afterthought once feasting on my tits became too explosive.

My pussy twitched at the distant memory. I tried a little girlish wriggle like the excited blonde niece. Oh yes, the feeling back then was always mutual. I only had to feel the flick of a tongue across one tight nipple to get my body singing. Sometimes the tongue was female. I wonder if anyone else has this obsession to feel a mouth inching nearer, licking, pulling the nipple in then biting and sucking till it hurts, to feel that shafting, aching pleasure shooting to my cunt, making it open and wet like a flower –

A door downstairs opened to more laughter. My breasts looked so big, so white. So bloody lonely. Those prim blouses hid them these days under their buttons and pin tucks. Who knew? Who ever looked? I pushed them together to make soft warm mounds kissed by expensive mulberry lace.

'We used to fantasise about seeing you naked.'

I froze, hands still round my breasts. A low shaft of sunlight dazzled me, so that the figure behind me in the mirror was shadowy.

'*Bonjour, mademoiselle.*'

The worn leather trousers creaked as Charlie leaned in the doorway, holding two glasses of mulled wine.

'They were wondering where you were.'

'Oh, they're all fine without me.' I turned slightly, locking my knees together. I kept my eyes on the house next door. The empty window. I'd known Hilde all these years, and I still didn't know which room that was. '*Bonjour,* Charlie.'

'So this is your boudoir.' He put the glasses on the dressing table. I could smell leather and sweat and alcohol. 'We used to sneak into the spare bedroom, that window there. Mum never went in there. She never guessed. Freezing cold. We used to watch you dressing. And if we couldn't see you, we imagined it. Even if you were just dusting or cleaning, we'd take our cocks out and wank ourselves stupid, watching you. We'd shoot all over the window pane, groaning, all star-shaped spatters of spunk on the glass. And you never knew.'

He sat on the wide sill and crossed his ankles, taking a swig of wine. I backed towards the bed and snatched up the blouse to cover myself. 'Dirty little tykes.'

He smiled. 'Hot-blooded boys, that's all, miss. And then I was the lucky one. Persuaded Mum that all that German at home was no good, I needed extra help with French, and I had you all to myself on Thursday evenings when everyone else was watching *Top of the Pops*.'

I laughed. I was hot all over now. Against the glare all I could see was the glitter of his eyes. 'Oh, Charlie, you were sweet. Innocent. And so hard working –'

'So hard, you mean. I was permanently erect, *mademoiselle*. Boys that age always are. Squirming in my chair next to you. Watching your lips move as you spoke French. Ever noticed how people from France people speak as if they're savouring something really delicious? Germans speak as if they want to spit it all out. I used to wait for your tongue to slip across your mouth, collecting crumbs of Mum's bloody gingerbread. I could see spasms rippling down your throat as you swallowed your tea. You used to twine that silky green scarf round your neck, but it was always unravelled by the end of the lesson.'

I was shivering now. 'That scarf there?'

He reached over and plucked it from a pile folded neatly on a shelf. He twined it thoughtfully round his knuckles. 'I fantasised about how it would feel to come down your throat, make you swallow my spunk. But what

42

the other boys talked about was getting a peek at your tits.'

'*Sois sage,* Charlie. Behave!' I turned my back to him, tried to get my arms into the sleeves. 'All very flattering, I suppose, but that's all over now. Look at me. My sister says I'm all shrivelled, and dry, and old –'

'She's just jealous and fat. You're still gorgeous.' He looked down at the scarf. 'Too thin, but – just the same once you get down to the skin. And only, what, forty-three?'

'Now you're really being cheeky.' I flicked my hand at him. 'Get out of my bedroom.'

He stood up. Really towered over me. Blocked out the light so now I could see him clearly. The same scar on his chin. A smear of bike oil by his ear. I clutched at the blouse, but he just took it and tossed it onto the floor.

'So then I'd go back to school and tell the other boys all about my private lesson. How we'd decline some verbs and then I'd rip open your dress –'

'You lying little bastard!' I gasped, trying to wriggle away, but he grasped my wrists and tied them together with the silk scarf. Goose bumps pricked all over me as my breasts pushed out into the cool air.

'Not so little now, *mademoiselle*. I can do exactly as I please.' He trailed his fingers over the tender skin of my breasts where they bulged over the bra. 'We'd sit smoking on the football field and I'd tell them how you let me feel your tits, like this, over your bra. God, bras were the holy grail then!'

His fingers hooked inside the bra, stroking down inside to find one nipple. It was impossible to ignore. Standing out, long and hard like a nut to show him my excitement even if I wanted to hide it. I moaned before I could stop myself. He circled that nipple, then hooked his thumb over the bra to push it right down.

'Then I used to tell them I'd undone it, you know, unhooked it from behind your back like we were always practising, and got them out, and how big they were, how juicy.' He bit his lip, making it wet, and undid my bra. My breasts bounced out heavily, thrusting into the dull afternoon light. 'And God, they are, aren't they? Big, and juicy.'

'Everyone'll be wondering where we are –' I breathed, but he took my face in his big grown-up hands and kissed me. A hard, rough, wet kiss, lips scraping against mine, tongue swiping into my mouth as if to claim me.

Downstairs they had found my Latin American salsa music.

'Fuck it. I'm not letting this chance slip. You have no idea how horny I am after that long bike ride. After seeing you again. And I'll be gone in the morning.'

My legs started shaking and he pulled me down with him onto the bed, unzipping my skirt as he did so. Christ, how many women had he undressed since he was fifteen? The leather of his trousers snagged on my bare legs, tugging at the tiny hairs. The pain shocked me into life. With my hands tied I couldn't even pretend to push him away but as I struggled against him I touched his flies instead and felt his waiting cock, hard and ready under the worn leather. My fingers stroked over its length.

'Someone will come looking –' I breathed, moving my mouth over his again, greedy for another kiss.

'So let them look, *mademoiselle*. Let them see what I've finally got my hands on. I would have killed to get a look at you.' He flipped me on top of him. I balanced my tied hands above his head and now my silky, wet knickers were scraping over that hidden, hard cock. 'So teach me.'

My breasts tumbled forwards, bouncing against his

face. I let them rest there for a moment, relishing the sensation of that mouth so close to my nipples. Then I raised myself up to look at him. I was rubbing myself against him without knowing it, hungry to get him inside me. Everything about him was irresistible, his eyes, his full lips, the little bubbles of saliva at the corners like a kid impatient to tell you something, the pulse pummelling in his tanned neck.

He reached under me and unzipped his trousers, hoisting his hips up to pull them right off.

'I wish I was the first,' someone, me, said into the quiet.

'You were always the first for me, *mademoiselle*. Now, give me those tits, so good, good enough to eat. Christ, I want to fuck you.'

'*Embrasse moi,*' I whispered.

He cupped my breasts, massaged them together, rubbed them against his mouth. I licked my lips like a porn star. After all this time I had this boy on my bed, a familiar stranger. I wanted to hold off the pleasure for as long as I could bear. Meanwhile there was other pleasure to be had. His cock, released from his trousers, was jerking upwards, banging against my stomach as I started to rock against it, letting my pussy open gently against its length.

He held my thighs open, my clit grazing his cock. I looked out at the darkening day, over to his mother's house and that empty window, shivering with all that returning pleasure.

'I want to suck your tits, *mademoiselle*,' Charlie whispered, threatening to lift me on to his cock. 'I want it all to come true.'

'So you can go back and tell the boys?'

I smiled at the fantasy, because it was mine now. Now

that it was safe. All those burgeoning boys creeping into the cold spare room, parting the curtains to spy on me, peeping toms one and all, hard young cocks in their hands, watching us.

So I leaned over him, letting the tip of his cock touch inside my lips, and dangled my breasts over his lovely face, juicy like fruit. My nipples were raspberry dark with desire. They were inches from his mouth and lips and tongue and teeth. He was my boy once, but now he was my very own man. And I wanted him to suck me.

I arched my back and thrust my dark, aching nipples towards his waiting mouth. The moment closed in around us. I'd forgotten how pleasure does that, presses down on you, obliterating everything else. All we both wanted, before the fucking, was this sucking, this sucking.

His hands came up from my hips, slid up my ribcage until they reached the outward curve of my breasts. I breathed in tiny gasps as his hands slid closer. I could hardly breathe. The room felt colder, but my skin was sizzling. His body was straining up under me. My nipples were swollen now, each one the size of the tip of his little finger.

'Let me,' he groaned. I rubbed one across his mouth. I felt as if I'd been punched in the stomach. His face flooded with red heat. His curly hair sprang with sweat.

I let my nipples hover just above his mouth, torturing us both. I felt his cock jump in my hands, his warm balls shrinking back.

Downstairs, more doors were opening to let out the noise. They were calling our names –

'Let's hope they find the *petits fours'*, Charlie laughed.

'And leave us alone.' I laughed, too. 'Now, where we were?'

I pushed my swollen breasts into his face again. My

46

nipple spiked up, poking against his palm. I went limp as his fingers closed round. I spread my knees to lower myself, my pussy opening, my breasts jumping into his face with each heart beat.

My stomach tightened as he played with both breasts, moulded them, squeezed until I could bear it no longer. I lay on him, smothering him, so that he had no choice but to nuzzle in between, press each breast against each of his hot cheeks. My breasts were heavy with wanting. I rubbed one taut nipple against his mouth again and again like coaxing a lamb to suckle. Just the sight of me offering it to him made me want to come. I jammed myself against his legs, my pussy tight with longing.

His tongue flicked out and I angled the tit right into his mouth. His lips nibbled up, tongue lapping round, then, at last, he drew the burning bud in, pulling hard, and began to suck. Sparks pricked at me. I closed my eyes as the sensations ripped through me. And yes, I admit, I pictured him as the eager schoolboy he was when I was his French mistress, eyeing me up secretly, wanting me, and me, finally, taking his virginity.

Charlie grabbed the other breast roughly and turned his head this way and that, lapping and sucking, snuffling through his nose to breathe, groaning, biting and kneading harder and harder as if he owned my breasts now. It wasn't enough for one breast to be suckled, they both had to be. That's what really does it for me. Suck one, pinch the other until they're both singing with pain. So the harder I pushed into his face, the quicker he learned, the harder he bit and chewed and pinched, and the sharper my pleasure.

'Fuck me,' a woman howled, and it was me.

'Show me,' he grunted back.

I wanted him to go on and on sucking and biting my

47

tits, but I wanted his stiff cock in my cunt, too, feel it ramming up me. But somehow I still kept it slow. I wanted him to remember every single move.

I planted my knees on either side of his thighs so I was straddling him, still crushing his head between my tits, still making him suck. I wanted him to suck and suck for ever, except that soon I would come against his leg, grinding against him like some randy bitch and what sort of lesson would that be?

As my nipples burned and throbbed, I slithered down onto his stiff dick. If I wasn't careful he'd come like a bloody train, before I wanted him to. I ground myself onto him, my toy, my boy, sucking my tits as if they'd make him stronger. I tilted myself over him.

'See how beautiful it is,' I crooned at him, rising to show him his cock slicked with my juices. 'See how well it's going to fit.'

He let go of my nipples, letting them sing with pain in the cold air, and lay back, spreading his arms out lazily. His hair tangled across my duvet. He never seemed to stop grinning.

'Like I said. Fuck me like I know nothing, *mademoiselle.*'

I aimed the tip of his cock towards my bush, let it rest just there, but it nudged into my wet lips and I shuddered as each inch went in. He lay there and watched me. I pushed my breasts at him, for more sucking, but he watched me, and that made me so horny I wanted to scream. I started to move up and down, relishing the way my tits bounced just above his face, rubbing the nipples across his collar bone, his chest, to get the friction, but going wild with the way he was making me work for my pleasure.

I couldn't hold on to it for much longer, and I let him

slide up inside, all the way to the hilt. It was tempting to ram it, but once it was right in I forced myself away again.

'Make me fuck you!'

We'd both lost the power of language. Fuck was the only word we knew.

I moaned in answer, tossed my head back, and down I went onto him again, holding onto his hips so that he was in as I ground myself down on him.

He filled me. God, there were years of wild lovemaking ahead for him and any woman lucky enough to have him. I swung my breasts over his face, saw the blood rushing there, his mouth dropping open as we started to jerk frantically and rock together.

I pressed one nipple into his open mouth, moaned as he took it and sucked it, pushed harder so that he chewed and bit and pinched at the other, sucked me so hard that it made me whimper joyously with the blazing pain

I was riding him now, jacking up the rhythm, rocking up and down his cock. I needed to ease the urge to come, but of course that only made it worse and more intense and I was getting tighter and tighter, holding him like a vice and his cock was getting even harder, harder with each frantic thrust, ramming right up inside.

'Tell me I'm the best of all the guys you ever had,' he suddenly shouted, grabbing my hips and lifting me off him. 'Want to hear you say it.'

'Shut up and fuck me, Charlie.'

His nails dug into me. 'Tell me, you bitch, tell me I'm the best!'

'You're the best, baby,' I said. And I meant it. 'You're my boy. Young, gorgeous, well hung, strong, eager, dirty, fresh, obedient –'

Then I flicked myself so that his cock slipped up inside

again. I was trapping him inside me and going at him so that we were welded together, releasing him so that he could draw back, trapping again as he tensed his buttocks and thrust inside, throwing his head back, pulling my tits with his teeth, thrusting faster now and faster, hearing my own crackling gasps of pleasure as I came and he saw me coming and he laughed with disbelief as he tensed and hardened to bursting point and shot it up me.

I slumped forwards onto his chest and listened to the drumming of his heart. I thought my head was empty, but I heard myself say 'I wish I'd been the one to break you.'

His laugh rumbled under my ear. 'Make me, you mean.'

I got off him. I went to sit on the chair opposite, my legs spread sluttishly apart. Although I was spent I still fondled my sore nipples, keeping them hard.

People were restless downstairs, moving about in the hall. We heard our names. Slowly he got off the bed, packed his gorgeous cock away, opened my door, beckoned to me.

'Did you really tell the boys you'd fucked me?' I asked him. 'All my pupils?'

'It was my secret.' He shook his head solemnly. Then he really grinned. 'But wait till they hear about *this!*'

And they all watched us tumbling down the stairs together, giggling like school kids and flushed and ripped and dripping wet with sex.

'Ever wondered how I got to be so fluent in French, Mum?' Charlie said, sauntering over to the punch bowl and lifting the ladle.

'What you talking about?' Hilde absently tucked a corner of Charlie's tee shirt into his trousers. 'Lovely party by the way, Mary *liebe*.'

Poppy's jaw was dropping. Chloe was sulking. The

nephews were oblivious. The men were looking at me with eyes on stalks.

'Mademoiselle Mary taught me everything I know,' Charlie said, pulling me over to him, running his hand up my spine. 'And that's why, tomorrow, she's riding on my pillion all the way to Paris.'

Cougar

THE GALLERY DOMINATED ONE corner of the Meatpacking District, turning its chic facade disdainfully away from the wind blasting off the Hudson River and instead facing a huge Abercrombie and Fitch billboard of a naked male torso in monochrome. Up above, greenery trailed off the rusting steel struts of the old High Line.

'You take that photograph, Sophie?' Stella asked, draping an arm around Sophie's neck as they stared out of the huge window. 'Looks just your style.'

'Honey, if I had we'd all be millionaires.' Sophie tapped her fingernails on the glass. 'I wouldn't be criss-crossing the Pond like this selling my wares.'

'You make it sound like you're some kind of tinker.' Stella handed her old friend another glass of champagne. 'This is art, girl. Your art. You've been taking classy photographs since we left school. And at last people are starting to get it. You've made more money this evening than that wheeler dealer husband of yours makes in a month.'

'How do you know how much my Martin makes?'

Stella ran her tongue over her blood-red lips and winked. 'Pillow talk, darling. You know, a few years back when you had other fish to fry and you lent him to me that long hot summer?'

Sophie laughed. The kind of laughter that came very

close to tears. 'OK, fair enough. You're the only one who can knock some sense into him –'

'*Fuck* some sense you mean –'

'OK, enough already.' Sophie held her hands up in mock surrender. 'You're only allowed to borrow him when he's gone too far with this open marriage lark. When even I've had enough of fucking his friends.' Sophie stared again at the monochrome six-pack on the billboard opposite and the traffic lights swaying in the wind in front of it. 'When he's taken one mistress too far –'

'So you find some friends of your own to fuck.' Stella turned quickly away. Too quickly.

'Well, he's promised to abstain while I'm here. It's a test. A big test.'

'Oh, quit fretting. He'll be good as gold.' Stella was distracted. I could tell by the way she was tugging at her dress. 'But in the meantime you'll have to make do with me for company. See that young sales chappie at the back desk, there? The one who's been flogging your work all night and is now adding up all those lovely numbers? Those numbers equal your success, girl. Enjoy!'

She waved her hand at the few remaining punters padding quietly round the gallery, gazing thoughtfully at the images framed on the whitewashed walls. At the red dots in the corner of nearly half the frames.

'That reminds me,' said Sophie, glancing at her watch. 'Jake and Seb are meeting us a bit later at the Gramercy rooftop bar.'

'It was a shame they were too busy to pop by this evening to support you.'

'I forgive them. They're tycoons in the making –'

'Just like Daddy?'

'And they're taking you and me out for a slap-up meal

later!'

'Oh, they're good boys really.' Stella nodded vaguely, but she had that look in her eye. That Italian mumma look, like she wanted to eat something juicy for breakfast. 'But isn't he just the cutest?'

Sophie glanced over at the guy behind the desk. Daniele, the gallery owner, had jetted off somewhere, leaving his assistant in charge. But she'd not really noticed him once the party started. He was cute, sure, in a squeaky-clean kind of way. Sleek and groomed, but still young enough, she noticed, to cut himself shaving.

Stella licked her finger and smoothed down one unruly curl. 'He looks like a young, just discovered Brad Pitt, no? When he was about to fuck Thelma. Or was it Louise?'

Sophie slapped at her friend's bare arm. 'Thelma and Louise is right, doll. We're old enough to be his mothers!'

'You reckon he can handle two mothers?' Stella put her arm round Sophie's waist. 'Well, you're the Susan Sarandon one, whichever she was. You've got the hair and the eyes and the tits.'

'Yeah, I'm a dead ringer,' Sophie breathed, mirroring Stella's gesture as the young guy ushered the last remaining guests out of the gallery. 'But she wasn't the one who got fucked by a boy in cowboy boots, was she?'

The cuddle wasn't just for show. She loved Stella. She loved her big, warm body, her warped loyalty, and her filthy mind. The guy glanced at them as he flicked the spotlights off over the door to show the gallery was closed. Stella couldn't resist it. She slid her mouth across Sophie's pale cheek and let her tongue flick out, like a snake's, across the other woman's scarlet-painted lips.

'Which means he's mine.' Stella chuckled. Sophie parted her lips very slightly, almost reluctantly, keeping her eyes on the boy, and delicately sucked at the tip of Stella's tongue. Martin would be stunned. She squirmed against Stella's hip. 'Ooh, fuck, I'm horny. Look at him. Box fresh. And he's got that young boy's mouth, you know, all red and wet and glistening, like he's only just spat out the teat?' Stella moved away from Sophie and tipped her spine so that her big breasts swelled out of her low-cut black dress. She actually purred. 'Todd? Or is it Grant?'

The guy gulped. His hands flew up to the knot in his tie. 'Er, it's Matt, actually.'

'Talk about Bambi caught in the headlights! You've scared the poor baby out of his wits,' Sophie hissed as Stella strained at the leash. 'Forget Brad Pitt. Those glasses make him look like Clark Kent!'

'So, Matt darling.' Stella swayed across the polished wooden floor. She was in full Sophia Loren mode. I'd seen grown men – my husband, amongst others – go pale when she bore down on them like this. And I mean bore down. I knew her favourite position was on top, because I'd seen her in action, crushing them beneath her warm, curvy body, working up a sweat, clamping them between her strong brown thighs like some kind of Venus fly trap. Suffocating them between her breasts, pushing her huge dark nipples, elongated and stiff with desire, into their eager, sucking mouths. 'What are you doing after you lock up here tonight?'

The guy clicked his pen shut, stared straight at the huge breasts curving out of Stella's tight dress. He smoothed his silk tie down over his crisp white shirt, plucked his jacket closed.

'Have to go over these figures with Mrs Epsom.'

Stella stopped and flung her hands on her jutting hips, Carmen-style. 'Well, hush my mouth! You turning me down, boy?'

'Signor Tremelli told me to be sure to get the figures checked.' Matt glanced past her bare shoulder at Sophie. He licked his lips nervously. Just spat out the teat, huh? Sophie's stomach tightened. Good. It reminded her to suck it in. The dove grey Roland Mouret dress and these teetering red Laboutin heels took no prisoners, after all.

'Daniele Tremelli has spoken, Stella. So put him down!' Sophie exclaimed, flushing hot. The dress felt too tight now, pulling in around her breasts, squeezing her bottom so all you could do was wiggle. Stella swore under her breath. Matt scuttled back to the desk and held the accounts book in front of him like a shield. 'Go make yourself useful. Get yourself to the Gramercy Park and tell my sons I'll be a little late.'

'Fifty says you're so busy obsessing about that no-good husband of yours back home you won't have this lovely boy's cock out in half an hour.' Stella crooked a finger through the window and by magic a yellow cab stopped outside. 'It's your big night, after all, honey,' she called, swaying out of the door. 'So don't let me down!'

It was like Stella had sucked the life out of the room once she'd gone. Sophie couldn't breathe. She stared at Matt across the half-lit gallery.

'You've gone way over Daniele's projected target figures, Mrs Epsom,' Matt said, perching on the edge of the desk and swinging one long leg. 'It's all good news.'

'All down to you, Matt, seducing the clients.' Sophie murmured, coming closer and staring at his flushed cheek. 'So which is your favourite?'

'Favourite what?' He took his glasses off wearily and pinched the top of his nose. 'Client?'

She stood in front of him. A baby spot light was beaming straight down on to her head. Sweat trickled down her spine. God, her feet hurt.

She swallowed the rest of her champagne. 'No. Photograph.'

They both looked up at the huge signature photograph dominating the wall above the desk. It faced the door, the world, when you first came in to the gallery. The one they'd used for the all the press and publicity. The posters. The flyers.

'That one. It makes me want to come every time I look at it.'

She gasped with shocked laughter. It was like he'd touched a burning taper to her cunt. He blushed red. Sophie clamped her thighs, not difficult under that dress. Her legs rubbed together, and she felt a slick of dampness seeping out of her pussy. Of course! She'd gone commando, the way Martin liked her. The only way to go in a dress tight as a second skin.

The picture was of a silhouette against a shuttered Gothic window. A female spine arched, lifting a bare female bottom brazenly in the air. What looked like a long tongue, its bright red the only colour staining the picture, extending in from behind as if it was going to take a long, wet lick of a dripping ice cream.

Sophie shifted on those infernal heels and leaned forwards heavily across the desk. Matt laid the book open in front of her and stepped behind her to take a better look.

'Where did you take it? Who is the woman? Whose is the tongue?'

Sophie was in front of him. Leaning on the desk meant sticking her bottom out at him, but she was so tired. She wanted to kick off the shoes, but then again they tilted her in just the right position, almost in the same way as the naked figure in the photograph.

'I took it in Daniele's *palazzo* in Venice. He wanted a portrait of his daughter. You ever met Maria? She's ferocious. One of these *vestali,* these vigilantes who stalk round the city dressed in black combat gear hauling tourists over the coals for lowering the tone.'

'Is that her with the bottom stuck out, gagging to be licked out?' His voice was quiet but she heard him swallowing, right up close behind her. Sophie tilted her bottom towards him a little more. The dress, too tight to rise or fall, stuck to her, sucked in between her butt cheeks. The edge of the desk dug into her belly, just above her pussy. There was a slight stinging as the urge to pee nudged her, and her pussy twitched in response. She thought of Stella's challenge.

'Hers is the tongue. But it's all done very tastefully, don't you think?' She giggled softly. Tasteful was the word, as she recalled. Maria's was the first pussy she'd ever eaten. 'And the bottom, gagging, as you so charmingly put it, to be licked –' she swayed from side to side, her legs straining against the skyscraper heels, the dress holding her in, only just concealing her no-knickers, every movement turning her on. ' – is mine.'

'That makes you one horny cougar, Mrs Epsom!' The breath juddered out of him. 'Christ. Can't believe I just said that. Sorry!'

'Oh, I forgive you.' She swivelled round on her heels to face him. 'So what's a cougar? Other than a wild cat?'

'A word we use over here for an older woman.' He fiddled with his tie again. 'A sexy older woman. Mature, you know. Gorgeous. Sophisticated –'

'And?'

He couldn't take his eyes off her. 'Like Samantha in *Sex in the City*. Hungry. Voracious, in fact. Goes for much younger men.'

'Like my friend Stella, you mean? Although she's not fussy if he's old, young, fat, thin – Husbands, sons –'

'Maybe not as addicted as that.' He stopped fidgeting and the way he was looking at her calmed her down. 'She's basically a cougar if she stalks, you know, hunts – wants – someone much younger.'

'Does that go for a younger woman, too? Because you know, that's what's going on in this photograph.' Sophie let the tension sizzle in the air as she swung one sore foot. His hands moved from his tie down to rest on the desk close to her. 'But I don't know if I'm a cougar, really, Matt, because Maria there seduced *me*. 'She swung round to look at the photograph. 'I wonder how we can find out if I fit the profile.'

Even her voice didn't sound like her own. It was a hoarse whisper. Not surprising, wearing a dress tighter than a corset. And not surprising, when the way she was rubbing meant she was about to cream herself against the desk.

'If the cougar doesn't know if she is, I wonder how her young prey knows? Maybe you just suck it, and see.' He came up behind her and rested his hands on her hips, started moving them down towards the hem of her short dress. Sophie tensed up with shocked excitement. But then he stopped. 'Oh, Christ. I can't touch you – I can't do this. You're married. And I have to tell you something –'

'Sssh, no you don't. You should see what my husband gets up to. Nothing to tell. You can blame me for misbehaving.' Sophie tossed her hair back impatiently and kept moving her hips from side to side. 'I'm a big girl now.'

Suddenly the vision of Stella and Martin flickered like a movie in front of her. Why had it never bothered her before? She'd encouraged them to do it that summer, for God's sake. Stella's gleaming body, brown from all the sunshine, straddling her husband, those dancer's legs gripping him, his strong hands lifting those broad hips on to him, his mouth biting and sucking those enormous nipples, his cock sliding in, that familiar, sweet-smelling cock, the two of them moaning and sweating and chuckling, joined by old times. Something – determination? Daring? Desire? – coiled and burned inside her. 'Your girlfriend won't know. We're just talking. You're not doing anything wrong –'

'No, it's not that – don't have a girlfriend –' He groaned, with a boyish catch in his throat. 'It's just – they never told me you were like this. Such a horny bitch. Christ, sorry, I shouldn't speak to you like that –'

'Daniele spank you if he heard?'

'Yeah. No. Not just Daniele. Your husband. The others. They'd kill me –'

'Who? My husband?' I liked the idea of the others, whoever they were, warning him off.

'Fuck. No one. Just, I've had a hard on all evening, just watching you working the room.' His long, clean fingers fiddled and tugged at the dress, stroking over the fabric, not daring to go closer. 'Go on, tell me about Daniele's daughter –'

Sophie shivered with frustration.

'It's so hot in Venice in the summer you know. So sweaty. Not the best time for an assignment. Everyone's cranky. The canals stink. But Daniele's an old friend, and I was fed up with my husband, and I needed the money. Anyway, I was crawling around on this big four poster, sorting out my camera. I had no knickers on. Just like now.' She reached between her legs and ran her finger up her crack, easing open her throbbing pussy to show him.

It was already wet.

He groaned softly and stroked his fingers tentatively over hers, just where they were tickling her buttocks.

Sophie laughed.

'So I was on this bed, setting up the shoot, thought she was off striking a pose, when suddenly I felt a pair of hands behind me, pushing my skirt up.' Sophie wriggled. 'You can touch me if you like, Matt.'

He paused, and then pulled the dress higher over her legs, up towards her bottom.

'Maria was stroking my legs, between them, you know? Up towards my pussy.' Sophie waited. The words sounded so dirty in the silent, dark gallery. 'It tickled at first, and I laughed, and thought she was just playing, but then it was shocking, and electrifying. It was so fucking sexy, Matt, being touched for the first time, all secret in that magical place, by a beautiful young woman.' Outside cars occasionally swished past. The occasional footsteps on the pavement. Sophie let her head droop a little. 'And I've never told anyone. It's true. Not even Martin.'

'Hey, hey, it's OK, ' he crooned, as she knew he would, all manly and strong and horny as she confessed. Then, as she also knew he would, he begged, 'Don't stop talking.'

'OK,' Sophie whispered coyly. 'But it'll be more exciting if you touch me.'

And at last his fingers were treading up, into the warm crack of her bottom, spreading open the cheeks, and he was breathing heavily. She was hot with desire.

'She touched me there, just there. But then, Matt, something warm and slippery was in there, licking up my thighs, and it was her tongue! Lapping up my leg, slowly, like a cat, and just that was making my whole body shake, and then it touched my –' she closed her eyes and

61

swallowed. His fingers stopped, too. 'My pussy. The lips, you know. She was licking me just there.'

Matt pulled her legs further apart. He was handling her more roughly now, more impatiently. He brought one hand up to her pussy to spread everything open.

'You ever licked a girl, Matt?' Sophie bit her tongue, tasting blood, and flushed hot red. The words hissed round the quiet gallery. Round this quiet corner of the city. It felt as if they were the only people in the world. Suddenly it felt weird, strange. She tried to close her thighs, straighten to get her balance on the high heels. 'Sorry. No. We should go. Christ, what am I like –'

'Fucking sexy, that's what you're like!'

Matt's voice was thick with lust. He kicked her legs open again and pressed her down so that she was lying flat on the desk, her cheek jammed against its smooth metal. Thank God she'd worked out before coming out to New York. Her legs would look long and taut from where he was standing.

'So what did she do next, this dykey Maria? How did she do it?'

Sophie couldn't breathe properly. She was squashed against the desk and the dress was like a strait jacket imprisoning her ribs.

'She licked me like a little cat –' It came out as a kind of death rattle. 'She licked me, and she made me come.'

'That's all I need.' He yanked her cheeks apart, stretching the skin so that it felt hot and raw. 'So that's what I'm going to do.'

The world shrank round Matt and Sophie, all focus on her cunt, bare, exposed there, throbbing like lit kindling. She was light-headed from lack of air. Humiliated, sprawled there like a dolly. And so, so dirty.

Sophie went tight inside as she felt first his fingers,

then his tongue, probing. Stella said he looked like he'd just spat out the teat. Well, he'd grown up a whole lot in the last five minutes. That fifty bucks was hers. She strained greedily towards him as he blew over her pussy lips, making them tingle, then started licking. She wriggled and gasped, spittle trickling from her mouth onto the desk as his tongue flicked at her clit.

'Oh, fuck!' she groaned, jumping and writhing.

'Just like the picture,' he sighed, with his mouth full.

She was stiff with desire now. His tongue started to circle round her clit, making it stand out and burn. She jerked frantically, but he held her still, his breath rasping against her skin. Then he closed his lips around the bud and sucked mercilessly so that tiny ripples of fire sizzled through her. The pressure was building. She started to grind herself against his face, to force him to lick faster and harder, and he nipped and bit until she squealed.

'Your pussy tastes so good.' Matt sucked and lapped, savouring her juices, and she pushed her bottom into his face. Sensations radiated through her but she wanted more now. And he knew it, because he pushed his tongue right inside, fucking her with it. Then his fingers thrust in. She could feel her cunt closing round everything like a little pulsating fist, and her knees gave way, weak with pleasure.

There were footsteps hurrying along the street outside. The crazy thought occurred that Daniele, or Stella, or any of the clients, or heaven forbid, one of her sons, could be rushing back to find her. But the footsteps hurried past. Sophie's body relaxed into the moment.

Matt pulled away to hoist her upright again, slamming her down against the desk, and the change in movement and rhythm altered the gear. Cold air rushed between them. There was a tense silence. She was more distracted than she realised. She blushed hot again, and tried to push herself up.

'Matt, darling, I really have to go. My sons –'

'Don't talk about them. Don't dare stop me now.'

She thought she heard the clicking of heels again on the pavement, but then he was undoing his trousers. Isn't the sound of a zipper the sexiest? Yanked angrily down the front of neat tailored trousers, the promise of the hard beast that's going to thrust itself out of there. The pause before the storm. He put his hand on her back again, more gently this time, then he was cupping her bush to lift her towards him, running his fingers down the slick wet crack. His knee pushed her legs open and then, oh God, there was the rigid length of his big hard cock pressing between her cheeks, rubbing itself up and down, those cute buttocks of his clenching to thrust himself against her, turning himself on.

'This is what you've done to me, Mrs Epsom. Now I guess this really makes me a mother fucker – and you're the mother I'd like to fuck.'

And there it was. His gorgeous young cock, banging at her for attention. How is it that no matter how many cocks you see or know, a new one, pulled out in the naughtiest of situations, is the biggest thrill of all?

Sophie gripped the far edge of the desk as if it was the bucking deck of a ship or a tipping raft as he lifted her bottom up to get at her, just like in the picture, and then with no more fuss or frills young Matt tilted her hips, opened her up, and pushed his cock into her, her sweet juices and his salty lick making it easy and then he was in and thrusting hard, pushing her across the desk, hurting her arms and chest. She had to lift her face to stop it scraping and her legs started to melt apart and falter off the heels as he went at her.

'Oh Christ, Matt, someone's out there!'

There was definitely something, voices, laughter, outside. She thought she heard the glass door rattle in the sharp wind.

'So they see the famous photographer at work, that's all! Perfectly posed, spot lit in front of the masterpiece.' He laughed hoarsely, all masterful now and yanking her hard so that his cock sank in up to the hilt. 'Now work with me, Mrs Epsom. Let me fuck you.'

And so he did, hard and rough across the desk, driving her onto spikes of pleasure and beyond as he fucked her and now she definitely heard laughter out there and saw something, a movement framed in the window, hands, mouths, eyes, watching.

'Better stop!' she practically sobbed as someone tapped gently on the glass.

'Not a fucking snowball's hope in hell!' he groaned, warm fingers gripping her, yanking her against him again and again as his hot cock pumped into her.

They'd see her white thighs parted, the dress up round her waist, Matt in his suit pulling back to fuck her, his cute butt thrusting rapidly like a dog, pushing her roughly across the desk, her throat arched with pleasure, his hands gripping her. They'd get wet or hard watching.

Matt's cock pushed on until she was burning with excitement. She slammed against him. And then he held her hips totally still, forcing them to pause again.

'Sexy mother,' he murmured. He pulled out the pins in her hair and messed it up, then smoothed it against her back as if she was a horse. Her body jolted with pleasure. Then he started thrusting violently, ramming hard, lifting her off the desk with the force of it.

She let myself go limp, enjoyed his youthful power, let him fuck her, felt the desk edge jamming into her belly, felt the pleasure expanding, thick, deep inside. His cock rammed faster and faster into her hot, tightening pussy. Someone laughed, and then so did Sophie, laughter and her thoughts scattering as she started to come, arching her back in a beautiful, perfect pose, shaking and moaning as Matt thrust into her from behind and with two more thrusts he came, shuddering and silent.

They stayed in position, stiff like dancers, Matt gripping her hips so as not to slip out and waste a single drop. His cock stayed hard. There was another pause, and then he lifted his hands away from her.

There was a ruffle of conversation outside, and then a ripple of applause. Matt pulled her dress down and held her against him. Pussy juice trickled down her legs as they stayed silent and at last the watchers moved away down the street.

She could feel his young heart hammering in his crisp white shirt. Idly she glanced at her watch.

'Christ! I'm late!'

Sophie turned, kissed that gorgeous mouth, and burst through the door into the street, empty now, and yanking her tight dress halfway back down she ran as fast along the sidewalk as her heels, and the stickiness squeaking between her legs, would allow. Behind her Matt was shouting something, but she relished that brief Cinderella moment, and the urge, suddenly, to show Martin what she'd done, too much to look behind.

She was born to stalk about in a place like this, sipping Watermelon Mint Martini, heavy on the Reyka vodka. The Manhattan sky was tinted violet, lights sparking around, above, far away. Below the terrace the trees in Gramercy Park whispered.

A few glossy people entered and drank and mingled

66

under the chandelier installation inside, laughing beneath a froth of glass bubbles, but out here there was no one. Sophie gave herself ten seconds out to relish the soreness of her cunt, fucked raw by young matinee idol Matt.

Her three sons and Stella were waiting, perched on blue velvet stools. Rickie, her eldest, and Stella looked oddly chaotic. He had lipstick on his neck, and her dress was only half zipped at the back.

'You look a million dollars, Mum,' said Rickie, handing her a flute of champagne. 'I hear the show nearly sold out?'

'Yeah, and talking of a million dollars,' she winked at Stella. 'You owe me fifty.'

Jake peered at her. 'You look feverish. Like, really flushed!'

'Matt not with you?' Seb looked over my shoulder.

Her heart lurched. 'Matt? How do you know –?'

'Great! Here he is now! Hi mate! You made our mum rich tonight?'

The boys high-fived and back-slapped him and here he was, walking towards her, neat as a pin, hand outstretched, her all-American boy.

'Hello again, Mrs Epsom.' He took her hand and kissed it. God, that tongue! The boys all whooped and elbowed each other. Stella was having a hard time keeping a straight face. 'Didn't the boys tell you?' Matt said, stepping away but grinning as if he owned her. 'We're all roommates.'

Behind the Scenes

CORPORAL PUNISHMENT MIGHT BE outlawed in school these days, but Mrs Caroline March, *commandant*, sorry, chair of the entertainment committee, was extremely skilled at slapping wrists. Not the kids' wrists. God forbid that she would ever put a patent leather toe out of line. No. It was the mothers who got the treatment. The dirty look, the brittle phone call. Being sent to Coventry. The flounce. And their crime? Oh, buying cakes instead of baking them. Refusing to high-kick and wave pompoms on sports day. Wriggling out of the activity weekend in Snowdonia.

Sara Singer had the reddest wrist. She might have been the most beautiful mother in the playground, but she was also the most idle and after endless pleading, cajoling and bullying, Caroline had no more truck with her. Until one steamy summer day near the end of term, staggering out of the town library with a stack of gardening books for the allotment club, she spotted Sara in the new art gallery next door. The lazy mare who claimed to be too ham-fisted to sew flamenco costumes for the dance committee's 'Strictly Classroom' competition was straddling a ladder, bold as brass, and deftly hanging a picture.

Caroline pressed her nose up against the window and watched as Sara stretched up to thread wire over the nails screwed into the wall. Her short summer dress rode up over her long brown legs. She cocked a knee on the next rung to steady herself, and Caroline saw a flash of bright pink thong, caught between two peachy buttocks.

Caroline's mouth dropped open. She was about to rap on the glass to stop the show, the *striptease* virtually, but Sara was so unaware as she moved about in there, all alone, showing her bottom to the world, if the world cared to look. So nonchalant. Caroline glanced round. The world hadn't seen. But she had. She could see her reflection in the window, goggle-eyed and gaping.

Sara bent slightly on the ladder and Caroline could see daylight glimmering between the tops of her legs and right through the gap to the neat bulge of her sex lips. Caroline felt her own pussy twitch sharply.

'Shit!' Caroline gasped, totally unladylike. Good thing the other mothers couldn't hear. 'Fuck!'

The silk gusset of her expensive French knickers felt sticky as a little dampness seeped in, pricking at the tender skin of her freshly waxed snatch. Sweat, surely. It was like she and Sara Singer shared a secret. Her breath steamed on the glass as she went on staring up Sara's flowery dress like a brazen schoolboy, at the way the thong sliced the darkness between those cheeks, the way the plump flesh wobbled slightly as Sara climbed another step to balance the frame. Even her butt was brown. Where did she sunbathe to get a tan like that, Caroline wondered? When did she have time? Was her garden sheltered from the neighbours' prying eyes? But now Sara was tilting her bottom, thrusting it out and away from the ladder as she absently reached a finger right into her crack to tug at the sliver of pink cotton caught up there.

Caroline jumped away from the window, dropping her books. Sara later remarked that she looked like she'd been stung. But back then Caroline always had the look of a woman chewing wasps.

Sara twisted round at the commotion. When she saw Caroline staring at her, out on the pavement, she frowned. But she didn't rush to smooth down her dress to hide the tiny pink triangle barely covering her crotch. Didn't come down the ladder. From here it looked as if, as usual, Caroline March was eyeing her with disapproval. So she slowly raised a hand to scrape her red hair away from her hot face, thereby lifting her dress even higher so that now Caroline could see the outline of her sex lips under the shiny pink cotton, God, even the sharp cleft dividing them. The thong was much too tight, that was the problem. It would be painful rubbing up there, chafing in this heat against that wet, soft surface. Caroline ran her tongue over her lips, which felt like paper. Sara must have borrowed that thong – surely only teenage girls wore such ridiculous garments –

Sara was crooking her finger to beckon Caroline inside.

'So, Sara, you look busy?' Caroline shouldered open the door and hovered on the step. The sun was hot on her back. The pile of books dug into her breasts. Her armpits in her floaty empire top were itchy with sweat. She swallowed and glanced at the huge pictures hung about in the clean white space. 'Didn't realise you worked here?'

'I don't.' Sara jumped down off the ladder. Her dress floated up for a moment, revealing one last glimpse of tanned thighs and more, a last flash of that cute, pouting fanny. 'I'm just hanging my exhibition.' She perched on the ladder, crossing one leg over the other.

The pictures were nearly all nudes. Glorious, spread-eagled nudes in mostly charcoal and chalk but with a gentle burst here and there of watercolour. Some were half obscure, backs turned, some full frontal, all sexy, but

70

all tasteful, Caroline could see. Even the huge one dominating the back wall, of an impossibly gorgeous naked man approaching a supine woman from behind, lifting her hips towards him –

'But you're so talented!' Caroline could make out the unmistakeable shape of the man's cock jabbing at the shadows as he lifted the sleeping woman, steadied himself on his knees as if his hard-on was knocking him off balance, ready to ease himself between her legs, ready to fuck her –

'Who knew?' Sara laughed softly, coming to stand beside Caroline. She smelt of fresh laundry and turpentine. 'See now why I've no time for fun runs or tombolas?'

'My God, Sara!' Caroline tossed her glossy hair. 'Surely it's illegal to depict a stiff, you know, penis, in a state of arousal like that, even for the sake of art?'

'Well, is it a thing of beauty or isn't it?' Sara placed her finger on her chin in a thinking pose. 'Don't we all love the sight of pliant, female haunches about to be pulled open and penetrated by a strong, horny male?'

'This is too weird. The way you're talking. I've got to go. Got to read up about seed planting.' Caroline backed towards the door. 'I always had you down as, you know. Innocent.'

Sara laughed, and held the door open. Her arm rested across Caroline's shoulders for a moment. Brown skin against pale bones. 'And I always had you down as frigid, Caroline. But seeing you creaming yourself just now in front of my pictures I know different, don't I?'

Caroline winched her shoulder away from Sara's touch. They had never stood so close to each other before. Or stayed so still in the hustle of the playground. Sara had freckles sprinkled over the bridge of her nose. Caroline stuck her own nose in the air.

'No, Sara Singer, I'm interested, that's all. Because I've just found the person who's going to paint the gypsy backdrop for our ballroom show.'

'Strictly Boring, you mean!' Sara snorted.

Quick as a flash Caroline's fingers were smacking down on Sara's wrist. They both looked down as two red streaks came up on her tanned skin.

Sara's green eyes glittered. 'I'll get you for that, Mrs March.'

'Brownie points, Sara. Just think of those brownie points!'

Her friend Marta, a genuine Spaniard in genuine frills, clacked her castanets. 'And she did barge into the private view of your exhibition and persuade all those hedge fund daddies to buy, buy, buy –'

'*Si, si, signora*!' Sara said with a sigh, hooking a tambourine over the spit of a makeshift fire. 'But this scene setting will never be finished. It's *opening* night, for God's sake –'

'Which is why we need to lace up your dress, Sara. You look like a cheap whore with it all falling off your shoulders like that.' Caroline was standing in the wings, one hand on her jutting hip. The other held an open bottle of sherry.

Sara flicked her previously smacked paw at her and turned her back.

'And you look splendid, Caroline! Quite the Spanish matriarch with that towering mantilla headdress!' Marta snatched the bottle and had a swig. 'And that ferocious cleavage!'

'Did you hear me about the dress, Sara? You may as well try to look the part –'

'What part?' Sara dipped an oversized paintbrush into a barrel. 'I'm behind the scenes, Caroline, slaving away, not doing the fandango out front! No one will see me!'

'You have to take a bow on the night. For all your hard work.'

'Yes, Sara!' Marta stamped dramatically about, lifting her scarlet petticoats and drumming her heels on the wooden boards. She handed Sara the sherry. 'You'll be an absolute siren all corseted up like a fiery Carmen!'

Sara took a swig, relishing the warmth surging through her brain, and climbed with the bottle onto a flaking Romany caravan to splash green paint onto its shutters.

'There's your intro, Marta!' Caroline waved her large lace fan towards the stage, where the local equivalent of the Gypsy Kings was strumming sly, sensual guitar chords. 'Break a leg!'

'*Ole*!' shrieked Marta, cantering out of sight to face her public.

'Right, now stop nagging, Caroline, and leave me to finish this painting –'

'Behave yourself, Sara! Just let me lace you up.'

Caroline had climbed up the wooden steps behind her. She pulled Sara roughly backwards so that she fell against her. Marta was right. Caroline did have a ferocious cleavage. Sara could feel it, pressing soft and warm against her shoulder blades. She could also feel Caroline's breath, hot against her neck. The music out front was getting faster, and louder. Some of the staff, wheeled out to watch the rehearsal, were clapping naffly in time. But back here, tucked in the corner of the back stage, there was a kind of frenzied silence. Sara couldn't move. Caroline's warm breasts were squashed against her bare back, rubbing from side to side, so slightly that she must be imagining it, but she could hear Caroline's breathing, hard and fast, as she started tugging closed Sara's plunging black bodice. The whalebone closed in tight around her ribcage, squeezing her breasts together, forcing them up and out, nearly falling over the lace edging.

Sara's heart started a low, fast drumming of its own. She felt light-headed from lack of air, her ribs refused to move as she struggled to breathe, so she had to open her mouth. As her lips parted twinges of excitement zigzagged through her. Her breasts bulged and pushed to escape, scraping her nipples over the rim of the bodice until they were sore.

Caroline took hold of her cinched-in waist and swivelled her round, so fast that she nearly lost her balance. Her skirts rustled, the net petticoats scratching her bare thighs. Caroline's ice blue eyes were smudged in thick dark shadow and outlined like a cat's with exaggerated black eye-liner. Her normally pastel-frosted lips were blood red and glistening as her tongue slipped out and ran over her mouth.

'You wearing that pink thong today, Sara?' Her voice, normally a kind of haughty bray, came from somewhere else tonight, deep and hoarse. She bit her lip. 'Whoops.'

They both stared at each other. Then down at the way their breasts were pressed up against each other, bouncing with each laboured heartbeat in time to some sort of tom-tom out front. Caroline's arms were still round Sara's waist and as she yanked her close, one of Sara's breasts bulged and fell heavily over the edge of her bodice, the nipple impossible to ignore, burning red and raw, stiffening in the cool air.

'Christ, Caroline, what are you like!' Sara's voice wavered out as a gasp. Confused, she tried to push her breast back in and at the same time knocked Caroline with her elbow and sent her sprawling backwards through the stable door. Her ankle in the high heeled dancing shoes twisted and she tumbled in a flurry of scarlet petticoats onto a pile of paint-spattered sacking.

Sara clapped her hand over her mouth. Caroline March, chairperson and parent *extraordinaire,* was flat on her back in a dusty old caravan, tangled amongst the props for her precious dancing show, black stockinged legs akimbo, one shoe off and one wrist bound by some nautical looking rope Sara reckoned looked suitable for harnessing the imaginary horses.

'You little bitch!' Caroline started struggling with the rope, kicking her legs and getting even more tangled. 'Get me out of here! I'm stuck!'

'God, I'm sorry, Caroline. Don't know my own strength. Come on. Let's get you up–'

She knelt down, hitched her skirts back, and started to crawl over Caroline's legs to untangle her. Caroline tugged weakly at the rope round her wrist, struggled a bit, then lay still and started to laugh softly. Her eyes gleamed at Sara under the theatrical make up. Her tongue came out again, sliding over her wet mouth.

'No, let's not. Let's stay right here, where no one can see us. I've been wanting to tell you –' There was that growl again, deep and sexy. She lay back, tossing her head from side to side, and arching her back, thrusting her big breasts up, one hand snaking over them and down her tight bodice to start pulling up her petticoats. 'I saw your pink thong in the gallery the other day, Sara. And your bottom. So gorgeous I wanted to bite it.'

'Too much sherry, Mrs March!' Sara yelped, face flaming. 'I can't believe you just said that!'

'Nor can I! You're a bad influence, Mrs Singer.' Caroline didn't look pissed. She looked as if she was in heaven. She kept her eyes on Sara, smiling her rare smile and shifting from side to side, parting her long legs, her thighs white above the stockings, her bottom rolling, squashing against the paint spattered blanket, lifting to show the black seam between her white buttocks.

Sara froze, hanging there on all fours. Her breasts swelled, and tumbled out of the bodice again. Her sensitive nipples shrank tight in the cool air and a thrill shivered through her.

Out on stage, they were doing the rumba.

'So are you, Sara Singer?' Caroline hooked her leg around Sara's back, tango-style, and pulled her lower. Her tongue was flicking back and forth with obvious pleasure. She tried to sit up, and started running her free hand under Sara's skirt, up her thigh. 'Wearing that pink thong?'

Sara leaned closer. 'No, I'm not, Mrs March.' Caroline was staring at her mouth, trailing her fingers over Sara's buttocks, tickling up the tiny hairs all over her skin. Sara shivered again, and now it was her turn to whisper. 'I'm not wearing anything.'

There was a short burst of applause and some wisecracks from one of the 'judges'.

'So you aren't.' Caroline's hand spread over Sara's pussy. She pushed herself up, paused, then brushed her red lips across Sara's. Sara stopped breathing. She closed her eyes. Christ, should she stop this, give Caroline a slap? But she couldn't move. Saliva was gathering in her mouth. Caroline's fingers were stroking at the crack between her butt cheeks, pushing them gently open, probing the damp warmth just as her tongue pushed between Sara's lips, running over the tender, tickling lining.

Then, as their kissing became more passionate, Caroline pushed one finger gently against Sara's tight closed arse hole. Sara tried to wriggle away but the finger followed her movements, and as it pushed further she went weak. This sensation was totally new to her. It should have disgusted her, but instead it was overwhelmingly dirty and gorgeous. She sucked greedily on Caroline's tongue as her hot little hole gave a little to Caroline's probing finger, teased like a tight little cunt as it opened slightly. It was shocking but delicious and her body started trembling as lust sliced through her.

Then, without warning, Caroline pushed the finger right in and up Sara's arse

'You filthy –!' Sara flinched away, breaking the spell, and pushed Caroline back down on the floor of the caravan, her legs waving in the air, and smacked her, hard, on the rump. The sharp sound reverberated round the old wooden walls. 'That's for touching me up, Caroline. For touching me there. Christ, that's for everything, actually! All your bloody bossiness!' Sara couldn't help it. She smacked her again. The prime, tender flesh rippled under her hand. She waited for Caroline to scream back at her, but instead she sighed sensuously and squealed girlishly. Not a sound any of the mummies had heard before. A livid pink hand print came up like a stain on Caroline's bottom. Sara felt power surging through her. A hot bolt of evil pleasure.

'Now look what you made me do!'

'I'm sorry, Sara!' Caroline whimpered, wriggling furiously on the old sheets. Her thighs slapped open and closed as she rubbed herself frantically against the rough fabric. 'You'll need to keep punishing me. Please smack me again!'

'That's better. Start feeling a little humility, lady.' Sara grabbed one of Caroline's ankles and without really thinking, lashed it with some ribbon round the leg of the little built-in table.

'Oh, I'm not a lady.' Caroline's voice was all husky. Sara's stomach clenched up with excitement. 'I'm a filthy little tart!'

'That's right, Caroline. A filthy little slut who needs a good slapping,' Sara murmured, and smacked her hand down again, loving the sharp sound ringing out in the tight little room, loving Caroline's responding yelp. The strange new power bunched up inside her, dark pleasure spiking right at her cunt, making it throb with desire. Caroline wriggled. Again Sara slapped, watching Caroline jerk, then slapped again. 'So keep totally still, filthy little tart, otherwise they'll hear you and then we're both in trouble.'

Out front the hip-wiggling salsa started. Caroline went rigid, exaggeratedly obeying orders.

'I'm a tart, because I stuck my finger up your arse, Sara, and I shocked you,' she said into the thick silence as the Spanish music swelled in the distance. 'Come here. I want to put it up your juicy cunt this time, finger fuck you hard up there –'

'You want the other mummies to know you talk like a back-street whore?'

Caroline smiled, and started stroking Sara's leg again. Sara's pussy went tight with ridiculous longing. 'Don't care. I'm sick of being good. You can tell them what you like!'

Sara was really struggling now. Caroline looked so sexy, writhing about there, her skirt right up round her waist now so Sara could see her flimsy silk knickers. 'No. You'll do what I want, Caroline. Not the other way round.' Sara smacked her hard again and shoved one knee between Caroline's legs.

'Anything, Sara. I'll do anything you want. Just let me

kiss you. Just let me touch you up there.' Caroline licked her lips and strained to sit up again. Even with one arm and one leg tied up, she was in charge. The husky voice, the spread legs, the fussy dress all rucked up. 'Untie me, and I'll show you what I can do.'

She was strong, and quick, and then she was kissing Sara again. Now her tongue was pushing inside, licking inside, sucking Sara's tongue until Sara groaned and fell down on top of her. Her pussy was aching now as she felt Caroline's breasts squashed beneath her. She lifted them roughly out of the bodice and kneaded them, rubbed them against her own bare tits, hard nipple against hard nipple.

'This what lesbians do, Caroline?' she whispered as they sucked greedily on each other's mouths, tasting sherry and coffee and wet saliva.

'No idea,' gasped Caroline, putting her free hand up to Sara's pussy and running one finger down the warm wet crack. 'Never done this before.'

Sara shivered as Caroline's finger caught on her swollen clit and then started to rub it, hard. Sara could feel her excitement pulsing, not far off. She wanted to open her legs wide and let Caroline make her come. The climax of the first act was approaching out there, Marta's professional flamenco. After that would be some judging and marks and they would all be piling off backstage for the interval.

Sara forced herself to pull away but Caroline just milked her hesitation by lifting her skirt right up and ripping away her knickers. She fixed Sara with those alien, painted eyes and spread her thighs, showing Sara her waiting pussy, the dark red slit shining between her legs. Sara crawled nearer and touched Caroline's legs. Her skin was so warm. Sara pushed her fingers up towards the pale sex lips and tangled them in the strip of soft blonde bush left there. Her own pussy was so wet she could hear the lips kissing each other as she moved.

'You going to smack me again? I do hope so!' Caroline bit the finger which had just been stroking Sara's clit, then licked it. 'Mm, tastes so good. Ever tasted yourself? Or another woman?'

Sara felt like she'd been electrocuted. She unzipped her skirt and flung it to one side. Her pussy was soaking now, and desperate, and she could smell her own horny scent.

She pulled Caroline's thighs further apart, saw the sex lips opening to show the vivid red promise of her cunt and without thinking she leaned right in and nudged the tip of her nose, forcing the lips further open, feeling the warm wetness on her face. A ripple of delicious shock went through her to smell the other woman's female scent. This must be what animals in the jungle do – but do the females go round sniffing each other's bottoms? Never occurred to her before. Forget the jungle. The scenario right here, in this daft little caravan, was enough to fill her with a special kind of madness. Christ, they were only a few metres away from all those worthies out in the school hall!

So what? Caroline's sex felt like slippery silk against Sara's nose. She was getting drunk on the smell of her. Caroline lifted herself up and there it all was, on a plate. Sara let her tongue swipe over the crack, sliding it over the red frilled slit, feeling Caroline tense and shiver as she swept her tongue once, twice up over the furls of her sex, tasting the salty sweetness, feeling the bump of the little clit standing up in there. She pushed the palm of her hand against her own pussy, rubbed one finger against her own clitoris, everything contracting and squeezing urgently to come, now, straight away. She snatched her hand away again, too soon, too soon, started lapping again at Caroline, lapping like a cat, making Caroline March twitch and groan with every stroke.

'I thought you'd be up for it, if I just found the right time,' groaned Caroline, pushing herself against Sara's mouth. 'Though maybe not the right place –'

Sara jerked away, angry at the interruption. Caroline pouted at her. 'Don't stop, Sara! You're a natural. So good –'

Sara bit her lip, tasting blood. She turned Caroline roughly on to her side, and slapped her hard on the bottom. 'For speaking you get punished. No more licking.'

'Please, Sara! I'm creaming myself here! Lick me, lick me!'

'You're here for my pleasure, remember! And you need to be punished.'

Caroline moaned and writhed, pushing her wet cunt up towards Sara. Sara wanted so much to lick it, to finger herself, to come with just a couple of flicks, but she was also enjoying this naughty game. She listened to the music out there, drowning for the moment the sounds of her slapping and Caroline's moans. Her challenge was to keep this going until the flamenco competition ended.

'Anything, anything,' Caroline moaned.

Sara smiled as a thought occurred to her. She reached into the bag she'd stuffed all her own clothes into, and brought out, yes, her pink thong. She feasted her eyes for a moment on Caroline, who was now shamelessly fingering herself, fanning her fingers over her pussy to open the lips, poking one long finger up inside, closing her white thighs over her hand, trapping it there until it had made her come. Quick as a whip she grabbed Caroline's free hand and lashed it to the other one, above her head.

'You wanted to know about my thong? Well, I have it right here.'

Caroline giggled, her eyes closed. Sara stretched the thong so that it was a taut string, then she knelt down on Caroline's thighs to hold them open and then holding each end of the thong-rope sliced it quickly up Caroline's slit. Caroline arched her back, pulling and tugging at the restraints, tipping herself upwards, offering herself desperately.

Sara scraped the thong down hard, knowing that it would be slicing right over the sensitive clit and all the flesh surrounding it, scraping at the most tender parts. She wished she could see better. In this semi-darkness she couldn't see how the pain would be turning Caroline's clit a brighter red. She started rubbing her makeshift prop up and down the other woman's cunt, faster and faster, thrilling to see Caroline bucking and writhing about on the scruffy floor, her elbows and knees flexing, her throat and back arching, her mouth open, tongue extended like a cat yawning.

And Sara was shocked to find that her own pleasure was rooted in inflicting just enough pain, that Caroline obviously wanted to be hurt, her squeals were turning into screams, but there was no fear there, just ecstasy, and Sara couldn't get over the way her own body was convulsing in response.

Caroline's screams were getting higher and louder. This was like being in a film, like watching someone else, another Sara Singer torturing a voluptuous naughty sex slave behind the scenes of the school show. Someone with no inhibitions whatsoever, the Sara she secretly must be. She couldn't hold her own climax much longer.

She yanked the thong away from Caroline, who

howled in animal anger and started trying to rub herself frantically against the sheets, opening and shutting her legs, to finish herself off. Sara balled up the thong and stuffed it into Caroline's mouth, enough to muffle her noise. Still Caroline wouldn't stop jerking about. The only way to stop her was to sit on her. She settled herself astride her slave, but as her over-heated pussy met Caroline's warm skin she nearly came there and then. She started rubbing her wet pussy against Caroline's legs, the other woman's body arousing her to madness. Now it was Sara who couldn't keep still. She crawled over Caroline, spread herself over her, pressed her breasts against Caroline's as she rolled every inch of her over every inch of the semi-naked Caroline, on she moved, crawling up until their faces were close. Caroline wasn't moaning so hard now that Sara had stopped with the friction.

'You want me to take the thong out?' she whispered. 'You promise to be quiet? They'll all hear you, if you go on mewling like an alley cat. They'll hear and they'll all troop out to see what's going on, and I'll show them where you are. They'll see you, tied up and spread-eagled, your cunt all red and wet and ready like you're a hooker ready for a gang bang, and who knows, maybe some of the daddies might like to have a go –'

They both grinned at each other, liking that idea. Sara hooked the thong out and Caroline's tongue flickered out at her. 'Time to let me go, Sara?'

'Oh, no. I haven't come yet.'

'But you just said, they'll be finished soon. They'll all see –'

Sara shook her head. 'They won't know you're in here, if I don't show them. I could keep you tied up in here all night. How about that? My slave, in her gypsy caravan, tied up here for my delectation. And anyone else's pleasure, come to that.'

'I want you, Sara, badly, but –'

'You started this, Caroline. You want me to gag you again?' She could hear her voice, thick with desire as she groped for what she did want.

'No, Sara. It tasted good, the thong. Tasted of you. And we can do this some more. Tonight. At my house! We can finish this properly, in comfort, in my Jacuzzi or my bed. Just let me go –'

Sara looked at Caroline's mouth. Now it was her turn to groan as she crawled up until her knees were either side of Caroline's face, her pussy inches above her mouth. 'First lick me, Mrs March. Lick me until I'm screaming as loud as you were.'

She lowered herself to sit on Caroline's face. Not squashing her, but hovering as best she could, feeling Caroline's warm breath on her bottom. And then the licking started. Soft, almost feathery caresses over her pussy lips, which pulsed quietly, and here was the wet tip of Caroline's tongue flicking up the crack then smoothing itself flat over the swollen lips.

Sara's head was spinning. She listened to the wild gypsy music, the applause, the laughter, imagined those faces if they could see Caroline pleasuring her behind the scenes, the adults leaving their seats, peering into the caravan to see Sara Singer's thighs spread over Mrs March's face, her white face jerking up and down between Sara's tanned thighs, her red tongue slurping at Mrs Singer's cunt.

Sara spread her legs wider, opening herself to more intense pleasure, moaning and straining as Caroline's tongue lapped faster, and then Sara wondered how often Caroline had done this before, who with, who in the parents' committee had she licked, and the thought of it turned her on even more, images flashing in her head, music and applause loud in her ears, sensations sizzling in her cunt as Caroline's mouth sucked at her while her tongue probed, forcing its way further in to her pussy like a cock, then pulling back so that Sara ground herself harder into Caroline's face, feeling her nose pushing above her pubic bone, into her bladder and now the sensation to piss started building as well and she thought she would go mad with excitement.

Now it was Caroline who was back in charge, torturing her as her tongue flicked mercilessly at Sara's clitoris, then started to encircle it.

Sara couldn't help it. She started to jerk frantically. She was on fire now, her clit burning, the waves building, her thighs shaking with the effort of holding her, and oh God now she was sucking again and again, so mercilessly. Sara rocked back and forth, opening her legs still wider to make a proper feast for Mrs March.

She could hear Caroline's saliva as she slurped on Sara's pussy juice and pushed her tongue right up, harder and harder, sliding over the clit as it thrust in and out. Sara rocked faster, her cunt and lips and clit rubbing against Caroline's tongue and nose and chin, her hips bucking more wildly.

The applause started to die away. Chairs were scraped back. Instruments packed into cases. No footsteps yet. Voices grew from murmurs to almost shouting to be heard. Caroline worked Sara to a final frenzy, her mouth and tongue lapping frantically. Here it came. Sara drew her hips back in a final glorious convulsion and her cunt, her whole body drew in on itself, grew tight as she moaned and started to come, pushing herself into Caroline's face, smearing her juices all over her, rubbing herself on and on over her face until long after the climax had faded.

At last she eased herself away, smoothed her petticoats down and stood up. Caroline's face and make up was all smeared now, with sweat and with Sara's juices, the lace mantilla all askew.

'What about me, Sara?' she whimpered, shivering from frustration and the cold. She pulled weakly at the ties, 'It's my turn to come. Or let me go.'

Sara thought for a moment. She was still out of breath, flushed and sweating. Under her skirts her pussy was still wet and twitching. People were mostly going out through the auditorium, but the orchestra and some of the staff came backstage. She jumped down, ignoring Caroline's hissing, and stuffed her breasts back inside the bodice. Everyone streamed past, the men staring at her, the women pushing them on.

Marta tripped through the curtain, panting with exertion, her dark hair in damp ringlets around her face. 'Where's Caroline, Sara? She was supposed to come out and give out all sorts of notices about the rules and the prizes.' She stepped towards the caravan. 'Scenery looks great, by the way. Looks fun in this little hidey hole? Go on, let me look!'

'You can't go in there, darling – it's still wet –'

She giggled at the thought of Caroline trussed up and naked in there, certainly still wet, inches away from an auditorium full of admiring parents, imagined herself dressed as a fortune teller, asking for money and beckoning them in to see what their future held –

'You OK? You look very flushed and sweaty, Sara. Coming down with some kind of fever?' Marta glanced again at the caravan. They both caught sight of Caroline's abandoned shoe. If Marta moved a fraction of an inch, she'd see Caroline's toes, too, wiggling frantically for help. Marta raised a jet black eyebrow. 'Or maybe inhaling too many paint fumes?'

Sara laughed. 'Swigging all that Spanish sherry.'

'You coming to the pub for another?'

'Oh, I can't, darlin. I've got to get this old heap finished off to my satisfaction so we can push it out on the stage tomorrow.'

She waited until everyone had admired her handiwork on their way out, and most of the lights were turned off. She wasn't ready to go home. She didn't want this game to stop. Not yet. Not while she had Caroline March at her mercy.

'I'm just going to tell your Graham that I need your help back here so you won't be home for an hour or so.' She climbed back inside, and sat down on Caroline's legs. 'Then I'll come back, and I'll make you lick me out all over again. And then if you're very very good, I'll lick you, too, till you're screaming for me to stop.'

'Don't leave me here!' Caroline reared against the restraints, eyes widening with fury. 'Someone's bound to find me! The headmistress. The carpenter. The caretaker!'

'They'll have something to show and tell, then, won't they?' Sara stroked Caroline's reddening face. 'Just think. Caroline March, ice queen, found tied up and butt naked in the caravan, offering her superior services to anyone who fancies!'

'You little ginger bitch!'

'Oh yes, that's me, honey.' Sara laughed and tickled the thong between Caroline's breasts, over the mound of her crotch. 'But I learned from the mistress. Right. When I get back I want you to suck my nipples!'

'Hurry back then, Sara Singer.' Caroline fell back, closed her eyes and wriggled sinuously. 'And if you're very good, I'll show you what to do with my cheerleader's pom poms.'

'I don't think so. I'm making the rules from now on.' Sara couldn't resist bending over and kissing Caroline's mouth, running her tongue across the other woman's teeth, tangling her tongue with hers. She pulled away, looked longingly at the curvy body lying there, just for her. 'And what's more, we've got all night, Mrs March.'

Good as Gold

WHEN I GROW UP I want to be just like Sophie. She's my idol. She knows it all, except how I feel about her. She's tall, clever, talented, beautiful, stylish. At her age you know she's been enjoying sex for a very, very long time and you can't help, or *I* can't help, imagining her at it. She knows it all, but I'm not sure she knows how amazing she is. And I never knew a totally red-blooded chick like me could feel like this about another, older, woman.

Anyway, she obviously loves me, too, because not long ago she asked me to undertake a very delicate assignment. Top secret. And fraught with danger. If I cocked it up, everything dear to us both could be blown out of the water.

'I don't care how you do it. Scramble across roof tops if you have to. I'll lend you a camera.' For now, though, she handed me a hammer. 'Call it arty reconnaissance.'

'Call it spying, you mean.' I banged in the final nail and hung the last picture.

'I can trust you, Suzanne.' She wandered over to the over-sized cream sofa in the corner of her sitting room. I love her house almost as much as I love her. It's all huge glass walls straight out of *Grand Designs* and they've both worked like dogs to get it. Everything is lush. Their bed is absolutely *built* for sex, right down to the mirrored wall opposite and the way the shadows flicker across the duvet. 'After all, this time next year you'll be married to my Jake. The little daughter I never had.'

'And Martin will be my father-in-law.'

'Whatever. I need to know what he's up to while I'm away.' Sophie crossed one long leg over the other and studied the way I'd hung her latest floral photographs. Their house was going to be used as exhibition space later in the year. 'Our marriage is totally open. You knew that before you signed up to join this family. But lately it's felt like it, he, is getting out of control. He seems more sexed up than ever. I can't keep up. It's like he's addicted –'

'Sort of like Michael Douglas, you mean? But he seems so – *calm*, always.' The thrill of scandal rippled. 'You think Martin needs therapy?'

'Who can say, sweetie? Maybe.' She shrugged. Her long diamond earrings swung against her shoulders. 'Certainly he'll go mad if he doesn't get laid as often as possible. Or maybe it's me, just getting old and paranoid –'

'Never.'

She bit her lower lip. Little teeth marks dented the tender skin then started to fill out again, redder than before.

'Your Jake the same? Permanently up for it? You know, permanently hard? Going at you morning, noon and night? I worry that he's just like his dad.'

I giggled, shocked at the question, and hitched myself up on to her quartz worktop.

'Oh, Christ, Sophie, stop it, no, not exactly morning, noon, and – Christ, I can't talk to you about *that* –'

I crossed my legs. I was wearing spotty stockings that day. She looked straight at my crotch and I blushed. Was she imagining her son going at me, right in there, up that hidden hole? Did she catch the fact that my pussy was bare, damp lips spread open where later she'd be blending mangoes for Martin's supper? My thighs felt hot as they stuck together. I turned her camera ignorantly upside down and pretended to study it.

She sighed, looking at my face now. 'I just want to test Martin, that's all. He promised he'd go easy while I'm in New York, to prove to me that he can.'

Sophie has endless legs, all taut and toned. She's been working out recently so she'll fit in with all those cougars across the Pond, but she's always been gorgeous. A while ago she stopped wearing trousers, other than jeans, when she's working, and now she wears these sensational fluid dresses and skirts which make her look sexy and young like a girl. Since Jake told me how he has a thing for Japanese anime schoolgirl cartoons I've ditched all my trousers, too, and now I only wear skirts. Except unlike Sophie's mine are very short.

'What about the age difference, though?' I tipped more wine into my glass. 'Won't he suspect something if he catches me hanging round here?'

'Come on, Suzanne. You're not a baby. I'm instructing you to think of something to say or do so that Martin lets his guard down.' Sophie smiled but looked sad. 'And I'll have you know we were childhood sweethearts. I was still a teenager when we had our Rick. Martin's only just fifty.'

'Yeah, but to a 22-year-old that's pretty ancient, no matter how cool he is.' I shrugged prettily to take away any edge of rudeness. 'But what I mean is, I'm a baby to *him*. Wet behind the ears. Thick. He's cleverer than me.'

'Ooh, but you're going to make such a cute little honey trap.'

Sophie patted the sofa next to her and next minute I

was cuddled up against the lovely soft breasts curving out of her caramel cashmere cardi as she wrapped her arm round my shoulders. Oh, God. That's when I knew exactly what my problem was. Is. It was like when I had that monumental crush on Regina Sanchez at school. I couldn't take my eyes off her in class, in games, at meal times. She was all flashing blood-red ringlets, Spanish swear words and silver bangles. I was all badly permed mousy hair, 10cc records and freckles. But I got to kiss her in a school play. Not quite the chaste kiss the nuns had in mind. God no. It made me wet my pants –

But Sophie? Do I have a crush on Mrs Epsom? I nudged myself up against her so that the curving side of my breast was touching hers. My nipples pricked. I could see them through my Hello Kitty tee shirt. I glanced to see if hers were hard, but I could only see a suggestion of her cleavage. I could smell her musky perfume and the tang of her lipstick where she'd bitten her lip. She's my boyfriend's mother, for Chrissake. So voluptuous and full and knowing and scented and unlike any other mother but so sweet as well and I wanted to touch and kiss her. Just like that time when I was pressed up, crotch to crotch, against Regina Sanchez. Then felt her tongue in my mouth.

'But what the hell are your husband and I going to talk about?' I couldn't do what Sophie wanted. But she squeezed me tight, up into the scented warmth of her armpit.

'Oh, sweetheart,' she said, in that low, ex-smoker's voice of hers, 'I'm not sending you on this assignment to *talk!*'

I thought spying would be the easy part. So I stalked Martin for the first two days after she'd gone. Mornings, lunch times, evenings, sometimes on the tube, sometimes hiding in their neighbour's driveway, watching to see if he was with anyone. He wasn't, but I took pictures anyway to study later for evidence. A mysterious woman lurking under the lamplight, maybe, or blowing kisses from a window. Actually I was really pleased with the way Martin looked in his suit, the way he sauntered with one hand in his trouser pocket groping for the house keys, his distinguished profile as he glanced up at the sky. The images were brilliant when I altered them to monochrome. Like stills for a *film noir*.

But on the third evening he wasn't there. At work, or at home. I prowled round the house and even climbed onto the roof of Sophie's studio in the garden to peer into their bedroom, but the lights were off.

'Fuck this for a lark,' I muttered to myself, stomping into the wine bar on the corner of their street. It was empty. A big-built girl in regulation tight black skirt and even tighter crisp white blouse, her white blonde hair coiled in Princess Leia plaits, was bending over the tables, lighting candles. Her hips thrust from side to side as she gyrated to the deep beat of the background music. I perched up on a bar stool and texted Sophie: *Zero to report – M good as gold.*

'Yah?' The *fraulein* glanced over her shoulder as if I'd said it out loud. She kept her bright blue eyes on me as she yawned, arched her spine, rotated her neck and stretched her arms above her head.

'A bloody enormous white wine, please.'

'Sure.' She marched across the wooden floor towards the bar. Her shins bulged like a dancer's. Her skirt slipped into the crack between her high, tight buttocks.

'And some slippery, slimy olives.'

'Good camera.' She leaned over the counter with the

hors d'oeuvres. 'Can I see the pictures?'

'There's nothing to see!' I tossed my phone down. 'Just need a drink.'

She nodded sharply like an SS officer, reached a muscled arm up to get a glass down from the rack above our heads. Bent down to the wine cooler, big breasts pushing together to make a deep cleavage and tumbling like a sensuous log roll against the few tiny buttons. Her strong, impatient movements were strangely comforting. I fiddled about on the stool, my own spindly legs splayed wearily apart. Mission unaccomplished.

'Bad day?' she barked. Every part of her body was toned and taut, and yet her breasts had a different life of their own. Now she was upright they had bounced upwards too, hoisted and contained inside the crisp white cotton. They were too soft to be false, but they still had a jutting, cartoonish perfection. Body builder Barbie. I thought of Sophie's breasts. I'd never seen them even half bare. She was far too sophisticated to flash her flesh. But she must have known how tantalising it was, the way the silk and cashmere she favoured clung to those promising outlines.

'Bloody awful, and frankly boring.' I fiddled with the mobile phone. Why hadn't she replied? 'Can't seem to do anything right.'

She took out a new bottle, beaded with jewels of condensation, and ran her hands up its cool green sides. She made it look like a sexy weapon, holding it like a policeman's baton, nudging it between her breasts as she unwrapped the seal. The cold against her skin made her nipples stick out. They were massive. My own tits are smaller than hers but exquisitely, painfully sensitive. Jake calls them his puppies, which has started to irritate me. When we're married I'll have to train him out of it. He likes me to walk straight in to the room where he's either working at his desk or sprawled on the sofa watching the rugby. He likes me to stand in front of him, lift my skirt like a lap dancer – always a skirt, like I said, for easy access, like a hooker – without a word, spread my legs to straddle him, and sit on his cock. I'm supple enough. I can still do the splits. I wrap my legs round his hips, grab him by the hair as he yanks up my shirt and grinds my tight nipples into his greedy young mouth, always wet with beer or the stinging juice from the grapefruit, or oranges, the citrus fruits he's always peeling and eating and which make him so glossy and healthy.

I closed my eyes in the wine bar, sucking on an olive, and the leather seat of the stool squeaked under my bare thighs. I wriggled at the thought of my handsome, horny fiancé's breast fetish. It was autumn, but I wasn't ready for tights. I lifted one leg to hitch my woollen hold ups over my knees. They were really striped hockey socks like something out of St Trinian's. I knew they were kinky, because men stared at them in the tube, the way they went over my knee and up my leg, just failing to meet my mini skirt.

I pulled the stocking up slowly, loving the scratch of the wool over my tender skin, then held my other leg up like a ballerina so the air circulating in the empty bar, no one looking, could tickle my bare snatch. Yeah. Commando Barbie. The habit started as a dare at school. Regina Sanchez of course. I'll never forget her lifting her school skirt in choir practice and showing us the luxuriant black Spanish triangle between her legs as Mr Soames took us through the Faure *Requiem* –

'Found the corkscrew.' The barmaid's voice sliced through the silence. I opened my eyes and saw her grasping the bottle between her knees and staring straight up my skirt. I kept my leg up and looked into her blue eyes then down at those huge breasts, squeezed tight together. She blinked slowly and looked down to fit the corkscrew into the bottle. I thought of my Jake grinning, licking his lips before taking in a nipple to suck but then suddenly it was Sophie's nipple he was sucking. In my tired mind's eye I saw her holding up her shirt or jumper in front of him, letting her nipples, surely they would be pale and elegant, grow hard and red in the cold air. Then weighing one breast in her hand, taking Jake's head tenderly with the other, she was pushing her nipples into his grown man's mouth.

The cork shot out of the bottle with a delicious pop, and as I thought about Sophie suckling her son my pussy popped, too. I lowered my leg and came, quickly and secretly with a tiny moan, right there on the bar stool.

'Now isn't that just music to the ears! And Christ, my little *pashka*, aren't you a sight for sore eyes in that twisted school ma'am dominatrix get-up.' The door banged shut behind the newcomer and he started to tug at his tie. His other hand reached across the bar to flick undone one of Olga's over-exercised buttons. 'Your boss ask you to dress like that to give us punters stiff ones?'

My lips had gone dry. I could only wriggle my damp pussy, and watch.

'No. I choose how I dress.' The *fraulein* leaned low towards him, her mouth glistening and open. Her finger trailed into her cleavage. 'And I dress only for you, Marty –'

'Hello! Stop! It's me!' I banged my knees closed. There was a loud squeak of flesh on leather as I tried to stand up, but I was stuck to the seat. Creamy wetness lined my sex lips, slicked inside my thighs. Under my warm bottom the seeping juices were like glue.

96

Martin turned sharply, his cheeks ashen beneath the dark shadows of encroaching beard. His eyes flared with shock, then anger. I'd never seen that look before, and it scared me. But just as violently it was gone, his face smoothed back into its easy urbane lines. 'Suzanne! Christ! What are you doing here?'

Olga glanced sharply from him to me. There was a high flush on her cheekbones as she splashed the wine into my glass. 'She wants to drink, of course.'

'I was – hoping you'd let me in to the house,' I stammered, spilling wine down my chin as I drank. Sophie would never swig like she was on the lash in Falaraki. I swallowed, and coughed, and my eyes watered.

'I'll have a Sauvignon, please, Olga.' He smiled at the bar maid. She poured him a glass and glared back. He held her china blue eyes for a moment as if he was taming her, and she did that slow blinking thing with her eyelashes.

Then he turned back to me and I wriggled uncomfortably, the stool suddenly too small, too high. And too wet. I realised I hardly knew the man. In the few months I'd been dating Jake, his father was mostly away on business. We'd certainly never been alone together. There was always Jake, and his brothers, and Sophie, and our friends, always celebrating something at their home or in a restaurant or in the gallery. I had never, for example, noticed he had a livid white scar across one eyebrow. Or how dark his eyes were, like slate.

'Jake wanted me to get a couple of things to send to him –'

'Touching. But they're in New York, Suzanne, not the North Pole. There are shops. Surely Sophie could have taken some stuff out with her?'

I sipped this time. The wine was singing nicely in my

head. I wanted more. 'OK. I confess. It was an excuse.'

The mobile phone lay idle on the bar between us.

'You don't need an excuse, Suzy. You'll be family soon.'

'I'm lonely without him, Martin!' Christ, where did that come from? Martin was watching me so intently, I found myself doing the eyelashes thing, too. The heat of embarrassment crept up my body. 'You know. I'm so frustrated at night.'

I crossed my leg, too late remembering that my fanny was bare, but he didn't flinch. Just kept looking straight at me like a very handsome, rather stern headmaster. I even felt a warm tear trickling down my cheek. It was like I was melting. Eyes. Yes, nose sniffling. Pussy still leaking –

'You miss sex with my randy son?' Martin drank some wine slowly and glanced very briefly down at my legs, crossed demurely now. I flushed hotter, wondering if the strip of thigh above my stripy socks made me look like a tart. 'Don't blame you. If he's anything like me he'll need it at least three times a night. But I'm still not sure why you came to *me*.'

'I think she was watching for you.' Olga had one hand on her hip, her Slavic eyes lasering us both. Her tongue ran slowly across her lower lip as if she was about to take a bite of a very tasty meal. 'She is in this street every day, like a little spy.'

'You'd better come home with me and sort yourself out,' Martin said, smile fading. He stood and took my hand. His fingers were warm but strong as a vice round mine, which felt tiny. He laid a tenner beside his already empty glass. Payment for my assignment, I thought giddily. 'Can't have my future daughter–in–law wandering the streets in this state.'

'Before you go, Marty.'

Olga pushed the camera over to him and slowly, calmly, he started to scroll through the display. I gripped the edge of the counter, whimpering. My heart hammered in panic. I was in deep shit. It was all there. Pictures of him calling goodbye to the security guys at his office, crossing roads, buying newspapers, paying taxis, pulling off his shoes in the sitting room at home, gazing out at the twilight before the electric blinds slid across the double height glass wall –

Martin slipped the camera into his trouser pocket, leaned his elbow on the bar, and rolled his sleeves up casually. 'Perhaps we'll stay for another one, dumpling.' He winked at Olga. 'While I work out what to do next.'

My body shuddered with relief. But my mini orgasm earlier had left me edgy and unsatisfied, and now my bladder was pulsing with urgency. 'I need to piss. Where's the ladies?' I had to work out how to get the camera back and me the hell out of there.

Olga opened her mouth to tell me but Martin put his hands on my shoulders, sitting me down again.

'Not so fast, young lady.' His arms were strong and muscled, like Jake's, and streaked with dark hair. 'You have some explaining to do.'

I went weak under his hands. 'Can I have the camera back now, Martin? Sophie leant it to me to – to practice some techniques she's been showing me. You know how much I admire her. Everything about her.'

He frowned and tapped his fingers on the bar.

'All pictures of you, Marty,' hissed Olga, her fingers touching his.

'Can you shut up and mind your own business? Olga?' I snapped, sliding off the stool. I turned my back to her so that I was between Martin and the bar. 'This is about my father-in-law and me.'

'Yeah. Give us a minute, *strudel.*'

A surge of anger boiled in my chest. He kept winking at Olga over my head as if I was some kind of minor irritation. She goose stepped or whatever across to the door and I heard her lock it. I pushed up against him. His body was big and warm and didn't budge. I started playfully to push my hands into his pockets.

'Oh, come on Daddy, give it back! Pretty please?'

He looked down at me with a strange, hot look, but this time it wasn't anger or shock. I froze, with my hands still grappling about on his hips. It was lust.

'Say that again.' His voice had gone really deep and rough.

I giggled. 'What?'

'Ask me again.'

What must we look like? Me, petite and cute in a chaotic Pixie Geldof kind of way. Dishevelled bleached hair on end, mascara smudged, tartan box jacket falling off my shoulder – and my arms wrapped round my fiancé's scary pin-striped father.

'Can I have the camera back?'

'Say all of it again. Say Daddy again.'

I took a deep breath and out came this little girlie whisper. 'Can I have the camera back, Daddy? Pretty please?'

He smiled and lifted his arms out sideways as if I was a copper about to frisk him. I reached inside his trousers, fumbling about awkwardly, aware in a flash like a hot rod shoved up my bum that I was in danger of touching his cock.

He swallowed, but kept his arms up. 'Keep looking.'

This time I did touch him through the fabric lining. His cock was rock hard. I felt like I'd been burned. The

100

camera, in his pocket, rested against it. I wrapped my fingers round the camera but couldn't resist, really I couldn't resist, running my thumb up that long hard shape, just to make sure. I felt it pulse in response. Martin was very still. I rubbed my thumb up again. His cock was huge. It extended up to his waist band. Excitement swelled in my throat. There was no thought of who I was any more, or whose cock it was. I was down to basics. Just a horny female touching a big, hard, male cock. It made me ready to copulate. Fuck like a bunny. A ball of desire twisted and rolled in my stomach as I rubbed the shape a third time and felt it shift.

And yeah, the fact that it belonged to someone so totally forbidden made it doubly, triply sexy.

I stared at the buttons on Martin's shirt as I forced myself to pull the camera, warmed up by his body, slowly out of his pocket.

'You've been a naughty girl, Suzanne.'

'I was bored.' I tried to give a nonchalant laugh, difficult while still squeezed up between him and the bar. 'Just a bit of fun.'

He took the camera easily out of my hand and scrolled through the pictures again. 'Very intense. Moody. But this wasn't a photographic exercise. Sophie asked you to spy on me.'

I shook my head violently from side to side like a child telling a lie. Now this really was like being in the headmaster's office. And now I really needed a piss.

'I just wanted pictures of you, Martin. You're lovely. I think I've got a crush on you.'

He lifted my face towards him. His fingers pinched my cheeks in painfully so that my mouth was squashed into a pout. Saliva trickled from one corner. Then he bent and kissed me, hard. My whole body gasped. He was

101

practically lifting me off the floor by my face, and I was electrified by the way his lips, barely moving, still kind of took hold of me.

Then he spat me out, turned me round, and bent me double over the stool.

'It won't do, Suzanne. For God's sake, you're engaged to my son.'

'But I love you all!' I whimpered, struggling to get upright. 'I love Sophie, too –'

'Touching. But let's leave her out of this.' He laughed and pushed me down again between the shoulder blades so that my stomach was squashed flat against the seat of the stool. 'Olga! Come here and hold the little pest down!'

Olga clicked back across the floor. She took my arms and stretched them across a second stool, so that my stomach was pressed down on one and my chest and head supported by the other.

'Lovely. Oh, look at this, Olga. Such a lovely bottom.' Martin flipped my skirt up over my bottom. 'And Christ, how dirty is she? No knickers!' He pushed my legs further apart. My sex lips kissed stickily. He stroked my thighs above my woollen stockings, hands moving higher. 'Jake know you go about like a little whore?'

'That's how he likes it,' I groaned. I couldn't breathe very easily, lying on those two hard stools. Olga kept hold of my wrists and started to stroke them. My eyes were on a level with her crotch. Her black skirt was stretched tight over the mound of her pussy.

'Well, he needs to know how naughty you are.' Martin's big hands reached my bottom and started kneading my cheeks, fingers spread wide as if to measure me, pinching and squeezing the plump white flesh and making me feel utterly stupid. I squirmed about, but all that did was raise my bottom higher in the air and put pressure on my bursting bladder.

'You can't do this to me!' I yelped. 'Not allowed!'

'We agreed we don't need excuses, didn't we, Suzanne? I can do what I like. And so you are going to get a bloody good spanking.'

'Don't be silly, Martin! You sound like a dirty old man!'

'Oh, you have *no* idea, sweetheart!' His drawl was as soothing as a snake's. 'Under this Jermyn Street tailoring I'm totally perverted, especially when it comes to naughty girls and their bare bottoms.'

Olga laughed, too, and it was an attractive, rattly sound. She bent down, still holding my wrists, and pushed her face close to mine.

'So sophisticated, isn't he? So charming on the top. But underneath he likes it dirty, Suzanne. Really dirty.'

My stomach twisted with excitement as her big red lips blew smoky air into my face before she ran her tongue over my mouth. But I had to keep fighting. 'I still don't deserve a stupid spanking. Come on, Martin! It's me, Suzanne! Not some little scrubber! I'll be wearing ivory lace in six months' time, making vows to your son –'

'And I'm giving the little orphan girl away, remember? So I'm the boss.' Behind me, Martin kicked his knee between mine so that they collapsed apart. He went on smoothing the tender skin on my bottom as if flattening a bed sheet. I could feel little goose bumps coming up on my skin as he stroked, and shivers deep inside my pussy. 'And if you want this wedding to go ahead, and this to be our secret, you'll keep very still for me. And if you're good, we can do this again. And again. Even in the church vestry, poppet, how about that? You in your ivory lace, all hitched up so I can spank you before I walk you up the aisle.'

I really did struggle then. His voice sounded harsh and rough like a stranger. Suddenly he slapped my bottom and I yelped with fury. It didn't hurt, but I could feel my butt cheek wobbling under the strike like jelly, hear the humiliating smacking sound reverberating in the air, and I wanted to die of shock and shame.

'Bastard!'

'Language, Suzanne. This is your fault for sneaking around.'

I made a pleading face at Olga, but she moved away as if I repelled her. Martin's tie whipped through the air over my head and she caught hold of it and lashed my wrist to the foot rest of the stool.

'Now, say it, Suzanne.' Martin's hands had stopped stroking. 'You're naughty, aren't you?'

'Oh, for God's sake, yes, I'm naughty.' My eyelids fluttered as I gasped for air. When I opened them again Olga had taken her skirt and knickers off and her snatch was inches from my face. Her lips were totally hairless, her snatch waxed so completely that everything was blue-white, almost see-through. I jerked in astonishment and the tie bit into my wrist. The sharp pain flashed a weird excitement through me.

'And now I want you to say sorry!'

'This is silly, Martin!' I twisted about, trying to lift my ribcage off the stool so I could breathe better, but out of the corner of my eye I saw Martin's arm lift in the air, palm flat. I opened my mouth to scream, but there was just a puff of hot breath against the leather seat. And then his hand came down really hard this time, the sting instant and sharp on my bottom. I jumped and squealed as the punishment burned.

'Stop it, Martin!'

'He told you to say sorry, bitch!' Olga pushed her crotch against my face and I breathed in her aroma of sex and piss and some kind of flowery soap. 'And when you've done that, you're going to lick my cunt. Can she lick me, Marty?'

'Oh, she can lick you, pumpkin. Just wait until I've punished her some more. I've got my own pleasure to come, don't forget.'

I twisted about frantically as they discussed me. I needed to breathe. The sting of the smack was fading. I was getting light-headed with the lack of air, the wine, and now the increasing urge to pee.

'Sorry. You asked me to say sorry.'

'Good. What are you sorry for, Suzanne?'

Martin stroked the spot where he had slapped me, lightly with his fingertips as if tracing his hand print. His voice was soft, hissing almost. I relaxed a bit, found myself staring at Olga's snatch as her fingers slowly opened the lips to show me the wet slit, and the plum dark frill nestling inside.

'For following you around –' I croaked at last.

'Good. Yes. And what else are you getting a spanking for?'

Martin's stroking continued, so gentle I could barely feel it. The sting of the slap had melted into a warm glow and I realised I wanted another one.

'For taking those pictures, Martin.'

'Yes, you naughty, naughty girl!'

Martin lifted his arm again, and there was a second slap, much harder. The stinging went deeper still, radiated further, on the already tender spot. I jerked wildly, unable to control myself, humiliation gnawing at first and making me feel like a little worm but then as the sharp heat spread through me the whole smacking thing started to make some kind of warped sense. The way it made me struggle helplessly, and squeal and wriggle. The way it made my supposedly sophisticated father-in-law grunt with warped satisfaction. The way it burned me, and hurt.

My pussy scraped against the seat as he smacked me again, and a vicious flare of excitement seared through me.

'Very good. Now you're being a good girl. But you still deserve more punishment for being a lippy little mare.' Martin slapped the other butt cheek, hard, and I couldn't deny it. Oh, yes. The slap felt good. The hot, vicious slap making me struggle and squeal, then the warmth spreading through me, felt so weirdly good.

'I'm sorry, I'm sorry, Martin!' I yelped, rubbing myself against the seat, turning myself on. 'Smack me again, Martin! I'm so dirty, and naughty! Please slap me again!'

'Oh, giving orders are we?' Martin chuckled, and pulled my bottom cheeks wide open. I could feel the hot, screaming sensation as the flesh split apart. 'Time to shut her up, Olga.'

Olga pushed herself into my face, burying my nose in the folds of her snatch, burying me in her smell. She smeared herself across my face. She was sopping wet. 'Lick me, bitch,' she whispered.

'Such a lovely white bottom, all sore now with my red hand prints all over it.' Martin crooned behind me. My head was spinning now. Their voices were like soft hissing spells weaving around me. 'I'm going to fuck it.'

He ran his finger up my butt crack and poked at the neat, tight hole. I went rigid with horror. I'd reckoned I was pretty street wise until then, hot stuff that Jake was lucky to have. But I had never been tied up or slapped before, and unlike the rest of me, my little arse was still virgin.

Martin was almost reading my thoughts. He slapped my buttocks again, and each time he did so Olga thrust herself into my face, holding her lips open round my mouth, and weakly I stuck my tongue out and took a tentative lick. Yes. Licking out another woman added to my list of never-befores.

Martin slapped me so hard this time that the shock and pain prodded right up my cunt. It was opening, twitching, and my bladder was swelling painfully, too, and oh God it was slackening, and now Martin was opening up my bottom with his fingers. Fingers I'd seen holding Sophie's hand. Peeling an orange. Steering a car.

Now I heard his zipper go, such a sexy sound, a pause, then it wasn't fingers but the round tip of his cock nudging at my hole, trying to ease open the little ring. I gasped. A good girl would have said no, no, no. But I couldn't, wouldn't move now. I wanted to feel more of it. More of everything.

The first drops of piss jostled, waiting to rain. Martin pushed his cock further inside. It was stiff as a rod. I moaned loudly. My little hole instinctively tried to close and push him out again and he smacked me hard, shoving me up the stool with the force of it. He thrust his cock harder inside until it bumped over the ridge of muscle and I was open, and he was in. That virgin passage felt packed tight with his rigid cock, strained to bursting, and I was pinned down like a butterfly.

He smacked me again and again as his cock went on swelling inside me, filling me, his balls slapping under me as the hot piss started to dribble.

'You dirty little girl, pissing yourself!' He growled in my ear, starting to fuck me. I could feel the shape of his cock ramming in so close to my cunt, just a few thin layers of skin away, and the excitement made me lick harder at Olga, who was suffocating me. The strange new taste of the other woman made me gag at first, but then I started to savour her dirty saltiness. I lapped harder and faster, locating the nub of her clit with my tongue and nibbling and sucking at it, and the more she pushed and the harder I licked, the hotter and wetter was the pleasure pulsating far away in my own cunt. She took my hair and yanked my head with it till it hurt, her big hips grinding into my face, forcing me to keep licking, and I knew I was doing it right.

Somehow as he fucked me Martin was smacking me at the same time and now the pain on my sore, red skin didn't get a chance to fade. There was no time between blows. He was smacking as if he was really, really angry, punishing my badness, but Christ, I was really getting it now, this whole perverted idea of smacking, the image of me tied across the bar stools with my bottom in the air, little skirt flipped up, woollen stockings up over my knees, red streaks on my cheeks, God knows what it was doing to him but me? Every part of me, cunt, arse, mouth, was being invaded and punished and every slap and smack from him and push and shove and yank of the hair from Olga was driving me faster to the end.

Olga was rubbing faster and faster over my nose and mouth, and I was licking and lapping faster. She was tilting her hips wildly and her flimsy white sex lips flapped at my cheeks, my mouth, my nose. Everything with Olga was about eating and swallowing and devouring and yes, now she was feeding me.

As the piss came faster, making my cunt clench desperately to stop it, I thrust my tongue up into Olga and felt her cunt tighten and grip. Olga groaned and writhed as my tongue pushed up her, smearing her juice against

108

my face as she came. That triggered my piss which shot a hot spray over Martin's cock and balls as he went on and on fucking me. The piss sprayed over the seat and stung down my legs, but the release and relaxing inside me was like a mini orgasm.

Olga staggered back against the bar, her fingers still stroking and poking inside her as she shook with dying pleasure. I'd done that to her. Licked the dominatrix until she came. Christ. Her panting mouth was open as if ready to suck cock but for now she pushed her sex-soaked fingers in to keep the climax coming.

Martin's cock swelled inside my bottom so that my body was impaled and stretched to ripping point. The brief distraction of Olga's climax over, he got to it again, grunting like some gorilla in a nature programme. The filthiness of his fucking my backside was crazy and exhilarating. I tried to get my free hand between my legs to finger myself like Olga was doing but there was no time and no need because I was coming now, rubbing against the seat, salty piss stinging my sore cunt.

Martin lifted my bottom in the air so he could pump harder and deeper into me, still slapping me viciously like a cowboy whipping his mount. I gasped for air as he shuddered inside me at last and I came in a short violent burst, climax shivering through me as I collapsed on the stool, my breath creaking in my chest.

Olga hummed a tune under her breath as if nothing had happened and swayed across to open the wine bar door and let in the world.

'What am I going to do?' I whimpered, collapsed on the stool, legs buckling like Bambi's as reality hit. My arse pulsed heavily after its brutal invasion. 'What am I going to tell Sophie? Oh God, and Jake?'

'You love them, don't you? So you tell them precisely

nothing, Suzanne.' Martin's voice was soft as he untied me. I felt his fingers swiping at my piss soaked pussy before he tugged my skirt down. 'You want to do this again?'

'I don't know. Yes.' I watched as he slowly licked my juice off his fingers. Of course I wanted to do this again. 'But it's so wrong. We've been unfaithful!'

Olga came up behind Martin and took his ear lobe between her teeth, moving her hands down his shirt front. A group of people pushed into the bar, demanding to know why it had been closed, and she just kept right on rubbing her palms over his softening cock before barking 'Yah?' over her shoulder and casually going to serve them.

'Touching,' Martin scoffed, handing me back the camera. 'But taking my future daughter-in-law up the arse doesn't count.

'Sophie know you're such a bastard?'

'Not the half of it, and she never will.' He yanked me to my feet, almost a gentleman again. 'You can tell her that we all behaved ourselves impeccably tonight.'

My mobile buzzed, right on cue, vibrating on the counter and making us jump. *Just finished private view. In Gramercy with boys. All well your end?*

I glanced at Martin. At his slate grey eyes. I looked at his hands, his fingers tapping the bar.

Like I said, I texted back, bottom stinging, stockings drooping round my ankles. *Good as gold.*

Second Honeymoon

ANOTHER DAY IN PARADISE. Poppy sighs and steps out on to the balcony.

As Frank says, what's the point of working your fingers to the bone all your life if you can't enjoy idyllic places like this? The hotel is an old converted pub standing on the edge of a Devon cliff. It may be off-peak right now and rather chilly (some even say it's haunted by smugglers), but the voluptuous Italian owner still fills her bar with fascinating locals. Anyone from tousle-haired surfers to distinguished old sculptors like Johnny Floyd, who's a bit of a celebrity. A couple of his figures recline on the grass outside their window, in fact. Two incredibly, what's the word, *debauched* female nudes clawing at each other and brazenly pushing their breasts out. One has her leg hooked round the other. Their heads are thrown back, mouths open, and if you stare for long enough you can almost hear them moaning, like they've given up waiting for a man to see to them.

'Well, Floyd was once based in New York, so what do you expect?' said Frank, when they took a walk on their first morning there. 'Debauchery probably runs in his veins.'

Floyd had told them that the figures were carved before his hands went. Out of driftwood he found on the beach. Old ships' timbers, he reckoned, which is where he got the idea of sculpting the women as big breasted figureheads.

'Pops! Time for a pre-prandial! Everyone's down in the bar discussing some Murder Mystery weekend!'

She doesn't turn round. 'I thought you hated fancy dress.'

'Not fancy dress, darling. Acting. *Character.* You remain in character the entire weekend. I rather fancy twirling my mustachios as the upper-class twit. And I can just see you as an arsenic-mixing flapper?'

She has loved Frank all her adult life, and will never stop, but these days his voice, even making the most innocent of demands, even when being sweet, tugs on her like a chain as if she was a dancing bear. He'll be waiting for her by the door, dressed for dinner and tweaking his cuffs. She's always loved his strong, hairy wrists and his big, warm hands. Just looking at them, knowing how it used to feel when they brushed over her skin and went up inside her, used to excite her unbearably. She still loves to watch them writing, gardening, making a point, cooking. They still hold hands as they fall asleep.

Otherwise he never touches her. Which is why this hotel room, designed for a second honeymoon, all colonial, polished wood, white muslin drapes, isn't paradise at all. It's more like a cage.

'I'll follow you down in a minute.'

Some reckon the garden sculptures are modelled on Floyd's aloof young wife Florence, but no one's ever seen her in the flesh. Frank thinks one of them looks exactly like Stella.

Ah, *signora* Stella! Even my Frank can't keep his eyes off her. She's like a sluttish Sophia Loren, he says. There's the shadow of the old sparkle when he looks at her, and I can't help glancing at his trousers to see if there's any life stirring down there, but even those enormous cappuccino-coloured boobs, squeezed into *broderie anglaise* gypsy blouses, sheened with sweat from all that cooking and scrubbing, can't get his dander up.

Impossible not to like her, though. Maybe my husband does ignore me and ogle her, but I also think she's lovely. And she keeps this place so well, just this side of bawdy. She brought peasant-chic decor and amazing food to the west country long before the likes of Jamie Oliver.

Poppy pats her stomach. She's allowed herself a bit of a pig-out. Hell, she's lost more than three stone since her toothpick-sized sister Mary told her at Christmas that she looked like Beth Ditto. And not in a good way. But what's the point of all that starving? Because along with all the fat, she's lost her *joie de vivre*. And Frank's not even noticed, certainly not commented, that she's found her cheekbones again.

Poppy comes slowly down the stairs. She still loves tunics, but they're not the tents she used to wear. OK, maybe there is a point in starving. She can wear these gorgeous clothes now. All metallic tones and satin fabrics which cling to her breasts and fall away over her still generous hips, and tonight it's a Cleopatra-style sheath with a jewelled neck and she's taking the plunge and wearing it as a short dress. She's hooked herself into some sensational new lingerie. Black opaque stockings, the kind nuns or Victorian housemaids wore. She still has the legs.

Every night since they got here she has sprayed perfume, drunk wine, played music, lit candles, the lot.

And *still* Frank has lost his libido.

'So, Poppy, is your Frank OK?'

The huge sofa sinks under Stella's weight as she plops down into the cushions. Poppy tilts towards her as if tumbling down a steep hill.

So much for fascinating locals. The bar is empty tonight apart from Ivan the silent barman. Frank reckons he looks like a James Bond assassin. All Aryan white blond hair, mean Slavic eyes and an expression as if he's permanently cursing your mother. His forearms flex as he polishes glasses and twists them under the spotlight to check for smears.

'He's fine, Stella!' The fire is making Poppy's cheeks hot. She frowns. 'We both love our room, and dinner was superb. Why? This all part of the service?'

Stella splashes wine into Poppy's glass. She pouts her berry-red lips and lifts her shoulders exaggeratedly like an opera singer. 'Service, honey? What do you mean?'

'You know, interrogating your guests. Surely the hotelier's job is to flit around in the background, fulfilling our every whim?'

Over behind the bar Ivan gives a low chuckle. The first sound she's heard him make since they arrived here. 'Flit? Stella? You seen her body?'

Poppy stares at him. His stony face is transformed by a beautiful smile. He has a look of a young Nureyev, but less scary. Very full lips, and very white teeth. The kind of teeth you can imagine ripping off first your dress, and then your knickers –

But Stella isn't laughing. She leans forward, one hand dangling between her open knees. Her feet are always bare, even though it's autumn. She looks like an extra from *Carmen,* about to roll a cigar on her bare thigh. Or Gypsy Rose, enticing punters into her caravan to gaze into her crystal ball.

Inside her blouse, black satin tonight, laced up the

front like a corset, her big breasts squeeze and swell with her breath like rising dough, catching her glittering red-stone necklace between the soft, sexy mounds. At dinner Poppy caught Frank staring as Stella moved among the tables, chattering to her guests, and when she stopped to bring them some bread he looked like a man dying of thirst, just ready to scoop one of her breasts out and suck it dry.

Poppy bites her lip at the memory. Because it had made her tighten with excitement, seeing that glazed look of hunger in his eyes. It was dead sexy, the thought of him fancying sex, even with another woman. Weird, maybe, but it meant there was a flicker of life in him, and hope, after all.

Stella's other hand trails absently into her cleavage as if seeking comfort.

'Whims are exactly my job, Poppy. *Our* job.' She glances over at Ivan, who has gone back to vigorously wiping down the bar. 'We don't interrogate, as you say. But I created this hotel to fulfil every whim, yes. Even if you don't know what you want. So, Frank. He's such an attractive man. Big, dark, a little rough. Just my type.'

'Funny, that. In another life he'd have had the hots for you, too.'

'Hmm, I wish.' Stella is like a great sinuous cat, never still, always purring. She's even licking her lips. 'So tell me, why does he go to bed early and leave you alone?'

Poppy lifts the glass and swallows mouthfuls of the mellow red wine as if it's fruit juice. Her head spins. The fire pops. Ivan starts to flick off the main lights.

'Because he doesn't want sex.'

Ivan slows his movements. He has his back to them, but the set of his shoulders, the way his jaw stops crunching the cashew nuts he has just thrown into his mouth, the way he thoughtfully and unnecessarily tucks his crisp white shirt into the back of his jeans, all tell Poppy that he's listening. She sits up straighter, crosses one long leg over the other.

'How far would you go to fix this?'

Poppy is sucked into the well of Stella's dark eyes. She hardly knows the woman, yet she wants to tell her everything. She leans towards her. She can smell sweet sweat, and musky perfume.

'You mean, try sex counselling?'

'Bollocks to that!' Stella shakes her head impatiently, earrings jangling. 'They just tell you to spend weeks touching and massaging, forbid any fucking, even with fingers –'

Poppy blushes, but she can't help spilling her guts now. 'I'd do anything, Stella. I love him! But I'm scared I'll dry up like an old witch. I've even thought about going with other men –'

'Ah, other men. My speciality.' Stella smoothes her hand down her neck, lifts her glossy black hair away from her skin as if it's making her too hot. 'Ever thought of letting another woman, ah, how should I say it, kick-start him? You'd go mad with jealousy, but it's very, very horny, especially if you watch. You see him in a new light.' She winks. Her eyelids are heavy, as if she's permanently drowsy. Her eyelashes are thick enough to catch a breeze. 'Believe me, it works.'

'I've never, not in my wildest dreams – oh God, maybe. But I can't lose him.'

Stella nods like a father confessor, but then fans her fingers over her mouth to try to hide the smile spreading there.

'Oh, forget it. We're all a joke to you, aren't we?' Poppy tries to stand up. 'You create this lovely place,

116

Stella, this haven, but what the hell do you know about the real world?'

'Sit, honey, sit.' Stella's descending hands spread warmth through Poppy's legs so that they buckle beneath her. 'I know plenty about reality, believe me.'

'No. You sit up here on the cliff like a queen bee, all gorgeous and enticing, screwing other people's husbands, no doubt you have your pick of all the tastiest male guests too, *and* the staff –'

Both women glance over at Ivan. He flicks the dish cloth over his shoulder and scratches his chin.

'Lucky me, huh? I tell you, that one, he's hung like a–' Stella holds her hands a foot apart and winks at Poppy, who splutters like a schoolgirl. 'Look, I'll leave you. Have this wine on the house. Don't leave this bar until you have finished it! That's an order!'

She brushes a finger over Poppy's hot cheek, down to the corner of her mouth. 'You've come to the right place, honey.'

Poppy stares into the fire and lets the wine, and Stella's soft words, wash over her. She can't move. A gust of strong wind blasts down the chimney, spitting sparks out of the fire.

'So, *signora*. Your husband won't touch you. He's crazy.' Ivan kneels in front of her, scooping escaped embers into a silver shovel. 'So let me touch you.'

Poppy goes rigid, pulls her knees together as she watches the muscles in his back rippling under his shirt. He lifts one of her feet to brush under it, fingers circling her ankle like a bracelet.

'You want sex, yes?'

Poppy's eyes smart. The wine burns hot in her throat. Her dress feels too tight. She's aware of how long her legs look, stretched out in the opaque black stockings, the

117

heels of her shoes catching on his jeans. Ivan has stopped sweeping. His eyes are moving up her legs.

'What a question!' She flicks ash off the arm of her chair. She feels as if she's melting, inside and out. 'Oh, Ivan, I can't remember. Yes. Yes, of course I love sex. Christ! I was lecturing my sister about being a cold fish less than a year ago, and now look at me. Fuck! Look at *her* –'

'What about her?' Ivan jumps nimbly to his feet like a Cossack dancer and perches on the coffee table in front of her. He props his chin on her hand. His eyes glitter blue in the firelight. 'She as beautiful as you?'

'Chancer! You sound like a gigolo.' Poppy giggles and blushes, but she is staring right back at him. 'You going to be a barman all your life, Ivan?'

'Part-time only. I'm training with Johnny Floyd to be a sculptor. That's why I like to watch people. And touch them, of course.' He runs his fingers down her bare arm. Poppy gives in and lets her skin shiver with pleasure. 'But tell me more about your sister.'

'She had no man for years, kept her house like a show home, and I'm standing in her kitchen last New Year's Day mocking her for being frigid, and the next thing, literally five minutes later, she's messing up her White Company duvet riding her ex pupil like a bronco while we're all supping punch!'

'So you're jealous because she has some adventure? Maybe Frank's jealous, too.' Ivan tosses the shovelful of embers back into the fire, which makes it crackle.

'What are you now? A therapist?' Annoyance coils inside Poppy.

He cocks an ear as wind whistles outside. 'Hmm. There's a storm coming.'

'It was Mary's face, Ivan. When they came downstairs.

118

All flushed, hair on end, buttons askew, *oozing* it, you know? Like she was high. And then her totally *edible* toy boy announces they're eloping. And when little sister Mary swings her leg over Charlie's motorbike you can practically smell it, the sex, she's like a bitch on heat, she's going to ride that throbbing bike behind him all through Europe, holding on tight, and every time they stop he'll throw her down on the ground and fuck her all over again.'

Ivan is silent for a moment. There's a rumble of thunder over the sea.

'That what you would like, Poppy? Someone to do that to you?'

Ivan leans forward and takes her face in his hands. The touch almost hurts, it's so unexpected, her skin so parched. They say you can kill with kindness, giving the starving too much to eat. His fingertips dig harder into her cheeks, pinch and mould her mouth. She pulls away but he holds on. In fact, he pulls her closer. Now he's running one finger between her lips, prizing them open, running back and forth till her saliva starts to make it wet.

She gulps. His finger pauses. 'We've come on this stupid second honeymoon to make things better, had walks and meals and lie-ins, I've wandered round in my new underwear, and still Frank –'

'Can't get it up?'

'Maybe it's me.' Poppy can taste the salt of his finger. 'I'm the one who's frigid. I'm numb. I think of being in bed with Clive Owen. I lie there beside my husband, stroking my silky new knickers up into my crack.' She blushes furiously but the way he's looking at her makes anything possible – 'But I can't turn myself on. There's nothing inside me, no excitement, no thrill. *Nada*, as my daughter Chloe would say. Zip.'

119

'Zip?'

'Zip.' Poppy zips up the air between them to show what she means, and Ivan laughs. Like Stella, he's infectious.

Then he stops laughing and takes her hand, and puts it on his crotch. She fidgets in her chair, but can't take her hand away.

'Zip,' he says, inching closer so that his knees are either side of hers and the movement makes her press harder on the bulge of his cock inside his jeans.

'Oh fuck, yes. Zip,' Poppy breathes nonsensically back, kneading that hard shape through his jeans before he starts to kiss her, brushing his lips over hers, pushing his tongue gently at her teeth and making her startle with excitement as she opens her mouth to let him in. He lifts his hand, freeing her to undo his zip and here's that swift, sharp, satisfying sound as it comes undone.

He pushes her back onto the sofa on the patch still warm from where Stella was sitting and now she feels helpless as Ivan climbs between her legs, pushing them open. She can feel his erection pulsing through the denim. She frantically pulls his jeans down, it's like teenagers groping at a party, clothes getting in the way but then his hot, hard cock is free and thumping into her hand like an animal. She strokes and squeezes it and he groans and kisses her again. These young guys, so ready. So flatteringly eager. And what was that about drying up? She's embarrassingly wet. Her juice is trickling inside her knickers. It'll smear over Stella's sofa. But Poppy wants Ivan's cock inside her. He wrenches her thighs open and her pussy lips separate stickily. All her senses zoom in there, to that small aching part of her, and she squirms frantically. All her itches want scratching. She grinds herself against him so that his cock nudges at her knickers

120

and she writhes against it, feeling it slip over the silky fabric, pushing between her wet lips –

A clap of thunder reverberates round the hotel and it's like lightning has struck Poppy too. Christ, what is she *thinking?* He's infectious, yes. But infection breeds illness. She pulls away, shaking. 'Shit, Ivan, I'm sorry, this isn't the answer! I'm a married woman and you're the – this is the hotel bar! Anyone could walk in! What if Stella, or Frank –'

'They won't.'

He nudges at her again, but she's all tensed up. So he sits back on his knees, leaving her sprawled there. Her stomach plunges with regret as he calmly fastens his jeans.

'I must go.' She pulls her dress down, whimpering with shame and regret. Oh, why doesn't he force her? Her cunt is throbbing with emptiness. Her mouth is sore with kissing. It wouldn't take much. But he's just looking at her. 'You're gorgeous, Ivan. I must be mad. There's women out there would kill to get naked with you. But –'

'Not stay for another drink with me?'

'I've got to be a good girl.' Poppy kisses his mouth, lets her lips linger there, wants to touch him, pull him down on her, be properly fucked, oh God – but then with a superhuman effort she pushes away, half hoping he'll follow, and stumbles out into the hallway.

The hotel is dead quiet as Poppy climbs the stairs, knees weak with wanting. No sound from behind her. The few guests must already be sleeping, because all she can hear through the rattling windows as she stumbles along the landing is the sea outside, churning angrily as the storm gathers.

Their bedroom door is ajar, and Frank has left the

curtains open. The room is full of noise. Rain and thunder rumble and batter like a horror movie sound track. How the hell can he sleep through this racket? Clouds are scudding thickly across a mean-looking sky, evilly lit as if by concealed strip lights. Poppy kicks off her shoes and drapes her dress over the chair in the little lobby area and walks to the window. There's another flash of lightning, which makes the statues down in the garden look as if they're leaping away from each other. Another flash illuminates her reflection in the French doors. Her skin is pure white and she's leaning there like a temptress outside a bordello, her black *balconette* bra supporting the weight of her breasts, still luscious after losing three stone. The French knickers are still stuck to her pussy, sucked in by her lips. Her stomach curls as she remembers Ivan kissing her. Remembers his hot cock heavy in her hand –

A crack of thunder makes her jump. The window swings on its hinges and now she can see, clearly reflected in the eerie light, Frank lying on the bed behind her. Or rather, just his legs. For some reason he's pulled the sheet away. He's naked, and his cock is standing up, stiff as a rod.

She gasps with astonished laughter. 'Frankie? Honey? You waited up for me?'

Her voice is drowned in the storm outside. She tiptoes round the corner and sees that one wrist is lashed, with the tie he wore at dinner, to the high wooden bed post. Her amusement turns to fear. She rushes to untie him but it's dark and she crashes into the armchairs and then the dim bedside light is switched on and she can see more clearly that he's not in trouble. Not at all. Not even struggling. Quite the reverse. He looks like he's in heaven.

His cock gives a great lurch as if it's bowing in greeting or worship and then Stella appears from the shadows on the other side of the bed and bends low over him. She's still wearing the black satin corset, but the rest of her is bare. Her big brown hips and legs look graceful in this light as she dances towards him, unlacing the corset top and licking her lips as she does so. She flicks undone the last hook and her breasts bounce free just inches from his face.

Poppy feels dizzy. They can't see her. That's her husband. That's her husband's cock, quivering like a bloody flagpole. But she can't take her eyes off Stella's breasts and the incredible nipples which are long, dark, stiff, and chocolate brown.

Frank says something and in a brief space between gusts of wind and thunder it sounds like *'buena sera, signora,'* but he growls it so sexily that Poppy thrusts her hand between her legs. Her pussy is throbbing.

'So, stopped fighting me now?' Stella laughs huskily and lifts one leg to straddle him. A flash of pink appears, slashing through the untamed curls of her bush. Poppy gasps, but nobody hears. Stella smiles, and Frank stretches out his free hand and runs it down the pink crack. Stella wriggles and tosses her hair luxuriously. Poppy can see the slit of pink as Stella's plump lips open and close.

Poppy kneels on the big armchair, watching them over the back of it. She wants to, she *ought* to, launch herself at Stella and scratch her eyes out, but she has no strength. She can't move. Doesn't want to move. Her body is frozen, yet buzzing. She's totally transfixed by what she's seeing. But she's locked outside, looking in. This is Frank, her man, but he's a stranger, a rough, sexy stranger tied up and loving it, with their hostess Stella sitting astride him, moaning with pleasure as she fingers her nipples, tweaking them so that they grow even bigger.

They really are sensational. They are ripe for one thing. For the first time in her life Poppy wants to know what it's like to suck another woman's tits.

'Now, Frankie, make me feel good. Suck them.' Stella settles her haunches on top of Frank's legs and puts her hands on either side of him so that her breasts are hanging over his face. His cock is bigger and harder than ever, standing up just in front of her pussy. 'Oh, Poppy's so going to thank me, darling. You'll be horny as hell when I've finished with you.'

Poppy is horribly jolted by the use of her name. She is ready to spring out of the armchair to stop the madness when a hand clamps itself over her mouth and pushes her back down on her knees. She struggles violently. She can't breathe. Her breath burns against the hand gagging her. But as a second hand comes up between her legs and rips her knickers off, she recognises the salt taste on the skin.

Ivan keeps his hand over her mouth. She tries to bite it. But he forces her head round to watch what's happening on the bed. But they wouldn't hear her anyway. The wind is howling like a woman in scary ecstasy. Stella is spreading her knees to lower herself over Frank, and there's that greedy slash of pink again. It's a cunt, same as Poppy's, but it belongs to the enemy. Stella rubs herself against Frank's balls like a mare scratching on a fence post.

Ivan is up close behind Poppy now, his knees forcing hers apart, pressing her against the back of the chair so that her breasts scrape against the fabric, making her nipples burn. On the bed Stella has taken one of *her* enormous breasts and is rubbing the huge stiff nipple against Poppy's husband's mouth. Frank tries to stroke her breast with his free hand, but Stella smacks it down.

He takes hold of one of her buttocks instead, and digs his nails in. Stella jerks, and smothers herself down on top of him and so he opens his mouth. His lips nibble up, Poppy knows how that feels, he used to do that for hours, his tongue flicks out and laps the hard point then he draws it in, sucking hard.

'See? He's not lost his mojo!' Ivan grunts into her ear as his hand rams up Poppy's cunt. 'Just needed the right woman.'

'You bastard!' Poppy tries to scream behind his gagging hand, flings her arm out, tries to hit and scratch him, but he catches hold of her in a dead lock, squeezes her arms against her ribs. 'Think you're some fucking gangster –'

'I've been in the army, if that's what you mean. So. You disturb Stella's work, and I have permission to gag you.' He shoves something into her mouth, jams it behind her teeth, not choking, but enough to muffle her. She smells the gag before she tastes it. Salty sweet. Piss, and pussy juice. Her knickers.

Poppy stops breathing. Her body goes steel-taut with excitement. Ivan's arm is like a vice. He has his other hand ramming up her cunt, pinning her down. She can't move. She can't escape. She's never been held fast like this, forced like this – it's intoxicating.

She nods her head. Now he has two hands he lifts her by the hips and tips her forwards over the arm of the chair. You'd think you could escape that position, if you wanted to, but again he's got her out of breath because the arm of the chair is now jammed into her ribs, so all she can do is hang there like a rag doll.

Frank is holding Stella's breast like a teat, pulling it long and jamming it into his face, biting and sucking at her nipple as if he's milking her. He's always loved breasts, but Poppy has never seen this kind of feeding frenzy before. But then Stella is like some sort of nurturing goddess, one of those fat, naked statues that Johnny Floyd might sculpt, crooking her finger to all and sundry to come and worship and, well, suck.

Stella is pulling and rubbing the other nipple, licking her lips with ravenous pleasure. Poppy reaches up to pinch her own nipples, hard, and they sing with delicious pain. Stella is swaying her big buttocks from side to side, her head tipped back with pleasure.

Poppy can't believe it's *her* husband, making Stella ecstatic. *Her* husband. *Her* sex god.

'So. You watch your husband fucking Stella and you still want to be a good girl?' Ivan hisses, opening her legs wider. His hand is still up inside her, probing, moving, promising more. 'Before, you push me off –'

Poppy groans behind the gag, the lack of air making her dizzy. She shakes her head and presses back against him. She can feel the long shape of Ivan's cock. The action on the bed is changing. Frank is trying to jerk upwards to catch Stella on his cock. But she smacks at him, yanks her nipple out of his mouth, and wriggles down his legs. She's pushing them apart, cupping his balls, and Poppy's stomach coils with shock as Stella takes his cock and starts licking it.

Frank falls back, totally surrendered. Poppy goes hot. She hasn't sucked his cock since they were courting.

'I fuck you now, if you want it or not.' Ivan tips Poppy roughly over the arm of the chair, and pushes his cock up into her cunt.

It's anger and jealousy and lust mashing inside Poppy as Stella sucks her husband's cock. Frank's yanking her hair up into his fist, lifting it off her face so that he, so that everyone, can see how her mouth looks working on him.

126

But Stella pushes his cock out of her mouth with her tongue, clambers back up, grabs his cock, wet with her licking, then she aims it towards her pussy, lets it rest, how does she control herself like that? Poppy is trying to push herself back onto Ivan's cock but he holds her in mid air. She gets it now. He's waiting for the signal.

The tension is ecstasy. But as Stella slides down on Frank's cock, so Ivan pushes his up Poppy and, boy, was Stella right. He's hung like a donkey. It goes sliding in for ever, making her squeal and shudder as it fills her and she wants to scream with excitement.

The storm is dying away a little, and the air is darker, so all the sounds in the room are clearer now. Stella starts to rock on top of Frank, and they set up an extraordinary sensuous, stately rhythm. That's when Poppy realises how fucking sexy her husband still is. She hears their flesh slap together, the wetness of Stella's juicy cunt gripping and releasing Frank's cock, their breath rasping, the bed creaking, as her buttocks squash down on top of his legs, the base of his cock visible as she lifts and falls, it's so huge and hard, thrusting up inside her.

So Poppy's riding Ivan, too, or rather he's mounting her, oh yes, she likes the horse analogies, as he takes her from behind, jacking up the rhythm as he yanks her hips and she rocks up and down his cock. The urge to come is so intense now. Poppy's cunt is getting tighter and tighter, his cock ramming till it hurts, she's sure her body will split with each big thrust.

Stella is flying up and down now. Poppy has forgotten how strong Frank is. She remembers now, on their first honeymoon, they fucked so hard they broke the bed. She was on top that time, just like Stella is now, she was so slim and wild on all the *retsina* they'd drunk at lunch time. They were staying in a cheap hotel room but it opened straight onto the Greek beach and they had scrambled in covered in gritty sand and oil, left the door hanging open in the hot, still afternoon because they'd been groping each other in the sea and had run straight up the beach into their room because they couldn't wait to get to it and later the hotel manager had a quiet word about the open door of their room and what people saw.

Frank may be tied up with one hand, but his buttocks are strong enough to toss Stella's curvy, solid body into the air like a shuttlecock. Her breasts wobble and bounce and as Frank gives one last almighty thrust, Ivan pumps rapidly into Poppy, shuddering as he comes, pulling her by the hips backwards, back onto him, skewering her until she comes too and then he pulls the knickers out of her mouth and lets her cry out, very loud.

Stella and Frank turn, but slowly. Stella is euphoric. She eases Frank's cock lazily out of her bushy cunt and lets it flop, still hard and wet, onto his stomach.

'He's all yours, honey,' she says, bending to pick up her black corset off the floor.

Frank takes one look at Poppy, out of breath, tits hanging down, wild eyed, still rammed from behind by the Aryan gigolo. Then he falls back and closes his eyes.

Poppy pushes Ivan off her and tries to stand, but her legs are weak as spaghetti.

'Oh, God, Stella, what have we done? He won't look at me!'

Stella just walks towards the door and beckons him to follow.

'See you at breakfast, lovers,' she laughs.

Poppy starts silently to peel off her black stockings. She's sore, and aching, and has nothing to say.

'Keep those sexy stockings on, and come over here so I can fuck you,' says Frank quietly, patting the bed. 'This is supposed to be a second honeymoon, after all!'

Poppy totters over and he pulls her down beside him, slides his fingers inside her wet cunt. She doesn't think she can, but she daren't say no, not after all this, and then he's hard again and up inside her and he's the sexiest man alive again, her very own George Clooney, and, oh yes, she can.

Later, when the storm has died down, Frank murmurs, 'Let's stay here a little longer, Pops. Let's stay for the Murder Mystery party? How about Stella as Miss Marple, all tweed cape, magnifying glass, Black Russian cigarette, teasing confessions out of us – oh ho, yes –'

Poppy slaps his leg, but half-heartedly.

'Ivan's an actor, apparently.'

'Actor? Sculptor. Gigolo. Whatever –'

'He'd make a good sinister chauffeur. Or spy. Or –'

'Yes, let's stay on,' sighs Poppy, shivering as the cold air blasts off the sea and her husband takes her hand. 'With Stella as mistress of ceremonies, it won't just be a classy party. It'll be one hell of an orgy!'

Frank falls asleep, and starts to snore.

Immaculata

IT WASN'T UNTIL THE leavers' midnight feast that Olivia learned what the other girls really thought of her.

Given Dutch courage by candlelight, joss sticks and the smuggled Spanish aniseed liqueur donated by Regina Sanchez, everyone was sprawled about in Olivia's room in their quilted dressing gowns, playing truth or dare.

'We never thought you could be such a laugh, Livvie,' Suzanne piped up, always the first. 'We thought you were always so haughty and aloof. A perfect head girl, in fact.'

'Yeah. An ice queen,' Chloe added. 'Always looking down your nose.'

'It's because I'm tall.' Olivia drawled hazily. 'And short sighted. Can't see a dickie bird without my specs.'

'Or even a dick!'

They all giggled, happy to be making friends, but she didn't give a shit. She wanted to leave them all to it, follow her more exciting friends up to their attic bedrooms for a last smoke before they disappeared back to their glittering lives. If only she could stand up. The thick, sticky liqueur, colourless but lethal, had gone straight to her head. Suzanne and Chloe and the rest of the pathetic 'netball team' sat cross-legged on the floor at her feet as if they were waiting for her to make announcements in assembly while she tried to stay upright, seeing double.

'Or maybe because you're all at sea when the Princesses have bigger fish to fry.'

'Oh, don't be such a boring little cow, Suzanne!'

Chloe nudged Suzanne with her elbow. 'Livvie's not such a laugh when she's pissed off, is she?'

'So where's Royal Regina now? And Salome? And Mimi Breeze? Too cool even to stay for prize day? All packed and ready to jet back to Madrid, or Buenos Aires, or wherever, without you?'

Olivia felt sick and fell back against the pillows. 'Thish, thish is why we're not friends. All thish catty stuff.'

'Olivia, you're so blind,' said Suzanne. 'You come on all high and mighty, but those bitches treated you like one of their maids.'

Boy, does the truth hurt. No way could she keep up with the posse of pouting Latinas from rich Catholic families who came and went on private jets as if boarding school was rehab. But she was mesmerised by their sophistication. They all were. The Princesses were fully fledged sirens long past their fat, beetle-browed, downy-lipped adolescence. By the time they arrived at school in their chauffeur-driven limousines they all had perfectly arched eyebrows, permanently glossy mouths, diamond earrings and *shaved armpits*. Maybe it was the hot weather back home or the oily food or the black-eyed, randy men, but they developed curves and knowing glances long before the gawky, pasty-faced English girls.

'They got bored, that's all, of you and your infantile chattering,' Olivia slurred, swallowing and gulping to get rid of the nausea.

'OK, come on, Suzanne, it's truth or dare,' said Chloe, ripping open a packet of custard creams. 'So tell everyone what you saw.'

'I think it's those amazing cheekbones.' Suzanne knelt up shakily and stroked Olivia's face. 'They make you look stuck up.'

'Oh, you're all so wrong,' Olivia moaned, brushing her hand away. 'I'm marshmallow, pure mush, inside.'

'Meaning that underneath it all you're a pussy cat?' piped up Annie, the smallest girl in the sixth form. '

The others tittered, their bare legs squeaking on the lino flooring. There was safety in numbers after all. Annie was all golden curls and round blue eyes, but she was far scarier than Olivia. The idiots couldn't see it. She had, has, what Olivia called Little Person Syndrome. The monstrous ego in the undercooked frame. She's one of the most powerful women in the City now.

'Oh, you know exactly what I am underneath, Annie baby.' Olivia felt a surge of power as the toxic liqueur loosened its grip. She licked her lips, and started to hitch her shell-pink antique dressing gown up her thigh. 'Remember when we were new girls and I showed you my fanny, like this?'

There was a silence in the room as the silk wrinkled up to her crotch. The candle flame bent sideways in the constant draught, as if it was eavesdropping.

'Yeah,' said Annie, voice hard with venom. 'You said, ooh, Annie, my neck's all stiff after that netball match. Give me a massage.'

Another silence. Downstairs they could hear the big wooden door leading to the nuns' cloisters banging in the wind.

'And did you, Annie?' Chloe, as ever, wanted to know everything. 'Give Olivia a massage?'

'Yes, she did,' answered Olivia, pointing her fingernail, which Regina had painted sapphire blue earlier that evening. 'And to do it she turned me over, and

132

straddled me, rubbing her pussy on my bottom.'

There was an audible gasp. Just then, out in the quadrangle, the clock tower bell tolled. The nuns had a code, like the dead who give one knock for yes, two knocks for no. Three dings and a dong for Sister Benedicta, two dongs and two dings for Sister Mary. One hard dong for Sister Ant, we used to giggle – that rumour about her and Mr Soames the music master never quite died, that he'd found her in the chapel one evening, clearing up after the procession and service for the Feast of the Immaculate Conception and he chose that moment, as she was bending to pick up the discarded hymn books and lily leaves and candles, to lift up her heavy black skirt and slide his piano-playing fingers in between her virginal, milky-white, opening thighs ...

'Oh yes,' Olivia chattered on, exhilarated by the attention. 'I liked it. It was the first time I really felt turned on. So, yeah.' She shuddered suggestively. 'Pussy's the word.'

There was a ripple of shocked amusement.

'Go on, Suzanne, truth or dare,' urged Chloe, pushing her mate so that she fell forwards onto her hands and knees. 'Tell how you saw Regina touching Olivia.'

'So?' Olivia's nausea had been replaced by a kind of shivering cold and she closed her eyes. 'We're bezzie mates.'

'Lezzie mates, more like.' Suzanne folded her arms round her knees. Olivia could see the other girl's knickers. White, sprigged with pink buds. 'Regina's definitely a lesbian, because she kissed me, once, with her tongue.'

The others tittered. 'So that makes *you* a lezzie, Suzanne,' declared Annie.

'No. Give me a boy to snog any day,' snorted Suzanne,

pouring more vodka into her Coke can. 'It was just a kiss, right in front of Mr Soames and the whole choir. But Livvie's a serious lezzie, aren't you, girl? Cos Regina was doing a hell of a lot more than that, and you weren't smacking her off. In fact you were both in lezzie heaven.'

Olivia and Suzanne were staring at each other now, some kind of unspoken battle going on. 'Yeah,' whispered Olivia. 'Maybe I am.'

Suzanne went on, 'I had to take some pins or thread or something up to their room, because Regina was sewing Olivia's wedding dress for *Trial by Jury*. She had Olivia's shirt off so she could pin the satin round her, and Mimi was doing the make-up, saying we were all such hideous little English scrubbers, it would take masks to make us look good, and Salome was fiddling with her hair –'

'They made me feel like a goddess,' Olivia butted in. 'Salome called me a pre-Raphaelite. A butterfly out of the chrysalis.'

'Ugly duckling, more like,' snapped Annie.

'You *did* look like a swan, Livvie, in that wedding dress,' said Suzanne softly. 'And you did get a standing ovation on the night –'

'Yeah, but what was Regina *doing* to her?' Chloe wriggled impatiently.

Downstairs the cloister door banged again and their eyes grew huge in the darkness.

'You wanna know? They got my bra off,' Olivia blurted out. 'They said it was to get the dress made. The Princesses were all there, puffing away. Then Regina got out her measuring tape and held it round my tits and accidentally on purpose brushed over my nipples. They went all hard, you know, and then Regina kind of flicked them and it was – oh, God –'

'Regina was stroking and pinching Olivia's nipples,

she wasn't fitting the dress at all, and the other girls were joining in. It was just an excuse for a massive lezzie grope!' Suzanne gurgled naughtily. 'All stroking Olivia, smearing lipstick on her, spraying her hair, touching her all over, as if she was some kind of pet.'

'If you'd been listening, instead of gawping, Suzanne,' Olivia said, lighting up one of Regina's Marlboros, 'you'd have heard Regina say that she was going to model her dressmaking dummies on my body when she becomes an *haute couture* designer.'

'Whatever. She had the tape tight round Livvie's tits like a bandage, and they, like, bulged out over the top. They're huge, did any of you know? And Regina was squeezing, not measuring at all, and Olivia's nipples popped out like nuts, and Regina looked ready to take a good lick and then you'll never believe this –'

Everyone held their breath, waiting for what Suzanne would say next. Olivia had no strength to stop her. She sucked smoke into her lungs, wished she had a hairbrush, shampoo bottle, anything to stick into the wetness springing between her legs.

'I didn't know where to look. I wanted to get back out, but the door was stuck.' Suzanne dropped her voice to a husky whisper. 'Regina said to Livvie, this is what Brazilian boys do, and then she shoved her hand down there, between Livvie's legs! Christ! Salome was behind Livvie, rubbing the satin material between her legs, all three of them touching and feeling her and fondling each other, and Mimi was over on the window sill just watching, touching herself, and moaning –'

'All right, all right, yes, who cares, yes, Regina Sanchez was touching my fanny, and then Salome kissed me, too, licked my mouth as if it was pastry, all those sensations, just like this, come on, you can watch me, oh

135

God!' Olivia moaned, rubbing faster and harder between her legs in the shadows. 'Go on, Suzanne, tell them more –'

But there was silence. And then a rap on the door.

'Olivia Preston? Are you smoking in there?'

'Fuck!' Everyone squealed in unison and scrambled to their feet. 'Sister Benedicta!'

'So, spill, Livvie. Are you a virgin?' Chloe hissed into her ear as they all froze in chaotic attitudes, unable to escape as the door creaked open.

What did it matter if Sister Benedicta caught them? They were all leaving in a week. Olivia felt weak as a kitten. She licked her aniseed-flavoured lips.

'Only if fingers count.'

'I thought better of you, Olivia. Drinking, smoking, lying around half-naked like some sort of tart,' Sister Benedicta chided, prowling the room after she'd booted the others out. 'Head girls are supposed to be infallible!'

'Only the Pope,' Olivia groaned, and was sick in the basin.

When she'd finished, and brushed her teeth, Sister Benedicta tucked her in to bed.

'Please just give me a couple of Hail Mary's, Sister, and keep it between ourselves?' Olivia shivered. 'I know I've been a naughty girl.'

Sister Benedicta stroked her forehead. Her fingers were like gossamer. She was so close Olivia could smell shortbread on her breath and see the piercing in her ear lobe where once as a lovely carefree woman she'd worn earrings.

'It's priests who dole out the penances, Olivia, not nuns,' she laughed softly, making the candle flame shiver. 'But you realise I'll have to come up with some kind of punishment.'

Rumour had it that Sister Benedicta was a dancer in Paris in her previous life. She had the faintest tinge of a French accent. She held herself beautifully and when she walked her hidden hips flicked restlessly at her skirts with a ballerina's reined-in tautness. But just then she was kneeling by Olivia's bed as if it was *she* who was going to confess. In the candlelight her eyes were a fathomless navy blue.

'Come on, Sister. No need to punish me. I'll be gone next week. You can forget all about me.'

The nun's hand paused on Olivia's forehead. 'How can I forget you?' Sister Benedicta bent lower over her face. 'I've watched you in the last two years, Olivia. All your talents, your singing, your painting. Watched you blossom. Those wicked Princesses have made a real woman of you.'

'You think, Sister?'

Sister Benedicta nodded and looked down, just like the saints that lined the cloisters downstairs. She had the most amazing long eyelashes. 'I don't trust them, particularly Regina Sanchez. She's a beautiful witch. She's the very devil, put in this convent to try us all. I know she's touched you, Livvie. Seduced you. Led you down that forbidden path.'

Olivia felt herself go red. She may have been eighteen, but she could still blush scarlet like a kid. The heat prickled right up her legs. Right into her armpits.

'How do you know, Sister, about Regina? Are you all-seeing, like God?'

'Not like God. I may wear a veil, *cherie*, but I'm still a woman with eyes, and ears, and all the other senses – anyway, I know what went on in that room. I know Regina likes sex with girls.' Sister Benedicta paused, in

137

that infinite, calm way that the truest nuns have, as if there's all the time in the world, no rush, no embarrassment, while all her shocking words sank in. She'd said sex. And *cherie*.

'Sister, will I be punished for that, too?'

'For liking girls? Maybe. Yes. It's all temptation.' The nun pressed a finger on her mouth. 'But I, too, was very nearly swayed.'

'She tried it on you? The bitch!' Olivia sat up. 'But, Sister, how did you resist her? She's so gorgeous! She's so strong, and voluptuous, she has this incredible smell —'

'Yes. Of knickers. And overblown roses.' Sister Benedicta coughed, and smoothed Olivia's hair away from her face, hooked her fingers behind her ears, down her neck. 'You smell of jam doughnuts, Livvie. Biro ink. And absinthe.'

'But what stopped you? Your faith, I suppose.'

Sister Benedicta stopped stroking Livvie's hair as if she'd heard something. The silence in the room was suddenly heavy, as if there was a crowd listening.

'She just didn't do it for me, Livvie.' She leaned forward, and kissed the curve of Olivia's cheek, just pecking at the corner of her mouth, pressing it slightly open. She left the faintest trace of dampness.

'Do that again, Sister,' Olivia breathed, lying very still. Her heart was pounding through the silky dressing gown, banging through the sheet the nun had pulled up over her chest. 'Kiss me again.'

Sister Benedicta paused, in that endless way, lips still pressed near Livvie's mouth. There was a flash in her eye. A totally unholy flash of danger.

But then she stood up in one smooth movement. 'In the old days, young lady, the smoking, the drinking, the messing about with Regina, would have earned you a

138

dozen lashes and some serious prostration.'

'Christ! You ever been lashed, Sister?'

'Oh, yes. Once. They used to save severe penances like that for the feast of the Immaculate Conception. The Immaculata.' Sister Benedicta lifted her hands to her mouth as if to hush it, but a smile was playing round her lips. 'They caught me having impure thoughts. When I was a novice. Doing impure things, actually. Touching myself. Just as you are touching yourself now.'

'Why are you smiling?' Olivia sat up straighter, but she kept her hands between her thighs. 'What did it feel like? The lashing? Did it hurt?'

'Like the fires of hell, Livvie. Literally. It's supposed to cleanse us of our sins. They make you lie on your face, on the floor of the chapel, spread your arms out, you're only in your slip, because you wouldn't feel the pain so keenly wearing this thick habit, and then they whip you.'

Olivia touched Sister Benedicta's arm. 'But why are you smiling? Is it because you felt clean then, and forgiven?'

'Yes, spiritually, Livvie, but also, oh God forgive me, I shouldn't be saying this, but–' Sister Benedicta gave an incredibly throaty laugh and threw her arms out. 'It's because it felt fantastic! I never knew euphoria could be so physical! Pain and punishment blowing your mind like that! Like being high on drugs! The first lash, oh, that's painful, and shocking, and you try not to jump and scream and you are humiliated and stupid in front of all those people and Mother Superior with her whip, but then the heat slices right through your skin, makes you feel alive, and then the next one burns more, because it's smacking down on the sore patch, but the sensation is just exhilarating! You feel elated, brave, tingling all over, burning, stinging, it's all so physical when for years

139

you've been forbidden – and then you're going mad because now you can't wait for the next thrashing, as if you're *begging* for the pain, it's creeping right inside you, you even shout please please please, though you're not allowed to utter a sound, and they think it's because you're so sorry for your wickedness, and while you're lying there prostrate on the floor and waiting there's this great ball of pleasure stacking up, like a bonfire, deep inside you, and when at last that whip hits you it's pure ecstasy, maybe that's what the saints felt, but the heat shears right up you, into your, you know, up inside your–'

'Your cunt?'

They both gasped and clapped their hands over their mouths, but shook with the hilarious wickedness of it.

'Yes. If you must. Up there. My pure little – pocket. It's like hot fingers, pokers maybe, prodding up inside you, opening you up, and then the pain and heat explode like fireworks, I wonder if that's the best way to describe it? It was the first time, really the only time, I ever had an orgasm, Olivia. Imagine that. Not with a man. Not with another woman. A whip. A punishment. That's all the pleasure I've ever known.'

There was that thick silence in the room again, except for their frantic, fast breathing. Olivia slid off the bed, shaking. 'Show me, Sister –'

The big wooden door downstairs banged again, and other footsteps could be heard stepping along the cloister downstairs. The spell was broken.

'Enough, Olivia. Back to this night's disgraceful behaviour!' Sister Benedicta jerked her head up. She swept her arm dramatically round Olivia's room. The bottles. The ash trays. The discarded slippers. 'I can't let this go.'

'So punish me, Sister.' Olivia took Sister Benedicta's

hand and kissed the pale skin. 'Prostration. Flagellation –'

'They don't do that any more. But you can stay back after the end of term. Report to me in the rose garden on the first day of the holidays for some hard labour.' She pulled her hand away, but gently, and glided out of the door. Again, that fresh, sweet smell of shortbread and linen starch.

'I'll do anything, Sister. To please you.'

Out in the corridor the nun paused beside a statue of Saint Theresa of Avila, writhing backwards, eyes half closed but cast heavenwards, throat arched as if swallowing something thick, sticky, colourless maybe, like a boy's spunk, mouth parted in blatant, breathless ecstasy. Sister Benedicta pinched back a smile. 'Well, you know, Livvie, sucking up will get you everywhere.'

Olivia watched her floating away down the corridor. Her black habit twitched above her invisible dancer's hips, making the votive candles in their blood-red holders quiver. The veil lifted over her shoulder blades, showing the tiniest glimpse of slender white neck.

But it was Sister Antonia who gave Olivia her orders on the first day. 'Sister Benedicta is indisposed. She's praying in her cell. You have one week to clear this and carry all the roses up to make compost at the top of the hill. It's a crying shame, but they're building a science block in the holidays.'

It was no fun any more trying to picture Sister Ant being fingered by Mr Soames. Not when everyone else had gone. Not when all she could think about, longed for, was Sister Benedicta. She had to work miserably on her own.

But the third day Sister Benedicta was waiting for her in the rose garden. Olivia's whole body leapt with a wild,

141

unexpected joy.

'Sister? Have you been ill?' She went up to her and touched her arm. The nun flinched. 'You're all stiff, and so white – you were so lovely the other night –'

'Couldn't let you do this on your own, Livvie. But let's get to it.'

They toiled with their wheelbarrows in the boiling sun, not speaking. The only sound was the insects fizzing, the buzzing of the blood in their ears, and the occasional tolling of the convent bell far below. And the snapping of the nun's habit as she disappeared into the cloisters each day without a word.

Finally, at the end of the week, Sister Benedicta dropped her spade and collapsed on the grass at the top of the hill. Here they were way above the bell tower, and could look out over the fields that shielded the convent from prying eyes, and the narrow road that wound through the valley. The only route out of their jail.

'If I wasn't going home tomorrow, I'd help you make a new garden up here, Sister!' Olivia looked at the neat piles of rose bushes, roots still healthy, flowers still blooming. 'It's a terrible waste, otherwise.'

Sister Benedicta frantically took off her grey cardigan and rolled up her sleeves. They were both sweating, but at least Olivia only had her netball kit to get dirty. Sister Benedicta was boiling under that horrible habit. There was a flush of sun on her cheeks. She lay back, and closed her eyes, gasping for breath.

'Speak to me, Sister. All this silence has punished me enough.' Olivia crawled across the grass. Not a wrinkle on the nun's lovely face. Her skin was smooth as silk.

'It's spooky here in the holidays, isn't it? So quiet.' Olivia started to whisper. It was her turn to bend low, stroke the other woman's face. 'There's no shrieking and prancing and bitching. No hockey boots scuffing across the quadrangle. No banging doors, scraps of music. No lessons, no bells, no deadlines.'

Sister Benedicta breathing was easier now. Olivia watched the rise and fall of her shapeless chest.

'Are you ill, Sister?'

Sister Benedicta's long eyelashes fluttered and she half opened her eyes. The corner of her mouth lifted. 'Been fasting, Olivia. To purge myself.'

'What have you done wrong?'

The sun edged behind the distant row of trees, taking some warmth with it.

'Impure thoughts, Olivia. Wicked. Evil. And all that flagellation has done no good at all, because here they come again.'

Olivia held her breath. Sister Benedicta's eyes were wide open now, blue as the night sky, and full of tears. Olivia smoothed her hand over Sister Benedicta's face, slippery with sweat. Her own body went weak as water. Sister Benedicta didn't move. They were both panting now. Olivia looked at Sister Benedicta's mouth, open now. She could see the tip of her tongue resting on her teeth, bubbles of saliva on her pale lips. Feathery strands of hair sticking out of her veil. Chestnut-coloured strands. And Olivia couldn't stand it.

She took the veil between her fingers, and pulled it off.

'I want to see your hair, Sister!'

Sister Benedicta flicked away across the grass as if she'd been stung, trying to cover her head. Her auburn-gold hair was hacked about, short, and flattened with sweat. But Olivia grabbed her hands and pulled them away so that everything was exposed to the fresh air.

'How dare you, Olivia!'

But all Sister Benedicta's customary calmness was

surging in to her. She pushed the nun back down on the grass, trapping her hands up above her head, and crouched over her.

'No. How dare *you*, Sister. How dare you hide from the world like this. From me. From God, even! Did you know that your face is heart-shaped? And your eyes are huge? And how without that stupid veil you look young, nearly my age? You're so beautiful, Sister. You kissed me before. Is that why you've been enclosed in your cell?'

The nun's dark blue eyes flickered, and there was that flash again. The snake bite of temptation. She let out a long, harsh breath, as if it was her last. They stopped wrestling, and Sister Benedicta went very still. Now Olivia could sense the nun's body underneath her. But she could see nothing. Not the curve of her breasts. Not the swell of her bottom. She could feel nothing under that stiff habit.

Olivia felt tight like a violin string. Bones and skin vibrating like flies' wings. Everything inside her was loosening. But although she was the younger one, she had to be careful. She rested her mouth on Sister Benedicta's, softly, and pressed a little, waiting for her to push her off or screech, but still she lay there quietly.

'Are you a virgin, Sister?'

'Cecille. That's my name from my life before.'

Olivia went dizzy, as if she'd been slapped. 'Oh, my God, Sister! You've told me your real name!'

'My previous name. Because you're so beautiful, and God help me, but I love you.'

Sister Benedicta pulled Olivia's head down, crushed her mouth, opened her lips softly, as if she was breathing her in. That day she smelt of mints. Olivia wobbled, unable to lean any longer on her hands, and she rolled onto her side, so that they were face to face, arms tight

144

around each other, Olivia's bare scratched legs tangled with the nun's heavy skirt, kicking between her woollen stockings, and now they were kissing each other, Sister Benedicta's tongue pushing into Olivia's mouth, exploring and tasting, and the excitement was like being drunk. They couldn't stop.

Sister Benedicta's cool white hands were already up under Olivia's sports shirt, stroking up her hot skin, under her bra strap, pressing her breasts, but Olivia couldn't feel any part of Sister Benedicta's body. As they sucked on each other's tongues she fumbled with her habit but all she found was endless buttons and folds and hooks and swathes of material, and she started to rip at it.

'Stop, my little *cherie*, stop. Don't rip it!' Sister Benedicta batted her away. 'I can't go back into the convent naked!'

Olivia felt as if a bucket of cold water had splattered over her. She let go and rolled on to her back. She was shivering with excitement and frustration and fury. A pulse was throbbing between her legs. 'Why the hell do you want to go back into that prison, anyway?'

'Open your eyes. Watch me, Livvie.'

Sister Benedicta was kneeling above her, blocking out the sun, and for a minute Olivia was dazed, but then she saw that with her long pale fingers her nun was undoing her buttons. Tossing aside the bib that covered her front, the apron, exposing more buttons round her neck.

'Let me do these ones.' Livvie knelt up behind and undid the endless tiny buttons down the back, and pulled her dress down, then unlaced the undershirt, and underneath that were surgical-looking linen bandages, binding and flattening Sister Benedicta's chest.

Sister Benedicta turned round to face her. They were both shaking now, even though the sun was back, still fingering them. Livvie's knees were buckling. Her pussy was weeping into her knickers. She took hold of the hideous grey bandages and forced herself to take it slow. The nun's mouth was open, her white teeth biting into her lip, as Olivia unwound the cruel covering. Her own breasts bulged and swelled with excitement and then she whipped away the last bandage and there were Sister Benedicta's breasts, firm and pale and soft, her nipples slowly changing colour from pale pink to an urgent, dark, red.

'Let me, now,' whispered Sister Benedicta, and much more easily she pulled Olivia's shirt off, saw her breasts bulging out of her bra, unhooked that quickly, and caught her breasts as they fell into her hands. The two women knelt in front of each other on the grass, feeling each other's breasts, their breath coming in uneven gasps of longing.

Sister Benedicta's fine, delicate features blurred and fused as she came closer and her fingers stroked Olivia's breasts, her back, her legs under the little netball skirt, sending ripples of pleasure through her. She closed her eyes, letting her head droop backwards as the soft caresses lulled her. Then Sister Benedicta's mouth bumped up against hers, just like it did in her bedroom all those days ago. They both waited, mouths just touching. Olivia's breath stopped totally. She couldn't move away. Her lips softened and parted. Sister Benedicta rubbed her mouth harder against Olivia's. Olivia slid her hands under the nun's heavy skirt, felt the white skin on top of those ugly black stockings, the voluminous cotton bloomers still there, and she felt a pressure of violence inside her and as Sister Benedicta's tongue flicked again inside her mouth she pushed her down on the grass, sucking her tongue in between her teeth, so that their faces were moulded together and their bare breasts and hard nipples were rubbing against each other, their bodies tangling together again.

This would be enough, Olivia thought. This kissing. Perhaps if this is all, we won't have sinned. We can go back inside the convent, and no one will ever know. But it was like setting a taper to a candle as they feasted on each other. She was smouldering from her feet upwards.

And those violent urges kept on coming. This must be how boys feel, she reckoned, when they want to fuck. She lifted Sister Benedicta's skirt up and there were the voluminous white cotton bloomers. She stroked her hand over them, over the mound of Sister's pussy. Sister Benedicta squealed, and smacked at her hand, but Olivia didn't care. She stopped kissing her and bent to watch what her hands were doing. She unlaced the bloomers at the waist and pulled them down over Sister Benedicta's narrow hips, running her fingers over the ghostly white cold skin pulled taut over her bones and her flat stomach. She wanted to see her pussy, but she didn't know what to do next. She was overcome with shyness. They both were. Sister Benedicta started to cross her legs, tried to pull Olivia's hand away, but the touch triggered the madness all over again. Olivia ripped the bloomers right off and there it was, the awesome chestnut triangle of hair, untouched, untrimmed, what would the Princesses say, already sporting their Hollywood waxes ready to please their glitzy boyfriends?

A manic giggle bubbled in her throat as momentarily she imagined them all standing round on the grassy hill in their tight jeans and cropped tee shirts, smoking, flicking their highlighted hair, swearing and slowly bending nearer to see more closely, biting their pumped-up, glossy lips, sucking excitedly on their long fingernails as she pushed her face into Sister Benedicta's russet curls, damp with sweat, edged her nose in between the hidden lips, breathed in the unmistakable sharp tang of aroused female. Her own pussy twitched frantically. Sister Benedicta took hold of her head and tugged her away, back up for another kiss. Olivia moved her face back over Sister Benedicta's stomach, over the rough folds of skirt, back up to her naked breasts, closed her eyes as she rubbed her face against the hard nipples, and then back to her mouth, her lovely, warm, wet, open mouth, and kissed her again, licked her mouth and pushed her tongue inside because that really felt the best.

But as she kissed her, she started to rub herself against Sister Benedicta's slim white leg. She couldn't help it. Her body was tight, coils of desire unwinding with all the sensations, and she couldn't help shoving her hand into the warm space between Cecille's milky white thighs.

Down in the valley the bell tolled.

Olivia forced herself to stop. 'Oh God, Sister, that sounds like your coda!'

'Fuck my coda!' Sister Benedicta growled, tossing her head from side to side, little bits of grass sticking to her short, cropped hair. 'Lick me, Olivia. Lick my sex. Bring me back to life!'

'Calm down, Sister! I'll lick you till you're begging me to stop!'

Olivia giggled softly, but anxiety pricked at her as the bell echoed round the hills and trees. Sister Benedicta arched her back defiantly and as the wretched coda beat through the warm evening air she grabbed Olivia's face and pushed her roughly so that she slid back down her long, slim body, down her stomach, and she opened her legs, hooking her thighs round Olivia's head, pulling her face into her fanny, and now Olivia's nose and mouth were sliding into her crack and it was already so wet, the secret chestnut hairs curled over it, tight with moisture.

Olivia closed her eyes and smelt her lover's new smell, felt the grass scraping her knees. Sister Benedicta pressed her thighs around her ears, trapping her there. Her fingernails raked at her shoulders, yanking at her hair, burying Olivia's face into her cunt, and then Olivia knew what she wanted to do. She lifted the nun's white buttocks in both hands and held her pussy up in front of her face like a gift. She saw the juicy treat opening stickily before her, curls of hair clinging for dear life to keep it concealed, then she dipped her head and ran her tongue up the dark pink crack to lick up that moisture, shocking her senses with the untried, sweet-salt flavour and almost coming with the thrill of it as Sister Benedicta started to buck and moan in response.

Once more the bell rang, echoing round the hills.

Olivia's tongue parted the nun's soft lips, probed deeper, past the tender frills of skin inside, found her tongue being sucked into the tight, never-touched cunt. It was all piss and sweat and honey in there, that dark wet place hidden so long from the world, and now she was going to deflower it. Her fingers hooked into Sister's buttocks and slithered into the warm crack between her cheeks and her own cunt flashed tight and loose with mad excitement as she burrowed her face into her lover's cunt and Sister Benedicta writhed and lifted beneath her, and then Olivia's tongue touched the little bump of her lover's clit, and when she swirled her tongue round it Sister Benedicta moaned and tossed herself about like a porn star.

Triumph surged through Olivia then, she was on it now, and she sucked hard, opening up the lips like petals, and the nun really screamed out then, reared upwards and slammed and thumped against the grass as she started to shake and as she started to shudder with her climax Olivia fingered herself quickly and roughly, as she'd done so often in bed, in the bath, in French classes, but this was something else, finger-fucking herself while she licked out the beautiful Sister Benedicta, and her cunt gripped tightly at her fingers as she came, too.

The sun dipped behind the trees and a faint breeze rushed like hushed voices.

'I want to stay here,' said Olivia, rolling up to kiss Sister Benedicta's slender, sun-starved neck. 'I think I've heard that call. That voice from on high that I've dreaded all my life. It means no sex. No boys. No clothes. No fun. But I want to stay –'

'With God?' Sister Benedicta tried to look stern, but then she kissed Olivia in an incredibly wanton, lustful rush, pushing her mouth open again, pushing her back on the grass, straddling her girl, pinning her there, her turn to be dominating. 'Or with me?'

Immaculata, immaculata, ora pro nobis

The chapel was empty after the service. Lilies, candles, prayer books. Olivia bent down to pick them up, and felt Sister Benedicta lifting up her heavy skirt, opening up her milky white thighs to push her long white fingers up inside –

'Lie down, Olivia. Lie down, Sister Benedicta.'

They stood up, straight as soldiers.

'Both of you have sinned.' Sister Antonia stood on the steps of the altar, hands folded into her sleeves. She didn't look beautiful and serene any more. She didn't look like someone who'd been finger-fucked by the choir master. She looked like the statue of some avenging angel standing at the gates of hell. 'We have watched you all summer. Prayed that this sinful infatuation would pass if we welcomed Olivia in to the realities of convent life, away from her friends, tried to separate you from Sister Benedicta. We hoped it would pass, drop away with the autumn leaves, but here we are in December on this special Feast day and finally we've caught you.'

'Sister!' Olivia fell on to her knees, her white novice's veil flapping awkwardly across her face. 'Sister Benedicta has been my guide, that's all. My guide to the holy life –'

Sister Antonia glared over her head as Sister Benedicta came up behind Olivia and placed her hands on her shoulders to calm her.

'Don't compound your sin by lying about it, Olivia,' Sister Antonia barked. The chapel door opened, and there was the swish of habits and the restrained tap of shoes on the polished flooring as all the nuns re-entered the chapel.

'You will both be lashed.'

Olivia gave a kind of whooping snort. 'Sister, lashing went out with the ark –'

Sister Antonia didn't smile. Instead she produced a slim whip from the folds of her habit. 'We can punish whomever, however, and for whatever reason we choose. And you two have sinned beyond endurance. Now, down on your faces. Father Michael will do the honours.'

Olivia felt tears blocking her throat. But Sister Benedicta's face was alight with excitement. Olivia remembered what she'd said. The elation. The stinging pain. The dark humiliation turning to darker pleasure.

She smiled back at her lover, running her tongue across her lower lip.

'I love you, Cecille,' she said, spreading her arms out on the polished wooden floor.

Eating Figs

THE MATTE-BLUE SKY closed in like a helmet being lowered over her aching head. Salome fanned the baking air with her guide book, waiting for her charges to scour the temple for final nuggets of interest before the carriages could trot them back along the *corniche* to their muslin-wafted cruiser.

She'd had her fill of faded hieroglyphics, soaring monuments to omnipotence, giant slabs of granite or limestone fashioned into strutting Pharaohs. What had started as a favour, become a hobby, wound up a very well paid chore, was almost over. This was the final private tour before she could start her *real* job.

A cold glass of petrol-tasting *Cru des Ptolomees* wine was beckoning from the boat, shimmering like a mirage. A shower, a last feast of roast pigeon and stuffed vine leaves, then a dip in the tiny pool on deck under the stars. And finally, of course, that cosy chat and fat cheque from Mrs Weinmeyer.

The Egyptian silence buzzed louder, swelling and blistering in her ears.

Sweat trickled between her breasts, wetness spreading through the gauzy turquoise top she'd bought yesterday in Luxor market. She'd attracted quite an audience as she twirled before the mirror held up by the lecherous stall holder. Even a couple of scruffy policemen, lounging near the heaps of terracotta spices, weren't sure whether to caress or arrest her as she lifted her arms, showing forbidden armpits and bare stomach, to drop the kaftan over her tiny camisole. Well, she was used to the staring. An auburn-haired, white-skinned Westerner got ogled and groped all the time. In museums, shops, trains. Hence her repertoire of fruity curses to send the men packing.

Not so easy when the clients came on to you. She could hardly tell the freckled Scottish professors, imported to give learned talks on Howard Carter, that they were the sons of camels. Or the sandals-wearing English daddies, giving their families the trip of a lifetime, that their mothers were whores.

And how to refuse Mrs Weinmeyer's vodka-fuelled and extremely tempting requests, every night of the cruise so far, for a threesome to jazz up her fading marriage?

She tried to swallow. Even her saliva had dried up. She swayed against the honey-coloured pillar. Her feet felt shackled to the dust, as if she was a galley slave. Sweat was matting her hair, pouring down her back, yet she was shivering. Hurry up, campers, for fuck's sake.

But the silence was absolute. No voices bouncing off the ancient stones. No scuffling feet. No clicking of cameras. Only the fresh white cotton of a *gelabhia* flapping above a brown foot. A man was sitting under the massive decapitated head of Ramses II drinking Seven-Up. Salome groaned, eyeing the beads of condensation on the lime green can.

'My group. *Fain?*' She waded through the heat towards him. 'Where are they?'

The man's eyes above a full black beard were brown and unblinking. Unusual. Egyptians were usually clean shaven. He shrugged, flicked away a fly, and tipped the can up over his open mouth. Salome would have sold her sister for a sip, but when the man held it out, inviting her to share, she felt sick.

'Change money?' the man asked gruffly, fumbling beneath his robe for some hidden pocket. She backed away with her hands up, but the man brought out a wad of dollar bills. He cocked his head at another man in jeans and a dazzling white shirt standing with his back to them in the shadows. 'Change husband?'

Salome's thoughts were jumping like grasshoppers in a jar.

'Not mine,' she croaked. She glanced towards the entrance of the temple, where ram-headed sphinxes waited in a row as if expecting Elizabeth Taylor any minute.

But the entrance wasn't there. Just a wall of stone. The silence and sun were suffocating her. The man with the Seven-Up had gone. The ground was almost white in the heat, sphinxes and statues casting shadows thick as pitch.

Then, in a far corner, she saw two silhouettes wavering in the heat like skinny candles. Between them she could see the glint of the river. Sweat dripped in to her eyes, but she was afraid to blink in case these figures, too, disappeared.

'We can go back to the carriages now, if you've all finished looking round.' Her voice wheezed across the emptiness, and she stamped across the dust. The silhouettes seemed to collapse together for a moment, merging like two streaks of watercolour. One of them waved a stick-like arm. She came closer. It wasn't Mr Weinmeyer, or Mrs Weinmeyer, or any of the other guests. It was the man with the Seven-Up. He was wearing sunglasses now. And the man with the Persil-white shirt. He looked as cool as if he'd just stepped out of the shower.

'I've put your people in here,' he said in a deep, terse voice. He pointed to a dark slit between two pillars. 'This is the sacrificial chamber of Sekhmet, the greedy cat goddess.'

'Yes, I know that.' Salome snapped impatiently. 'But what are you doing?'

'Eating figs.' He held out a straw basket, his hand dripping with juice. 'Do you want one?'

She stretched out her hand towards the gleaming fruit, licking her dry mouth, but suddenly he pushed her through the doorway and she fell to the ground, grit scratching her elbows.

A sour draught licked through the chamber. She didn't recall it being so small. Shadows shifted and whispered. One of them was bending over her, fingers like tentacles sinking in to her arm.

'Let go of me!' she hissed, trying to shake it off. The pinching stopped, and something scuttled away in the sand. 'Now, can someone tell me what the *fuck* is going on here?'

'Salome, thank God, you've got to get hold of the ship's captain or something!' Mrs Weinmeyer was gasping. 'These guys are after some kind of ransom.'

The others crowded round, jostling and questioning. She pushed her way back to the two men.

'*An iznak?*' she barked at the two shadows blocking out the sun. 'Excuse me. What's going on?

The men folded their arms. Someone behind her began to cry. 'They say there's scorpions –'

'I can't breathe –'

'Salome,' said Mrs Weinmeyer quietly. 'They've taken us prisoner.'

'Correct,' one of the men said. 'Rich foreigners. Your captain or your families will come looking for you and then we will tell them what we want.'

Salome felt the panic, thick as blood in the hot space. So thick she couldn't breathe.

'No, you bastards, I'm in charge here, not you.' She stood up dizzily and jabbed her finger into Mr Seven-Up's face. 'You want a hostage, take me. These people hired me as their private guide. You let them go. They'll get you money, or guns, or whatever you want.'

There was a pause. Another scuttling in the sand. Then an arm came round her throat and started to squeeze.

There was moonlight outside the louvered window. The slats printed lines all over her, binding her in hoops of shadow. Every so often someone flickered past, near enough to touch. She shifted her leg and there was a weird clank of heavy metal.

Outside there were noises. Echoes off water. Cockerels. It must be early in the morning. The cockerels were crowing frantically, as they do before the knife comes.

But it couldn't be morning, because there was also music coming from somewhere. It was the same as last night's entertainment.

The sexy belly dancer had undulated around the tables offering a basket of freshly split figs on a bed of basil leaves. Her band of musicians sawed and sweated. The male guests lapped up every sequinned, wobbling inch of her, their lust undisguised, because her movements blatantly said *this is what I look like when I'm fucking*. Or maybe that was just the drink. Mrs Weinmeyer had been plying Salome with French champagne in yet another attempt to seduce her. Her pale hands, weighted with diamonds, had stroked Salome's back while Mr Weinmeyer, all steel-eyed Aryan beefcake, had watched silently from the bar.

Then the dancer had beckoned the two of them up to the front. She'd wrapped her velvety, mocha-brown arms round them to wind their hips with sparkly scarves, pushed her soft, warm body against them as she flirtatiously dragged their tee shirts up to bare their stomachs, then everyone had gone wild because Salome had this skill licked, cocking her knees, tilting her hips, wiggling her tits, letting her fingers ripple in coquettish invitation –

'OK, she's awake. Now we can get to work.'

Someone lit a lantern in the corner of the room. The flame sputtered then settled onto its wick. Evening, then. Both kidnappers were there. The bearded one had taken off his *gelabhia* and wore desert fatigues. Muscles bulged under his black tee shirt.

The lantern swayed on its hook, as if the whole place was on the move.

The Persil guy's white shirt was sticking to his torso. Not so cool now. And apparently unarmed. Sweat streaked his upper lip. Salome looked at his jeans as he swaggered into the room. When the time was right, the obvious place to strike was in the balls. Make him double up so she could escape.

'You're all tarts, you English. Always half naked,' he spat onto the floor.

'Half Cuban, actually.' They'd taken her white trousers. She was sprawled on the floor, legs open, wearing only her underwear and her turquoise kaftan, ripped now and filthy with dust. 'So why undress me?'

'Why do you think? No point having a hostage if we can't play with her.'

He handed her another basket of figs. As she leaned forward to snatch it, something bit into her ankle. Her foot was shackled to the floor with an iron ring. Salome yanked and pulled but it only rubbed her skin raw. The fig juice spurted stickily over her chest as she stuffed the fruit into her mouth whole.

'What's this round my ankle?' she mumbled, spitting pips.

'It's my version of a *khuul khaal*. You know, the precious badge of the married woman.'

'But I'm not –'

'No, but it marks you as mine.'

Salome's heart was pounding. Sweat and fig juice dripped between her breasts, and seemed to crystallize on her skin.

'Did you tell your clients how you can cast a spell by rubbing basil leaves between two leaves to create a scorpion?'

Salome's neck prickled with new fear.

'*Yeh,* Ali!' The other guy muttered to him in Arabic.

'Khaled wants to stop with the small talk. And I agree. I promised he could have you as his prize until your saviours get the money. And who knows? Maybe after that, too.'

The other guy squatted down and stared at her, hard, like he had at the temple. Salome tried to focus on the miniature reflection of herself in his eyes as he looked at her mouth, her throat, her breasts. But she couldn't help staring at his red, wet mouth, splitting the piratical beard. He licked his lips, then ripped off her kaftan. Her breasts fell heavily forwards, covered only by the flimsy lace of her dirty, sweat-soaked bra.

'After that you'll have to let me go.' Salome's voice shook as she tried to cover herself. 'Mrs Weinmeyer will do anything –'

Her stomach twisted sharply. Would she, though?

158

Maybe Mrs Weinmeyer didn't give a toss. Salome had turned her down, after all. Every night. Refused to climb into the huge circular bed in their imperial cabin to pleasure her rich blonde client and her silent, blond husband. How hard would that have been, for God's sake? Any minute now some gun-toting terrorist was going to screw her on a rough, dusty floor when she could have been spread out on Mrs Weinmeyer's satin sheets, totally in control, inviting Mr Weinmeyer's long, pale cock to thrust inside her while his wife lowered her waxed, perfumed cunt onto Salome's face –

There was another deafening burst of music. Curiously, it sounded nearer than before. A CD, playing on the deck outside the window. The same tinny, snake-charmer flute, the rhythmic, banging drum. The room, or boat, or whatever they were on, dipped and swayed violently as if in the wash of a much larger vessel.

'You can shut up now!' Ali drawled. 'Can't bear females chattering on.'

Khaled took hold of her legs, and opened them wider. He stroked them as if she was a dangerous pet, pushing them apart so that his hands could run up inside her thighs, up towards her warm, sweaty crotch.

'Get away from me!' She shifted frantically, trying to escape his probing fingers. Her breath caught in a rough gasp as he took hold of her and pushed her onto her back. 'Not seen a white woman before?'

'No point struggling.' Ali laughed scornfully. 'You're easy meat. Khaled here thought he was going to have ten fat tourists to deal with. Not just one cute tour guide.'

'They'll throw away the key –'

'Whatever, princess. Khaled gets ugly when he's roused.'

Khaled grunted, and grasped at Salome's hips, ripping

159

at her knickers. She tried to close her legs, slapping weakly, but he pinned her wrists over her head.

'When are you going to let me go?' she bleated, faint with heat and the slow slide of surrender.

'That's up to your friends. Depends how much they value you. Quite frankly, we've got plenty already. Raided all the rooms while you were off cheer-leading. I've got a comfortable cabin upstairs and a willing skipper. And his even more willing wife, all ready to cook and scrub and do whatever I want. Very cute, she is. Lovely wet, pink cunt all wrapped up in a big brown arse. Just my type. And gagging for it. You know, she let me fuck her senseless in the galley just before we went over to Karnak to catch up with you lot. Got me going, you know, really got me in the mood for a fight. And I know her husband was watching, because I saw those eyes peeping through the port hole, saw him having a good wank –'

'Oh for God's sake!' Salome pushed the sweat out of her eyes. 'How long are you keeping up this charade?'

'No charade, princess. I'm deadly serious.' He took out a beer. 'May as well get used to it. The Nile's a very long river. This trip could take hours. Days –'

'Let me go! I have to get back to New York –'

'You're going nowhere!'

Khaled smacked her, viciously, on her bottom, and she yelped with pain and fury.

'Get on that phone and find out what's happening out there!'

'Don't tell me what to do.' Ali leaned forwards. His black hair was falling over his eyes and his hooked nose, dripping with sweat now. 'You're still our prisoner.'

She bit her lip. 'OK. Let me go up on the deck, then. I can help the woman. I need air, Ali. I need light –'

Ali said, 'Just go ahead and fuck the bitch.'

Khaled's laughter choked in his throat. Fuck. A word everyone the world over understands. He unzipped his fly with his free hand. He pulled out his cock, which was almost erect, and circled his fingers round the base of it, ran them lovingly up to the knob, then down again. The foreskin wrinkled away, smoothed out over the surface as blood pumped through. Salome thrashed about on the floor beneath him and struggled for air and escape, but something awoke inside her, something toxic, coiling greedily at the sight of the thickness growing in his hand, aching to penetrate her. She thought it might be adrenalin rushing to equip her for danger. But it was something else. Mad, wild excitement. She was nothing, just a hot, empty cunt. He was a stiff, ready cock with only one place to go.

The mad, hypnotic music was inside her skull now. Khaled bit his lip as he massaged his cock, watching it grow stiffer, his pirate's face intent on what he was doing. Salome closed her eyes, stopped struggling, giving herself up to the music. Fine. He was going to jerk off over her bare pussy. Let him. Whatever.

But then he thumped down between Salome's sore thighs and with his cock still gripped tight in his fist he started to push its blunt tip in to her. She gathered all her strength to scream blue murder but instead, when his cock edged through her sticky opening and slid inside, the sensation was blinding and her moans dwindled into pure, lustful pleasure.

As the discordant music wailed, drums beat faster, Khaled pulled his haunches back, then thrust his cock further in. She thought of bulls or lions mating, she couldn't help it, clumsily, urgently thrusting, just like this, not even speaking. Copulating like animals on the

161

splintery, dusty floor. Her legs gripped to pull his groin into hers but he wasn't interested in what she wanted, kept pulling back, banging himself into her, out of time, no rhythm, no finesse, just wanting to get his bloody rocks off, the sheer rampant roughness of him making her want to scream with laughter, the only thing stopping her was his dark head holding steady above her, jerking slightly with every thrust but staring. Always staring.

There was a sound outside the door, what sounded like the metallic drag of a heavy chain or anchor. But still the music wailed.

Khaled thrust harder, and faster, still staring into her eyes, his tongue sliding across his mouth, pumping and fucking her like a dog. Salome's back scraped on the wooden floor, but the stinging pain kept all her senses acutely alert.

There was no kissing, or licking, or touching. Khaled still held her down with one hand, but the other was taking his own weight. There was just his cock, and her cunt. Muscles flexed constantly in his arms, his neck, his thighs, and suddenly he shifted his position, sitting back on his buttocks. He dug his fingers hard into her bottom and flipped her up towards him so that her back was to the watching Ali. He might have been masturbating as he watched, groaning, coming for all she knew, but the boat's timbers seemed to be creaking and rocking and the music was deafening.

They were face to face, her straddling Khaled's knees with her legs still wrapped round his waist. The chain round her ankle made a little echoing rattle of the one outside. Khaled's cock was aimed into the small of her back. His face was close to hers. His breath was hot, and surprisingly sweet.

'Kiss me, you bastard!' she hissed.

She pushed her face forwards, rubbed her mouth against his, felt the scratch of his beard, the wetness of his half open mouth, but although that brief touch made her hysterical with excitement he didn't kiss her back. But nor did he pull away. He just paused for a moment, panting loudly into her face, the excitement mounting uncontrollably. Someone started clapping outside, on the radio, in the room, she couldn't tell.

But then he pulled back and gave a kind of rising yell and then he slammed into her, hips back, arching, slamming again, both of them shuddering with the jarring impact of bone on bone, the captor and the captive, and before she was ready he was coming, face dark with the effort of holding back, growling obscenities into her mouth and though she wasn't coming she screeched triumphantly, feeling his body tense up. She bounced her butt across his legs, tightening her muscles round his cock and her legs round his waist, thought she was coming any minute, but then it was her turn to screech with fury because she couldn't keep up, he was pumping violently into her, she'd done too good a job, his eyes were blazing, never blinking, watching Salome as she arched angrily away and he roared out his climax.

They tumbled chaotically apart, crashing on to their backs. Khaled's cock slid out, pulsating heavily to a halt across her leg. She watched until it stopped lifting and spurting, and as she curled crossly into a ball, her cunt clutched with frustration.

'Never had white women down as cold fish. Our big brown cocks not good enough to make you come?' Ali tossed a box across the floor. 'Try these on her, Khaled. A kinky lot, those Americans. We found these sex toys in the cabin of Frau Weinmeyer. More like weapons of torture, I'd say. Or maybe I'm just very innocent!'

163

Khaled snapped on a pair of nipple clamps and they pinched her viciously. It was as if her nipples had been bitten by something very sharp, or stung by a venomous insect. The sting eased into a red-hot throbbing, deepening to a new, dark excitement.

'And my God, what's this?'

Ali held up a belt with a kind of truncheon attached to it. Salome's cunt pinched shut, then open again, as she stared at the brutal length of it.

The music suddenly stopped, and there was a knock on the door.

Salome tensed herself to scream for help, but Khaled, reading her again, covered her mouth.

A woman's voice called, 'Please?'

The triangle of light from the door illuminated a voluptuous figure in a long, glittering skirt.

'Mona, darling. *Habibti*,' Ali crooned. He kissed the woman on the mouth. 'Come and meet my prisoner.'

Khaled lowered his hand and Mona gave a little gasp of laughter.

'Salome from the American group! I was teaching you the belly dancing!' She thrust her breasts out, tassels whirling, and wiggled her hips sensuously. 'You were very good!'

Salome tried to signal her fear but Mona just smiled at her, allowing Ali to run his hands over her, bumping her belly-dancing hips against him.

'I'm a hostage, Mona!' Salome hissed desperately. 'Help me!'

'You've got it all wrong, Salome.' Ali laughed. 'She's not your friend. She's the one who got us in. So, *habibti,* try this contraption on for size.'

Mona made a face but he slapped her roughly, yanked up her long skirt, and strapped the harness round her waist. He bolted and buckled, ran the straps round the tops of her legs, bent her over so that the lavender strip between her butt cheeks opened briefly to show the little purple hole. He pulled one very thin strip so hard that it sliced through the untamed bush of Mona's pussy, making her toss her glossy black hair and run her incredibly long red tongue slowly over her mouth, then he yanked her upright and she stood there, proud as a queen.

Except that now, poking through the emerald green folds of her skirt was a great thick penis made of leather, rearing at an angle as if growing out of her. She jerked her hips obscenely so that the leather cock jumped at Salome, and yet again Salome's cunt pinched tight with an evil longing.

'So, *habibti,* dance for us. And Salome, wasn't she the dancer of the seven veils?'

The music started abruptly and at the same time the boat rocked sickeningly. Mona stepped towards Salome, wiggling her shoulders, and pulled her to her feet. Salome yelped as the iron ring yanked her backwards, but Mona just smiled. She had incredibly thick lips, and her tongue was flickering as she circled, stepping from foot to foot, flicking and rolling her hips, thrusting her wobbling breasts in the green sparkly bra, and all the while the brutal penis jumped eagerly between the silky folds of her skirt.

Salome stepped dizzily in a small circle, allowing Mona to put her hands on her hips to make her dance, too, and they started to step and whirl together, until Salome couldn't see straight, the blood was pounding in her ears, and all at once Mona fell to the floor in a kind of over-dramatic swoon, laughing and pulling Salome down on top of her.

The chain clanked, and the men shouted and clapped.

Mona's huge brown breasts squeezed over her sparkly bra as she caught her breath, and she pulled Salome towards her and started to lick at her with that long tongue, lapping at her mouth, her face, along her cheek towards her ear.

'You'll enjoy it, I promise,' she whispered. 'These guys are a pair of pussies. We can escape whenever we choose.'

Her hot breath tickled Salome's ear. Her body tightened with a mixture of excitement and relief. Then there was no more talking, just Mona's mouth and hands, taking charge, the men standing back to watch. Mona's arms were imprisoning Salome as her thick, wet tongue rammed into her mouth, forcing it open, forcing her to suck it. She'd not tasted a grown woman. Not since they'd mucked about at convent school. She liked it. And found herself thinking, this is what Mrs Weinmeyer wanted. Would she taste like this?

Mona was like a sensuous restless snake, she couldn't, wouldn't stop moving, her head was tossing from side to side as if she was already in ecstasy. She gyrated like a water-bed under Salome, moving her body as if they were dancing on the floor. Salome was too weak and dizzy to resist, and her body moved with Mona's, skin on skin, sweat on sweat, Mona's breasts rubbing against hers, her plump, hot body and her strong hands weaving a tight sexy web.

As they ground against each other, her legs parted and now her pussy was wide open, scraping the sharp sequins of Mona's skirt and, oh God, rubbing up against that huge leather phallus poking at her stomach.

She tried to whisper 'OK, when are we going to get out of here? When?' but Mona was lifting her now, so that her aching breasts, nipples elongated and tortured exquisitely by the clamps, dangled over her face, and as Mona's long tongue came out of her grinning mouth to flick one nipple she hoisted Salome right up and with another deft thrust of those agile hips pushed the leather dildo up inside her, so fast and so hard that Salome rose with the force of it, knocking her breath out of her.

Ali squatted against the wall, hands in his pockets, maybe reaching for his cock, swelling quietly in his trousers. Who knew? Mona was fucking her with Mrs Weinmeyer's dildo, and with every push Salome bounced helplessly on top of her, knees scraping, chain jarring at her ankle bone, every inch of her aching and raw but alive with shame and shock and excitement.

Mona thrust the dildo in with her strong dancer's hips and sucked on Salome's sore nipples, tongue tweaking and flicking at the merciless clamps. Salome fell forwards, impaled by the thick weapon and by the searing sensations, helpless as a puppet.

Now other hands were pulling at her buttocks, prizing them open, making the delicate dividing skin sting in protest as it was stretched open. The fleshy cheeks wobbled as Mona tossed her. Sparks jumped in front of her eyes as she realised what Khaled was doing. Her bottom hole clenched tight as a fist as he wrenched her open and started to push his cock at her.

She was already being pumped to bursting point by the dildo, what the fuck was he doing, Christ, he was ramming himself between her cheeks, penetrating that tight resisting ring and making it melt open for him.

And now Ali kicked off his trousers and came to kneel over Mona's face so that she was forced to fondle his balls and stick her fingers up his backside, spreading his buttocks so she could lift her strong neck and lick his arse hole with that amazing tongue of hers, and as Salome gaped at what they were doing and bounced on the dildo, Ali aimed his cock, straight and hard, at Salome's face and with no word, and at the same moment as Khaled penetrated her bottom, Ali pushed his cock into Salome's mouth.

'At last. She's silent,' he grunted. Salome's every orifice was brutally forced, and filled, bursting and burning with pain, shame, and a dark, dark desire.

All three of them possessed her, a perfect team. Khaled's breath was hot on her neck. Mona was strong as an ox, no sign of stopping. Ali fucked her face and mouth. She couldn't stop bucking and grinding, chasing her pleasure and grunting like the animal she'd become.

The nipple clamps were like terrier's teeth, worrying at her, the exquisite pain now real agony, somehow numb and acute at the same time, shivering down to every nerve end, making her lift and plunge on to the dildo, grind harder onto Khaled, bite and suck on Ali's cock.

Mona in particular gripped her like a limpet, long sharp nails digging into her skin, the phallus pushing further and faster, loosening her for Khaled, too, so that each time he went up her backside, the dildo went up more easily, everything lubricated by her juices. As she rocked forwards she was shafted up her cunt, as she rocked backwards it was up her arse, so her insides were melting too, she was opening her legs and buttocks as wide as she could, Mona and Khaled had her wide open, using her like a toy. Her jaw was cracking with the effort of taking the length of Ali's urgent cock.

The boat bumped hard, as if it was coming alongside. What if the police were here? What if the tour group were about to storm the store room to rescue her from terror and torture, only to find her loving it, impaled by not two but three huge cocks, pinning her as if she was on some kind of rack.

The thought of them watching her made her arch wildly with pleasure as her climax crashed through her. She was feverish with the madness and danger of it all and let her body grip and slacken, fast and slow, until the men were moaning and grunting and spurting up her arse, down her throat, using every part for punishment and pleasure.

The heat and silence in the bare cabin was total, time stretching like frayed rope. The boat swayed and rocked under them, making Salome sick, dizzy and delirious at the same time. She thought, through the window, she could see a fluffy cloud in the sky, just like England.

And in the corner a hard black shape, about the size of an avocado, flickered in the basket, dislodging the fruit, and one of the figs rolled out.

Ali's mobile phone rang, and he answered it, his cock still in Salome's breathless mouth.

'Money's here,' he drawled, snapping it shut. 'But it seems the group won't be going back to the States for a while. They're all holed up in the Winter Palace. Gone down with some kind of poisoning.'

He kicked Salome out of the way and laid Mona out beneath him like a feast. He wrenched the buckles and straps undone, and threw her skirt up so that it floated down over her body like a parachute. Mona squealed and squirmed with pleasure.

'Your turn, *habibti*. You've earned yourself a good fucking.' He took his cock and nudged it up into the thick black bush covering Mona's pussy. He glanced over his shoulder. 'Still here, bitch?'

Salome sat back on her haunches. The metal ring had warmed to blood heat round her ankle and fitted like another bone. Out of the basket of figs the shape scuttled onto the floor, its tail curved over its back like a question mark.

'Yes,' said Salome, fingers trailing up her hot, sticky thighs as she settled down to watch. 'I'm still here.'

Vivaldi's Girls

IT'S USUAL FOR SERENA and the other novices to be guided across Venice in the dark, shielded from the glare of daylight and men's stares. They are always taken to instruction or singing practice in the middle of the night. But she has no idea why. Their regulation grey cloaks conceal every lovely hint of burgeoning breast or hip as completely as any *yashmak,* so who's to know they're female?

After all, the girls were out, *sans chaperone,* when they first drew her under their wings.

But she knows she shouldn't question. The very reason she allowed, no, *yearned* for them to entice her into their silent, incense-flavoured world was to stop all the questioning.

So here they are, creeping obediently through the streets. They've fastened the drooping cowl hoods over their hair, not yet shaved off but pulled into viciously tight ballerina buns. Like so many Grey Riding Hoods they glide one behind the other in a delicate crocodile. The lit-up shop fronts glitter with glass trinkets, or glow with expensive leather. *Trattoria*s and bars flash music and voices as they pass, then fade behind them. Eyes down, watching the tips of their bare toes kicking out from their heavy skirts, growing stiff and cold.

Tonight feels different, though. It's Carnivale and she

can smell spice and madness in the air.

Their minder, Carlo, plucked just three of them from the dormitory tonight, rousing them from their wooden beds high up in the attics of the Palazzo Tremelli. As they step through the cobweb of alleyways, they seem to be skirting dangerously close to the Rialto Bridge and the louche revelry spreading through the city. They have been told that if they ever venture out unaccompanied, Carlo will treat them to one of his infamous, prolonged floggings.

Serena hasn't dared disobey, but others frequently do, because she's heard the lashings. The rush of the whip through the air and the reverberating slap hitting naked flesh. The initial gasps and screams of shock and pain behind the wooden door, choking into what she imagines must be the low, shivering moans of exhaustion and surrender. Carlo's low curses, his rhythmic grunts of effort as the lash rises and falls, answered by the victim's moans, makes him sound like a man fucking. All that is behind her now. But it still makes her fidgety and hot as she listens.

But of course he's not fucking them – he's there to punish them. She's seen the stripes of shame across the bare bottoms of her sisters when they've returned, swaying wide-legged like cowgirls, a weird smile playing on their zipped lips. She assumes they're smiles of gratitude because the punishment has made them purer. Eyes bright with secrets. Then they've silently lifted their grey skirts, making her recoil with prickly embarrassment as they've bent over to make their bottoms open slightly, showing the lavender crack, and shown everyone the hot red welts.

So there's no danger of Serena wandering anywhere. In any case, she's totally lost. She may as well be playing blind man's buff.

And that's just the way she likes it.

Earlier, Carlo marched them down the back stairs of the *palazzo*, through the little garden permeated with lemon scents, across the slippery jetty and onto to the gondola which rocks temptingly on the green water, rippling very slightly beneath their shuttered windows, promising adventure.

But you don't want adventure, Serena tells herself, getting sweaty under the cloak even though her bare feet are freezing on the paving stones. That's why you're here.

In the Bar Florian, three weeks ago, her friend Alissia picked up her bags and stared at Serena as if she was deranged.

'You paid a fortune for this dating weekend, you've got guys all over you like a rash, and you're letting us go home without you? Vince is livid, you know. Christ, you even had that horny glass-blower up against the wall like a hooker!' Alissia tapped the side of her head. 'And now you want contemplation and solitude?'

'Button it! People are staring!' Serena pressed her finger to her lips. 'Scoot. You'll miss the plane.'

'I don't get it –'

'It's not yours to get. I just want my life to change.'

When Alissia and the others had gone, Serena closed her tired eyes to bathe in the muted gold lamplight. She breathed in the aroma of hot chocolate mixed with sweet Marsala and wondered what the fuck she was going to do next.

A soft noise made her open them again. A group of women appeared beside her banquette, emerging from a mirrored panel. They pulled soft grey hoods over their faces as they glided through the crowd across the marble

173

floor.

They all looked incredibly young. A glimpse of severely pinned hair made their long necks look swan like and vulnerable. As Serena drained her gut-simmering *sambucca* the door kissed shut behind them. A weird panic gripped her. The tendons at the top of her thighs twanged as she stumbled out after them.

To her right the golden façade of the basilica San Marco gleamed through the winter mist. She could almost see the ghost of herself with the glass-blower last night, running hand in hand across the deserted piazza. He'd pulled her into the shadows behind the church, deep into a creepy dank alcove which was pitch dark and dripping wet from the recent floods. As he slammed her against the wall the bricks seemed to vibrate with loud remembered organ music.

The glass-blower stared at her for a moment. He had slanted sea-green eyes. She grabbed his head to kiss him and tangled her fingers in his long silky hair.

His buckle jabbed at her flimsy skirt as he ground against her and she wriggled into him. After hours of drinking and flirting she was wired. She let him prize her mouth open with his tongue, sucked on his tongue, opened her legs to rub herself on the bulge of his cock.

Shafts of excitement shot up the back of her legs just remembering it. Alissia was so wrong. Last night she was hungrier and hornier than any cynical old hooker.

Her head had banged against the wall as he kissed her harder, if you could call it kissing. More like devouring. Her knees started to buckle as he tugged her silky dress up. He ran his fingers underneath and sank them into the soft flesh of her butt, lifting her quickly so that she was forced to wrap her legs round him. Her pussy slicked open, sticking to the lacy knickers as her dress floated up round her waist and her thighs strained to grip him.

He bent his knees slightly to balance them both against the wall and then his fingers were ripping off her knickers and diving deep into the damp crack between her cheeks, searching and sliding inside her tender flesh. She couldn't tell whether it was sweat, wetness from the wall, or cream from her pussy, but she was seething with excitement now, opening wider for his fingers, to grip him, grinding her cunt against his jeans, wetting them with her pussy juices.

He groaned unevenly as his fingers slid in and out of her, releasing her urgent, musky scent into the cold air, driving her wild with wanting. She slid her hand down to scrabble at his belt, grinning at the sexy wet noises they were making, their ragged gasping, as her legs parted and his hot cock thumped into her hand.

There were footsteps, echoing off the walls, whispers skidding across the khaki water of the narrow canal beside them.

The glass-blower lifted his head, lips wet with saliva, and they stared at each other like babes in the wood, eyes glittering in the freezing gloom as watchful silence closed in again. Serena was quivering violently now, with the cold and the desire and the effort of gripping him. His tongue pushed hungrily in again and he hoisted her so that she was tilted backwards into the alcove, then with a sexy jerk of his hips he pushed his cock smoothly inside and started to fuck her.

Serena's pussy pulsed just to remember it. She had barely felt the scratch of rough bricks against her back as he pulled her towards him and away, thrust his cock harder inside her, faster and faster, so that the wicked excitement of the cold, wet open air rushed over her and she came far too quickly, clinging and shivering behind

175

the church on the last night of her holiday. She didn't even know his name. Just, yes, just like a last-chance hooker.

A grey swirl caught her eye as she hovered outside Florian, remembering. To her left there was a copse of marble colonnades, and she started walking towards the group of nuns or whatever they were. They looked as if they were playing hopscotch, but she now knows they were skipping on the spot while they waited for her, because of the cold on their bare feet.

'You look lost.' One of them touched her arm. Serena looked at the strong, olive-skinned fingers resting on her red suede jacket, then up at the calm face shrouded by the hood. At the base of the girl's throat was a silver cross, jumping lightly with her pulse.

'Do you have somewhere to go?' She had huge brown eyes. The others gathered behind her and gazed at Serena, inclining their heads stiffly like sombre birds.

'No, sister. Nowhere.'

'Why don't you let us take care of you tonight? We always love a visitor.'

Their breeze wafted Serena in their wake, out of the square and into the knitted maze of streets.

'What were you doing in the cafe Florian?' she asked the brown-eyed girl as they walked.

'Singing for the Vivaldi choir.'

'It still exists? I thought that was for the abandoned daughters of courtesans. And centuries ago. Not for nuns?'

'People can call us what they like. We're Vivaldi's girls.'

She took Serena's hand and they hurried through the city. Serena was just wishing she could unwind a skein of thread to find her way back when one by one the nuns

176

popped through a tiny arched door, like doves into a dove cote, and led her into a dark garden peopled with lemon trees.

'Where are we?' Serena watched their shadows on the wall as they climbed some stairs and passed into a formal drawing room which smelt of sherry and peppermints. The others drifted away through doors and up other staircases. 'Is it a convent?'

'I guess you could call it a place of retreat.' The girl untied her cloak and dropped it on to a huge velvet sofa. She smoothed a coil of black hair off her forehead. 'Just what you're looking for, no?'

She gave Serena a huge goblet of dark red liquid and as she fell into a hazy sleep it made all the sense in the world to let the girl with the brown eyes lay her down and take off all her clothes.

Their senses are battered now by violent revelry. Masked figures, jerking like puppets or deathly as corpses, parade across the water and over the spindly bridges. Even Carlo is dressed strangely tonight. He has on his customary leather mask, the one that makes him look like an executioner. The girls secretly giggle, when he's locked them into their dormitory at night and thumped away down the stairs, that underneath it he must look like Shrek.

But tonight beneath his long cloak they can see he's wearing elaborate patent dancing shoes with gold buckles beaten into the letter C.

When they stumble across a shadowy, ill lit *campo*, leopards, witches and eagles lunge at them and fall away, cackling.

Serena's heart is pounding and she grabs the brown-eyed girl's hand. Her name is Maria. Carlo doesn't see them touching, otherwise he would take both girls aside into a corner, there and then, for a quick punishment. As Maria tucks her hand up under her sleeve and strokes her wrist, Serena wonders when her time for that will come. He seems distracted and rushed tonight. He pushes them all up a wide dark stairway, much like the one at the Palazzo Tremelli, marshals them into a row, then vanishes.

A door in front of them creaks open. They are sucked in to a room where jewel-red bulbs splinter their seductive light through cracked glass shades. Ball gowns hang from rails, gilded mirrors endlessly reflect the walls. A heady perfume lies like mist across the ceiling, and it fills their skulls.

'Ah! Vivaldi's girls!'

A vast woman with black hair coiled in a tower bears down on them, licking her thick purple lips. She rips their cloaks off as they stand around, blinking like a bunch of Bambis, eyes huge in the bright light. They stagger in their little herd towards a vast mirror propped against the French blue painted panelled wall.

'And those hideous dresses! Off!'

'Maria? What do we do now?' Serena looks round. Maria is their leader. Their Sister Superior. But she and Lucia have weirdly gone into little girl mode, wrapping their arms round each other's waists for comfort. They whisper and shake their heads at their reflected themselves.

'We can't take them off. We're, you know, protected.' Serena speaks quietly. Her voice is a hiss in the huge room. 'We're not even supposed to speak, let alone be seen. We're trying to live the holy life.'

'Oh, is that what they're calling it now?' The woman cackles, from somewhere down in her belly, and her bosoms shake like huge jellies. 'I'll go along with that, just makes it all the kinkier.'

The woman takes hold of Serena, who has been abandoned by the others, looks at her, and reaches round to unpin her hair. Serena snatches her head back. 'Carlo will be back, and if he sees us talking, let alone undressing –'

'He'll get a massive boner, if I know Carlo!'

Serena's mouth drops open. She manages to croak '– we'll all be in massive trouble.'

At that the woman laughs all the louder. Maria and Lucia giggle behind their hands, geisha style, and start to unbutton each other. Fingers of fear crawl up Serena's spine.

'Carlo brought you here as the entertainment. Didn't you know? He promised me the best.' The woman twists Serena round, and swiftly unbuttons her dress. 'And he never disappoints. Eh, Maria?'

Maria smiles, head bowed, and steps out of her dress. Instead of the plain white linen shifts they usually wear, day and night, she and Lucia are wearing diaphanous see-through baby dolls.

'Maria?' Serena pleads across the misty room. 'Say something!'

But Maria just puts her finger to mouth, making a dent in her plump red lips as Lucia unpins Maria's dark hair and combs it out with her fingers. It ripples down her back. Then she unpins her own, and pulls Maria close to her again. They could be twins.

The room is cool, and the sharp air bites at Serena's nipples through the linen, making them stiff.

'Just do as you're told, like your sisters,' says the woman. 'And call me Signora.'

She lumbers about the room, selecting various

garments to hold against up against the other girls' cheeks, pulling their hair up again, but into baroque, tumbling structures involving bows and butterflies' wings. She swivels them this way and that, and as they are pushed together in front of the mirror their little nightgowns ride up and Serena's eyes are drawn towards the neat triangles tucked between their legs.

Next Signora plants herself between them, trailing her hands down their throats, fingering the young swell of their breasts while Serena watches, her body prickling with the remnants of fear and a new, creeping curiosity.

The thought flashes like a trapped bird. How far removed she is from Alissia, those accountant guys, the dating agency. Even the glass-blower –

'Come here, my lovelies.'

Maria and Lucia are drawn to Signora like chips to a big black magnet. Although she's vast and severe, Signora's touch seems soothing to the point of hypnosis. Their mouths fall open and they shuffle closer. She presses their dark heads into her heaving, flushed bosom, which bulges out of a corset shiny as ravens' wings. It looks like a huge embrace, but then they nuzzle into the crack of her cleavage, eyes closed as they breathe in her heavy scent and lick at her glossy skin. Their fingers start groping under their nighties, exploring each other's cute bodies, stroking and squeezing each other's bottoms, fingering their pussies –

'Oh, why does he keep you to himself? Why can't I have a taste of you more often?'

Signora's hands are restless, roving over the soft dent in their bent necks, smacking their hands out of the way so that she too can run her fingers down their spines to cup their high, firm buttocks. Lucia wriggles and blushes, cleaving closer to Maria, aiming quick kisses at Maria's neck. But Serena, watching out in the cold, sees a new, sharp gleam in Maria's eyes, which are fixed on Serena. Maria is not giggling or wriggling. While Signora is groping them both openly now, lifting up their garments to take a look at their breasts, their pussies, their bottoms, shifting her own heavy hips from side to side as if she needs to wee, Maria is very still, letting the woman touch her all over but circling one arm around Lucia's hips so that her hand comes to rest possessively on Lucia's crotch.

Suddenly Signora tugs at her own bodice to free the wobbling ocean of her bosoms. Her breasts roll out, velvety and brown, sheened with sweat, and her large brown teats poke out stiff as conkers. Serena's stomach tightens with sick excitement. A new throbbing sets up in the hot place between her legs. The last person to touch her there was the glass-blower.

Lucia squeals. Maria's eyes shift from Serena to stare at Signora's huge offering. Serena expects her to pull away in disgust. But as Signora lifts the enormous breasts towards her face, muttering in Italian and offering them to suck, Maria's eyes gleam again. The woman arches her back, wraps her arms round their necks, and pushes both girls' faces in between her breasts, rotating their uncomplaining heads against the cushioned flesh until their red, wet mouths open readily.

'Go on, now. Suck me.'

Signora's head falls back. Her tongue comes out to swipe across her purple lips. Maria's hand disappears under the folds of Signora's skirt and by the flexing of her arm Serena knows that Maria is touching the woman up. Serena falls back dizzily against the glass dressing table heaped with jewels. Although the groping, touching, kissing and sucking are mostly silent, the peace of the last

181

three weeks has been well and truly ripped away. Because all Serena wants right now is someone to suck *her* burning nipples.

There is a rap at the door. Not the door where they entered, but one that is concealed in a medieval tapestry on the opposite wall. Music beats from the other side.

'Signora! Bring the girls in now!'

'Shit. Others are waiting for you,' Signora growls.

She pushes Maria and Lucia roughly away from her. Their mouths leave her nipples with a wet smacking sound. She sighs and hoists her breasts, nipples hard and wet from their licking, back into her corset and steps across the room to shake out two identical ice blue dresses from a rail. She tips her chin at the girls and they start to raise the lacy hems of their nightgowns, up their slim brown thighs. Lucia tries to close her legs to hide her bare pussy. Maria tips her hip like a catwalk model, brazenly thrusting her crotch out for inspection.

Serena's head swims deliciously as if she's drunk the perfume. Her tongue is trapped between her teeth, urging her sisters on now, off, off, off, itching to see them totally naked. As if reading her mind Signora yanks their nightdresses roughly sideways and in doing so shreds the thin fabric. She drops the torn slips to the floor, swirls round clutching the silk ball gowns, and stops.

Maria and Lucia have wound one arm round each other's waists and are glued hip to hip once again in front of the mirror. Perhaps the perfume has intoxicated them, too, because they appear to be in a trance. Everyone stares at the apple roundness of their breasts, perched high on their rib cages. In the cool air of the room their nipples have puckered to sharp points, and each girl plays her free hand across the plump skin of the other's breast, pinches a nipple experimentally, watches it redden and stretch.

Maria smiles directly at Serena in the reflection, and her tongue slithers across her lower lip.

Serena feels as if she's reached up inside her rib cage and started to squeeze. She can hardly breathe. Nothing like this ever happens back home in Fulham.

The harridan Signora pauses behind the two girls, eyes round with greed. They are like a marble statue of the Fates, carved from the same stone, smooth young limbs poised in identical posture. But she slaps their caressing hands away. Deftly she drops the dresses over their heads and hooks them in, so that they become fledgling duchesses. The dresses are cut so low that their young tits don't quite fit inside the whalebone, the dark brown nipples totally exposed and popping like chocolate drops over the tight bodices. The full skirts of the dresses are slashed at intervals from the waist, so that as soon as the girls move the material falls away, revealing the jut of their hips and the shadowy dip and cleft between their legs. They sway towards the door, exaggerating the movement so that the blue silk alternates with flashes of tawny skin. They wait there for instructions, running their hands up the expensive fabric, admiring each other in their new finery.

Serena's hands are roaming up her legs as she watches their transformation. Her fingers burrow through the sturdy linen of her shift, find the sticky warmth of her pussy, and as no one seems to care what she does she pushes the material in, scraping it up the tender crack until it touches the concealed kernel of her clit and makes it throb. The material gets damp. Her lips beneath start to open like a flower. She spreads them further and her finger probes deeper.

Suddenly Signora looms up in front of her, holding up a crimson dress.

'Your turn now, beauty,' she croons, then sees what Serena is doing. She traps her wrist and winches it up and down as if pulling a bell rope, so that the heel of Serena's hand goes on rubbing frantically against her pussy and her mouth drops open at the hillock of excitement building there. Bubbles of desire pop and fuss inside and threaten to boil over. Serena squeals and Signora lets go of her wrist, clamping her hand over Serena's soft bush to still the quivering.

'Hold that sensation, pet,' she murmurs, her hand big and warm. 'You are well prepared for your initiation ahead.'

Serena is tamed. She raises her arms and Signora pulls off her nightdress, tossing it aside and making Serena stand there, naked, in the cold. Signora lets out a hiss of air.

Compared with the other two, Serena's English skin is snow-white, all the more so for the weeks incarcerated in the *palazzo* by day and cloaked by night. Her hips are broader than Maria's or Lucia's, though her waist is slimmer. Her breasts are almost too large for her frame, full and ripe, swelling round to the sides as well as beneath but firm enough to lift proudly so that against the white skin the hard, berry-red nipples thrust out expectantly, impossible to ignore. Still burning to be sucked.

Signora presses up behind her, smoothing the palms of her hands up Serena's sides, lifting her breasts higher. She pushes them together for a moment, creating a deep cleavage, allowing the nipples to scrape against each other. Sensation swoons inside Serena. Signora moulds her breasts with one large washerwoman's hand, and pinches both nipples until they are rigid and pointing forwards like sharp missiles, sending quick tingles of pleasure to join all the other tremors making Serena's knees knock.

When she smiles, Signora smiles back and her face lifts and is suddenly extraordinarily beautiful. Serena is lost now, happy to let the other woman arouse with her big strong fingers. Signora pushes Serena's legs open, and there's the moistness lining the velvet lips, and it's throbbing in there, wet and wanting –

But then Serena's suddenly drowned in crimson taffeta. Signora laces her up tightly in to the bodice, so tightly that she can hardly breathe, and her breasts swell desperately as she gasps for air, threatening to tumble over the edge, nipples only just covered and rubbed to aching point by the stern material.

Signora fusses with Serena's skirts, taking every opportunity to slip her hands through the slashes in the skirt to touch her thighs and bottom. There is another loud rap at the door.

She claps her hands. 'Now that you are excited, signorinas, you are ready for your public.'

She herds the trio, transformed from vestal virgin to sultry seductress, towards the tapestry doorway, and flings it open.

The overwhelming noise and colour and movement outside makes the quiet, mirrored dressing room full of nakedness seem womb-like. If this was some giddy secret party back home – another period, another planet – they would all be yelling *surprise!*

Serena is dimly aware of some kind of wild gypsy music abruptly silenced as she is shoved headlong and caught in a sea of masked faces and sumptuously dressed bodies. The mouths that are visible stretch into grins. The arms and hands, all trailing lace, rich velvets and long black gloves like so many tentacles, reach out of the crowd to wave and finger and grab and pull at the newcomers.

The ballroom beyond is dazzling with chandeliers and the shifting, searching kaleidoscope of masked figures. She spins round, but there seem to be no doors or even windows. The walls are all sealed with seamless tapestry. The air crackles with expectancy.

The crowd parts before Vivaldi's girls. They file into the middle of the room. How different from their dark, silent midnight walks! A low murmuring starts up and people press round.

A violin tests its strings and then the orchestra swings into a mad, galloping, gypsy-style waltz. Lucia gives a little whimper. Serena is grabbed and tossed across the sea of bodies, and briefly sees that Maria and Lucia have been surrounded by a group of mainly male guests who would be like a pack of wolves were they not up on their hind legs and clothed. They spin the girls round, touching, feeling, tasting, gloved paws going up and under their dresses, scooping out their breasts for a squeeze, velvet fingers poking up into their fannies, before flinging them like tasty morsels to the next partner. People turn them round and lift their ball gowns and prod the bodies beneath as if it is some kind of meat market.

Maria's expression is blurred as she is tossed about in the throng but Lucia is closer and her face, after some initial terror and confusion, starts to shine with excitement, then triumph, until she is actually pulling open her dress, thrusting out her breasts as the filthy reality of this scenario starts to hit home. She spins on the floor, in the air, dancing, flying, and spreads open her arms and legs to say *come and get me*.

Hands smother Serena now as she dances. A man covered in green feathers grasps her buttocks. His fingers

186

scrabble up the warm crack dividing them, jabbing into the button hole of her anus which tries to squeeze shut. She jerks with shock, her leg curling round his to keep her balance, but then he vanishes, his finger sliding smoothly from her hole, and another figure in a top hat spins and rocks her from behind, scooping her bouncing breasts out of the scarlet bodice with a shout and a flourish so that everyone can see them.

His white magician's gloves offer the ripe handfuls to the audience and everyone has a feel, then two men with cat masks advance, clawing at one tit each, drawing the dark nipples between their teeth until they are elongated and stinging with painful pleasure, then the two mouths suck hard so that spots dance before Serena's eyes but she leans on their shoulders, thrusting her nipples further into their mouths, loving the pain, the filth of two men sucking her, other mouths and hands touching her, and all the men, oh yes, the cocks packed into their breeches, bulging against the velvet and lycra and leather, waiting to be exposed to the crowd and massaged into life.

She wants everything to hurt. She pushes the men easily down to their knees, falling on top and straddling them, her pussy opening stickily, her tits dangling over them where they can suck and chew like kittens.

Her dress is whipped up over her bottom again and huge hands grip her hips from behind. Other hands part her thighs, fiddling up and down the soft skin there, up between the sex lips which are throbbing and leaking pussy juice as electricity darts from her tortured nipples. A big thick cock nudges between her cheeks, into her wet cunt, nosing in like a battering ram, and her knees start to buckle with excitement. The cat men are still biting her nipples, now following the cock up inside her with their velvet fingers.

All around her faces push up close to see, glittering, eyeless, featureless masks peer and pry, turn to each other, slide over each other's costumes, turn back to Serena, mouths agape with lust, elbows jostling for a turn.

The tempo alters to a wild gypsy dance. Serena's body jerks forwards as the stiff cock enters brutally from behind, forcing its way up the centre of her body. Its hugeness fills her and as it starts to pound into her, slowly at first then faster, the people start to clap in time with her invisible lover's thrusts.

Across the room Serena can see Maria lying on her back, legs splayed across a velvet *chaise longue* as a man in clinging snake skin swipes his narrow pelvis into her. A weird twinge of jealousy pierces Serena as she sees Lucia, her face ecstatic as a saint's, hooking one bare leg over the end of the chair and lowering her pussy on to Maria's face, holding the pale blue silk away from her legs so that everyone can get a clearer view of Maria's tongue flicking up for a lick.

Serena allows herself to go limp, smothering the cat men as they claw at her soft breasts and feed on her nipples, lets the urges inside her drive the orgasm closer. A scream escapes her as the man behind her slams into her again, faster and harder, lifting her off her knees. The clapping and stamping has accelerated to a frenzy. She grinds her nipples into the mouths of her worshippers as the cock explodes, and although she's not coming yet there's an answering wave of ecstasy surging inside her. She arches wildly to lock in the sensation for a moment longer. She knows there'll be other men. Other cocks. Any minute now it'll be her turn to come, and the thought makes her want to scream with pleasure.

She slumps forward into the crowd. Her bare foot hooks momentarily round the ankle of her invisible lover, and as she disentangles herself, she sees that the gold buckles on his shoes are shaped like the letter C.

She tries to spin round, pushes the cat men away. Their mouths are wet from sucking her nipples and other women descend on them like birds of prey, screeching and ripping off the men's tights and bending to suck on their swollen cocks. The tightness of her bodice has made Serena weaker than she realised. She can't stand, let alone turn round to find the man who fucked her, and as she starts to collapse someone else catches her and carries her away from the jostling bodies, through corridors and archways and courtyards and outside where it is raining.

The stranger sets her on her feet and pulls her along the slippery stones until they reach the edge of a canal. There are rows of empty gondolas tilting on the water, disturbed by some faraway wash and corralled like wild horses to stop them escaping. One rocking gondola is familiar because unlike all the others it's been stripped down to basic wooden seats. That's where Vivaldi's girls perch when Carlo steers them through the mist. She knows it's theirs because a silver cross glints where it's fallen on the planks.

So. After pacing invisibly round the city after Carlo, eyes down, he's brought them full circle, back to Palazzo Tremelli.

The stranger pulls her onto the nearest gondola and it veers violently as they step through and over it, along to the next one, until they reach the furthest craft, a proper one with sinister dark prow and curtained canopy. He drops her into the cushions and pushes off and as he steers them up another canal and under a series of low-arched bridges, she sees that he's wearing rich green breeches and a splendid gold-frogged jacket. His face is painted chalk white and it splits into a grin beneath an emerald-spangled mask with a long hooked nose.

'Didn't make you come, though, did he?'

Serena lies back, gasping for breath. Sweat trickles between her sore, exposed breasts although cold drizzle is falling.

'They said you were staying in Venice,' he mutters, running his hands over the rustling silk of her gown which has opened out over her legs. 'But I didn't have you down as a Vivaldi girl?'

'Who said I was staying – how do you know who I am?'

'The only woman in Venice not wearing a mask.'

The gondola rocks violently as he settles between her legs, pushing her billowing skirt up. Serena is too weak to move even if she wanted to. Fresh pleasure squirms inside her.

'So if you're not Carlo – who the hell are you – Christ, not Vince from the singles weekend?'

The water slaps beneath the underside of the boat. It could almost be slapping her bare buttocks, spread open on the cushions. Presumably in Casanova's day they wore delicate lace drawers. Or perhaps Casanova's conquests came to him well prepared, *sans culottes*. She could lie here for ever –

Some revellers run over the spindly bridge above their heads, whooping and shrieking.

'You want me to make you come or not?' His mouth presses down to silence her. She reaches up to keep his face close. His hair, tied back in a velvet bow, is incredibly silky.

'I know you,' she whispers. 'The glass-blower.'

'Fuck, get me out of these trousers,' he mutters, and pulls back, tugging at the tiny buttons running down the swell of his velvet fly. She squirms with renewed impatient pleasure, watching him unpick each button, the corner of his shirt sticking through the opening, then more corners of shirt and more slices of bare skin. Serena lifts her legs and rests them on his shoulders so through the slits in his mask his glittering eyes can see her open, wet cunt.

And then he's ready. Laughter lines groove down either side of his mouth as the mask eyes her silently. The trousers are somewhere round his knees, like a boy caught short, but that's all the better. Vivaldi's girl is fully clothed apart from her skirts up round her waist.

The green velvet falls open and there's his cock again, and it's up under her skirt and thrusting into her. The gondola bows sleepily at first, then nods into life, then with its slow, steady rocking it shows whoever's watching, and there's plenty of watchers on the bridge above, what they're up to. The glass-blower thrusts into her, deep and hard, pushing her into the cushions. She lies there, loosened in every sense, doing little, saying less, a good Vivaldi girl. She gasps for breath then gasps with pleasure as fast and furiously he fucks her and yes, he makes her come, and come, and come.

As she writhes under the glass-blower, milking the last drops of pleasure from him, a huge shadow falls over them. Fists clenched at his sides.

'Up, signorina. Up the stairs to your room.'

She starts to laugh. 'Don't be ridiculous. I've jumped the wall. I'm free to do whatever I like.'

The glass-blower sits back on his haunches, idly tucking his cock back inside his breeches. He lifts not a gloved finger.

'Vivaldi's girls never escape,' growls Carlo.

He yanks her up by the elbow, ties her cloak tightly round her neck.

191

'Stop him! Help me!' she shouts, but the glass-blower has jumped out of the gondola and is running up on to the bridge. 'I thought he was rescuing me –'

'You made your choice.' Carlo marches her across the wet paving stones towards the lemon garden. Already lined up there are Maria and Lucia. 'He knows. Everyone knows. You belong here now.'

'Your turn for a thrashing!' Maria hisses as Carlo pushes them all towards the stairs.

Serena watches Carlo's massive shadow, climbing the wall behind her. The buckles of his shoes clank. She remembers his hands on her hips, his cock ramming her from behind, the sounds he makes when he's fucking. Her sore cunt clenches sharply.

Carlo pushes them all into their room and locks the huge wooden door.

Mother Figure

YOU'VE HEARD THE PHRASE all mouth and no trousers? Well, my fantasy made flesh is a man who's all trousers, no mouth. The silent fuck. Spooky if you like endless sweet talking, but if you like to be in the driving seat, cut to the chase, get down and very dirty before *Desperate Housewives* comes on, the silent fuck is the business.

My old friends in the old town wouldn't recognise me now. I was the perfect wife and mother. A whore in the kitchen, maid in the bedroom, whatever it was Jerry Hall said we should be to keep our very own Mick Jaggers. And a sergeant major at the PTA meetings. They used to call me the *commandant* behind my back, but I didn't care. I *relished* the role. Back then it was only my public face. Now somehow that dominatrix has come home with me, and in the shadows my slut side is having a ball.

We were all happy as pigs in shit until poor Graham caught me playing away.

I blame Sara Singer. It was her fault the school caretaker's lad stumbled over me one Saturday morning behind the scenery. I was butt naked, whipped red raw and tied up in a half-built gypsy caravan when he came to take the Strictly Classroom props down. So it was her fault that my husband, combing the premises for his missing wife, found her being fucked by a monosyllabic but stupendously endowed boy in overalls who couldn't believe his luck.

Graham got a good eyeful, though, before he hauled the boy off me. The second time he forgave me actually, because that was when he caught me with Sara Singer herself. We were lying on the grass behind the wine tent at the open air music festival in the school grounds. It was a hot night, but very dark. Sara had her white Louise Sandberg kaftan hitched up round her slim tanned thighs and was sitting on my face. I can still remember the sweet juice of her pussy. The first and last I've ever tasted.

The third time was the worst, because it was at our house. In our bed. Graham caught me with Sara Singer and her gorgeous Dutch husband. Well, mainly her husband. Sara was squatting at the end of the bed, filming us. At the opening of her last exhibition her husband and I were projected, fucking in monochrome slow motion, all over the walls of her art gallery.

Graham upped and went back to Sydney, and the kids flew the nest with him. Oh, I go down under occasionally. They visit. But they prefer me at arm's length. Thank heavens for Skype. I can speak to them wherever I am in the house. Whatever I'm doing.

Sara went back to Amsterdam. So I left the old town and with my very generous settlement came to live in this cute mews house in South Kensington. I'm still on committees galore, but I ditched the pearls and the Alice bands, had a little work done, and none of them, not even Sara, would recognise me now. Oh, I kept the blonde hair. It's the only natural thing about me, other than my voracious appetites.

My little sideline is taking in foreign students. For the cash, and the company. They get my profile from the language school, and I wonder what they envisage? Gloomy little house? Grey-haired harridan with a rolling pin? Well, rolling pin's almost right, as you'll see. They could choose big host families with dogs and noise and daddies if they wanted, and some, the girls, do. But I get a constant stream of boys. And men. All single, at least while they're here. All quiet. The ones who speak no English at all are the best because they're, obviously, silent.

Have you any idea how sexy a totally silent man can be?

So they know what they're getting, at least in outline. And what an outline! Their host mother is an older single woman, sure, but you just watch when I open the door to my little house round the corner from the Natural History Museum, greet them after their long flight from Tokyo or Peru, or their shorter flight from Naples or Moscow, and their eyes fall out of their sockets. Who needs Sydney when there's so much fun to be had right over this threshold?

Still wondering what I'm like? Madame Whiplash, perhaps? Close, but no cigar. I'm not so crude. All you need to know is that no one's ever complained. The students never squeal to the school. I suppose they'd have to chide me if they knew what goes on behind my Kelly Hoppen shades, but they couldn't fault my teaching technique. And the students, if they were really shocked, could demand another host mother. But they never do. Why would they? The first guy came close to leaving, but eventually I realised that was because he was frightened his cock was going to burst out of his pants every morning. It's the slippery peacock blue silk dressing gown I always wear to serve breakfast. And the way I did his full English.

His cock was the only part of him that ever really moved. He rarely even used his hands. Which was marvellous. It made him my sex toy, and he was the blueprint for how I wanted to mould the others. So I persuaded him to stay the full duration.

I've got a feeling you're thinking seaside postcards now, so if I tell you that Marilyn Monroe is my heroine, will that fill you in?

My first guest, the guy with the every-morning horn, was Japanese. Shiny suit. Smaller than me, and I'm petite. Handsome, chiselled, very pale almost sickly face, and a very full, purple mouth. Black, hooded eyes. I wondered what made his stare so very deep. After a few days I figured it was because I couldn't see his pupils. From the moment he walked through my front door his eyes on me never wavered. Any idea how sexy that is? Your every move watched, never missed. Cooking, sleeping, bathing, pissing, he was always there, watching me. I told you I liked them silent? Just once he tried to speak so I gagged him.

My front door closed the two of us in. This stranger and me alone in here, and the silence and heat seemed to crackle with electricity. It almost paralysed me. I'm usually like a cat on tacks. I can never keep still. Why pole-axed by one small Japanese bloke? It wasn't him. Not immediately. It was this situation, so new, and intimate to the point of claustrophobia. My small house transformed into a designer den. A glittery cage, locking us both in and shutting everyone else out.

I showed him his room, prattling on as I always do with the new ones, to cover the shyness, then gave him his supper, still prattling. He looked at my face for a bit, my mouth, made me blush and bite the blood up into my lips. Then his round black eyes swivelled towards my breasts. Well, you can hardly miss them. There should really be a dress code if you want respectable host mothers. Fisherman's sweaters, perhaps. Painters' smocks. Dinner-lady housecoats.

He stared as I was leaning over to pour parsley sauce onto his gammon, and my nipples hummed under my red satin blouse. My nipples are big, and super-sensitive. No question of any surgery there. I couldn't bear the lack of sensitivity. My husband used to call them his ripe cherries as he bit into them. Poor boy. Anyway, Kyo's eyes grew very wide. They were like X rays, lasering through my blouse. I couldn't help myself. I leaned over him a little longer, aware of my deep cleavage inches from his face, scented heat pulsing off me.

Then I sidled away, but the kitchen is tiny, and the more I stirred sauces and shook salt and shined surfaces, the harder he looked and the stiffer my nipples grew, poking through my bra, poking through the satin.

I left my bedroom door open that first night. I wanted him to see me touching myself, wanted him to come to me across the hall, but he didn't come in. I got it. After that I always went to him.

It happened the next morning, and I made him late for school. I turned round from the coffee machine and he was staring at the huge plate of eggs and sausages and bacon as if they were the enemy.

'I know you eat rice in Japan for breakfast. Maybe a little raw fish.' My thighs squeaked as I wriggled myself up on the kitchen stool. I always wear stockings and suspenders, but I rarely wear knickers. They spoil the kinky line of those straps and buckles. I had just showered, but already I could smell fresh excitement. 'But this is what we eat in England. So eat.'

He picked up his fork and watched me as I blew froth across my *cappuccino*. Then I sat back, crossing one leg over the other with a swish so that my dressing gown fell open. Peeping up between my thighs he couldn't help but see my bush. That was the Sharon Stone moment that made me the exhibitionist I am today. The naughtiness. The silence. The gleam in his eyes.

But you can't have an exhibition without an audience. He didn't have to look, did he? He didn't even have to stay.

But stay he did. Kyo ate his sausages, one by one, his big lips opening and closing, all the while staring at the place where my gown was open. I sipped my coffee, opened my legs, tilted my pussy a little. He chewed, staring openly as a schoolboy. I spread my waxed sex open with one hand to show him the pale pink frills inside. My English cunt. Oh, that made me shiver with real delight. His first, maybe his only, English cunt. What were the pussies like back home? Butter soft lips opening to frills that same dark purple as his mouth?

I stretched two long fingers up inside, the nails scraping painfully, making me flinch, as they went in. He didn't budge, or quiver. Just chewed. Didn't even twitch his feet, or fidget the fingers grasping his fork. My fingers went in, and the breath came out of me, hot, as my cunt closed around my fingers and sucked them in. I pushed them in hard, wanted to hurt myself, started frisking myself, in, out, faster, wet slipping on my fingers, jerking about on the bar stool.

I thought, Christ, wouldn't a normal man have done something to me by now? Run out into the street screaming, or called the embassy? Or slammed me onto my back across the granite breakfast bar, ripped open my silk gown and fucked me senseless?

But that's not how they do it. He watched, as they all do, and that's how I like it now, what I make them do, and the more silent and still he was, the wilder I became. My thumb massaged my clit roughly as my fingers fucked me and then I came, in a kind of ragged burst, and at the same time I gave a strange little ladylike screech which shivered off into a sigh.

He forked the last bit of runny tomato neatly into his mouth. Then he leaned forward, still staring at my cunt, pulled my fingers out, sniffed the salty scent into his nostrils with his eyes closed, as if that heightened his senses. Then he nodded. A sharp, decisive, approving Japanese nod that was more like a salute. Or a subject's bow before a queen.

Then he'd gone from the table. I listened as he moved about upstairs, opening drawers, moving furniture, turning on lights, then showering. Again. God he was so clean. Or maybe I made him feel dirty. I was convinced he was packing to leave.

'Kyo? You'll be late for classes.'

There was no sound.

'I'll understand perfectly if you want to find another host mother after that – little display.'

I heard the creak of his bed. In his doorway was his rucksack, stuffed with books. On his duvet he was lying, white, shiny and naked, like a kind of mini but muscular mannequin. A blow-up boy. *My* blow-up boy toy.

I stepped nearer in my feathered mules. One arm was thrown above his head as if in surrender, but the other hand had wrapped round his cock, pulling it into life. He was wearing soft white gloves, the kind that a waiter or a clock maker or an archaeologist might wear. As I got to him he threw that hand above his head, too, leaving his short cock rearing out of the jet-black nest of hair, stiff as a baton.

My pussy squeezed greedily. A new delicacy, prepared just for me. My own *crudité*, laid out in a finger buffet. I

199

reached out to touch it, watched it spring back briskly.

That was when I suddenly remembered my ex-husband's story about a business trip to Tokyo when he and a colleague had been ambushed in a bar by a group of frisky, drunk Japanese girls. They had dragged the two men into a booth and ripped their trousers and boxers off, giggling and shrieking like homing sparrows and demanding to see if British men's cocks really were as big as the rumours said.

But when they saw what Graham and his friend really had lurking in their pants, an electrified hush had descended over the group. Their black eyes and red-painted mouths went all round and open like, well, like astonished little sex toys, because, Graham explained proudly, even when they were semi-erect, British cocks were evidently at least double the size of any they'd ever seen.

It took a lot of nagging and wheedling to get him to tell me what happened next, because he tried to deny it at first. Said it was his colleague who ended up misbehaving with all that Japanese totty, not him. But eventually, when he saw how turned on I was by the scenario, he admitted the whole hog. How the dreadful pop music had drowned the girls' wriggling and giggling. How the glitter balls and flashing disco lights in the bar had dazzled him. How the girls had pinned him and his mate down on these sweaty leatherette banquettes and started touching their big British cocks with their tiny white fluttery hands, taking turns to stroke them, wrapping their delicate fingers round them and pumping at them until they were standing up rock hard. How one of the girls had lifted up her pleated gym skirt to show him her Hello Kitty knickers and her spotty thigh socks, spread her legs and started to lower herself –

'And then?' I asked him. I was packing sausages into a lunch box at the time. Graham was knotting his tie, getting ready for work. We looked at each other. Only our offspring crashing about in the hall stopped us from grabbing and humping frenziedly then and there on the kitchen floor.

'And then we went back to our hotel with them. Christ, Caroline, you don't want to hear this. I shouldn't be –'

'Tell me, Graham!'

And so they'd gone back to their skyscraper hotel room, he couldn't remember how many girls there were, they were all drunk on saki, and these girls, still giggling and wriggling, had used their kinky thigh socks to tie the two men down, side by side on the bed, and then taken turns in lifting up their skirts, kicking their knickers off, all identical little black triangles between their white legs, then clambering on to the men's cocks and bouncing up and down on them all night.

'What did it feel like? Fucking them? What did the girls feel like?'

I remember Graham tugging at his cuffs, picking up his briefcase, both of us glancing at the bulge in his trousers.

'Like being forced by little tarty aliens. Oh, they were cute as buttons. White, when they were naked. Flitting about our room, flicking through the porn channels, emptying the mini bar, so white they were transparent. And light. You couldn't feel any weight, like they were acrobats. Maybe they were holding each other up. It was like they were spinning on top of us. And so tight. Their cunts felt like kisses at first, then when we were inside they sucked and gripped tight like wet little fish mouths. And all their movements so fidgety and quick. Slithered

201

up and down like little pole dancers. Like we were the toys, and they couldn't get enough of us.'

So. Let's see if size really does matter.

The dressing gown slithered off me and I knelt on the bed. I always like to keep my bra and suspender belt on. Apart from anything else it conceals any imperfections. Well, I'm a cougar, not a kitten! And the whalebone accentuates my Sixties-style figure. It's tailor-made with ferocious, satin-covered corsetry. It makes me both sexy and scary. It's my battle dress. My uniform. My armour. Most peculiarly of all, I've discovered since that morning with Kyo how all that silk and satin and whalebone promises and gives intense pleasure, even if it never comes off. It hides you, holds you in, pushes you out. And a sex toy never touches anything unless he's told to.

That first time we were short of time. Since then they've learned to set their alarms, because I'm horniest first thing. Fuck me before *This Morning*.

I approached with caution, in case he jumped up and ran away.

I slung my leg over his straight thighs, brushing his cock as I did so. It quivered, then was upright again and still. I caught it in the folds of my pussy. I held myself above him and then had the nerve to look him in the eye. He blinked just once. I looked at those big, thick lips, and my pussy softened, knowing exactly what it wanted.

I crawled up his stomach and chest, letting his cock bounce away from me, and hovered for a moment over Kyo's calm face.

'Lick my cunt, Kyo.'

I didn't mean to hiss at him all roughly like that, but I was having trouble breathing. He was laid out beneath me, taut and ready and in my power. But I could tell he was happy. His cheekbones lifted, stretching his face into a smile-free beam, and his black eyes glowed.

We were alone in my little house, hemmed in by the shadowy buildings. Neighbours often flickered at their windows, sometimes pausing to gaze into my back yard. I wanted them to see me. Next time I would push the bed closer to the light.

Kyo nodded sharply once, and opened his mouth obediently. There was his tongue, long, thick and quivering out between his strong white teeth. Those thick lips were soft and pillowy like a woman's. They closed round my pussy, sucking my hot sex whole into his warm wet mouth and holding it there as if his face was an exotic fish pulling us both down to the bottom of the ocean.

He was doing something amazing with his mouth. He was massaging my swelling, pulsing sex inside it, and as his lips squeezed and nibbled and sucked, his tongue roamed up between the lips, insinuating itself up the tight wet crack and sliding inside, probing through, tasting the next layer before circling my clit.

Christ, forget deep-sea fish. It was like he had a forked tongue, flicking every which way, like a snake.

I moaned and juddered violently as he tapped and flicked and then licked my clit. His white-gloved paws fluttered round and landed on my buttocks. I gasped again. His hands were small and soft, but I guessed they were powerful, used to quelling animals, people, food, machines, and I liked that. Maybe back home he was a ninja. Maybe he could break trees, or opponents' necks, with just one snap.

Somewhere outside a sash window scraped up. I heard my neighbour's bracelets chink as she watered her flower box.

My silent warrior was holding me completely still on

my bed. I watched him sucking me. I was totally mesmerised. His hands manipulated my bottom as he sucked at my cunt, pressing my butt cheeks very lightly as if he was testing it for reactions, but it felt more like a warning not to move. Hell, I wasn't going anywhere. I was frozen above his face, my head tipped back in a kind of melting ecstasy, my own tongue flickering obscenely like a porn star as he worked at my pussy. The more I challenged myself to stay absolutely still, the more intensely every flickering sensation was heightened. Spot-lit in the cold silent morning.

My stomach started to coil and tighten with excitement, but I roused myself before the climax got going. I didn't want to come just yet. I wanted to feel that small white prick inside me. See what it was made of.

His suction on my pussy was so strong but I pulled away gently, and very reluctantly.

'Fuck me now, Kyo,' I breathed, and the order was soft this time, not harsh at all.

His mouth released me with a delicious wet sound, my sex lips flipping against his lips as he spat me out. As I slid back down his chest, letting my pussy slide wetly across his white skin, he licked my juices off his lips then closed them quietly, as if he'd just finished speaking.

His hands came away from my bottom and I placed them like two white flowers on my breasts, jutting out of my corset. He rotated them slightly over the material, and my nipples pricked up hard with desire. I wanted to feel that big purple mouth sucking on them. I pulled one breast out, and fed it to him. I'd meant to keep that treat until later, another day maybe when we had more time, but I couldn't help it, his mouth was a huge hot wet pleasure zone all of its own, and yes his lips closed round my breasts taking in the sharpened nipple and the sparking flesh around it and he sucked it in like a lovely wet powerful Hoover and I felt the nipple scrape on the roof of his mouth, and so did he, because then he bit it, and it hurt, and I screeched with delight, and crushed his face into me, scrabbling to get the other breast out, holding it, heavy and warm, in my hand as I pressed it against his wide cheek, rubbed the nipple against his mouth until he turned his head and started to nibble on that one, too.

As I arched my back to push my breasts into his face I caught the flash of a white curtain outside and my neighbour's watching face, her hand still holding a little silver watering can, the petals of her red flowers dotted with droplets. Her window is to the side of my yard. She was staring into my lodger's bedroom, saw me suckling him, stuffing my nipples into his mouth while my hand reached round behind me, under my bottom which was just sitting over his thicket of straight black hair, and I took hold of his smooth white cock, guided it to slide between my buttocks, thought the shadowy dampness there might really shock him, got even hornier at the idea of making him do something really dirty like fuck me up the arse and not letting him show it.

But there was all the time in the world to introduce his cock to my arse. So instead I rubbed it across my hidden clit, wet and singing from where his tongue had been.

I nearly came there and then at the touch. I was so worked up now.

I moaned and writhed, rubbing his cock again and again across my pussy, feeling it bump against my clit, my own special toy, keeping it as delicate and slow as I could, while his face disappeared between my breasts, his small hands roaming over them because they couldn't manage a whole handful, caressing them with those soft white gloves, how sexy was that, clinical but sexy, while those thick lips kissed and sucked.

And then I leaned over him, on my hands, watched my breasts dangle heavily over his face, his black eyes fixed on them and I wriggled down on to his cock, felt it lock into me and jut up inside, so weird and new the way it didn't grind and pump and fill me like a big one would but rather *introduced* itself, explored me as it slipped inside, eased up far enough to have my cunt close greedily round it, and then waited.

Here was that stillness again. I floated there, his cock resting inside me, plugging me tight. Yes, that's it. It wasn't much longer than, sorry to say it, perhaps a large gherkin, I suppose, but I'm here to tell you that anything can give you crazy pleasure if it's the right shape, touching the right places in the right way. So he was plugging me, closing me in, not going anywhere. Yes, owning me. And he was all mine. I could hover there, squeeze him tight inside, until I was ready to move. He didn't move, pump, jerk, didn't thrust, didn't fuck me in the usual manly way, just waited, locked in there, lying beneath me, my white mannequin, my sex toy, but before I moved a muscle his cock started, not to pulsate, not even to throb, but to *vibrate,* God this was something else. It was just like that. Vibrating inside me. Slight, tiny, imperceptible, shivering pulses, but steady enough and strong. Growing stronger, like a light burning brighter. Like, well, like the best, newest, shiniest Rampant Rabbit you can imagine.

And so it took a while. He missed school, I'm afraid. Because this incredible vibrating penis increased the pressure so slowly, and so slightly, and my body tightened round his cock so slightly in answer, that we inched in sensuous slow motion towards our climax, as his mouth sucked on my nipples, because I wouldn't allow it to end, and it got more and more delicious, and I knew for sure now that my neighbour was watching, and I wondered if she was touching herself as she watched, because all she could see was my head tipped backwards, my breasts smothering a small white man with a small white cock, but from her angle she would also have seen that as our bodies started to melt together he let one of his hands drift gently behind me and as I was starting to go faint with ecstasy he inched his gloved finger in between my buttocks and jabbed up into my little arse hole, which opened softly to let him in, and as his finger started fucking me, hard, up the bottom, we twitched into life and rocked together, very quickly, lightly, whitely, tightly, just like those little Japanese girls did when they fucked my ex husband in that hotel room above the roof tops of Tokyo, and then Kyo and I came, him spurting inside me but silent, me, sighing, whispering, perspiring a little, and, after a long pause, winking both at my neighbour and at the web-cam bolted into the corner of the room.

But I had to remember that I was his host mother and I had duties. So after a few minutes I lifted myself off his cock, which was still as stiff as a spanner, hitched my stockings up again, wagged my finger at him and said, 'Tomorrow morning, Kyo, you must be ready to fuck me before breakfast. Then you won't be late.'

And when he'd scuttled off to school, I fired up my laptop and showed my Graham, far away in Sydney, what we'd been doing.

The next student was a quick learner, too. He was taller than Kyo, but on his first morning I found him in my sitting room hanging up all these red and gold dangly charms.

'To bring my host mother good luck.'

He had huge black eyes and Gok Wan hair. I thought he might be gay until he told me about his black belt in *taekwondo*. Everyone in South Korea, he told me, has a black belt. They learn it in the military.

Yes, but he could still be gay … so I asked him to put on his *taekwondo* uniform and show me his surge fist and dragon punch.

'Those are from computer games, Mrs Caroline. Not real moves.'

The real moves, especially when I persuaded him to perform them naked, was all I needed to know. Every morning I would strut into the kitchen and he'd be ready. He'd show me his cock, short, slim, white, and perfectly stiff, jutting out of his white suit. Then once he'd eaten three fried eggs and two rashers, he'd stand up, kick his chair back, just like I'd shown him. Then he'd have me right on this kitchen table, riding me, tight white buttocks jerking as he fucked me, plates clattering to the floor, mouth open in silent climax. My neighbour filming from the patio. Me hysterical with pleasure.

And watching in cyberspace all the way from Sydney, my ex husband becoming aroused and very, very interested.

In amongst my alabaster army of silent house guests there was one exception. My Arab boy. He was very royal, very devout, and very virgin. He had silky skin the colour of *cafe crème*. Which is why I spent much of his short but delicious stay in my care licking him, very slowly, all over.

What he also had, and the jolt of lust that shook me the first time I disrobed him proved how much I still relished a thing of beauty, was a very big, brown cock. My job was to show him what to do with it.

At first I decided just to be the perfect mother figure. There was danger written all over this one. His family were strict and powerful, he was engaged to a princess whose bare face he had never seen, and he had the permanently wary look of a handsome, muscular Bambi.

But I'm afraid he started it, because he broke my only rule and wandered one night into my bedroom.

He knew it was a mistake as soon as he saw me sitting at my dressing table. As our eyes met in the bevelled glass of my Venetian mirror and his eyes wandered over my naked shoulders, I doubted he'd ever seen this much female flesh.

'Sorry, Mrs Caroline. Sorry. I want ask you for clean towel –'

He shuffled his bare feet on the carpet, but he didn't move. He was half asleep, as always. He was also half naked, and, as always, squeaky clean. He wore designer jeans falling unintentionally low over his hips and I could see the jut of them, the young, permanent bulge in his crotch. He crossed his arms over his hairless, muscular chest like a surly kid and leaned in the doorway.

I decided to take it very slow, which I regret, looking back. I stood up. Unlike all my other boys, he'd caught me unawares. Because it was night time, I was naked as the day I was born. Like him I was as clean as a whistle. No war paint. No armour plating. If you walk in the right way your breasts will always look good as new. Just bare, and heavy, let them bounce a little. So I stepped closer, my breasts tilting at him, nipples shrinking into bright red inviting hardness. Graham's cherries. My hair was wet from the shower, freshly blonde. All I wore was my stockings. Always the glossy nude sheen, the lacy tops leading the eye up the thighs to my fanny, waxed, smooth, girlish, my flash of pink smiling an invitation.

He couldn't move. I'd never seen such genuine innocence in an adult male. Such paralysing shock. And such a genuine, male, reaction. Eyes, mouth open. Mind frozen. Body on fire. Jeans straining and pulling round his cock.

'*La'a, haraam,*' he stammered, holding his hands palms up as I sashayed up to him, idly caressing my breasts. 'Can't. Forbidden.'

'Oh, it may be forbidden, my love, but I happen to know that you have your desires just like any white man.' I cupped my hand over his crotch and had his flies undone quicker than you could say 'Pharaoh'. 'I saw a long brown Arabian cock once before, you know. I was 20 years old, and walking down a back street in Cairo one hot afternoon. There was a man sitting in the shadows, watching me, and he lifted up his *gelabhia* and jerked himself off, just as I was walking by.'

He frowned, not understanding perfectly. I caught hold of the surrendering hands easily and led him to my big, white bed. I glanced to make sure the curtains were open. Ever since Kyo, I had developed the taste for being watched. I liked the cocoon of my own home, but the thought of being watched, being known from outside, also turned me on. My own bedroom looked across the front of the cobbled mews. These chi chi little houses are very close to one another. Well, they used to be stables, didn't they? Full of horses, and grooms. Then cars, and chauffeurs. Not designed for detached, aloof living.

Opposite my window anyone could be arriving for dinner, departing for a journey, watching for an awaited lover, getting ready for bed themselves.

I glanced to make sure the web cam was angled correctly. Well, both cameras, actually. I'd added to my equipment in recent weeks.

And then I pushed my boy on to his back, easily like a dandelion, and pulled his jeans off. He was shaking. I kept stroking him, smoothing his skin, soothing myself too, and I just wanted to lick him. And sniff him. He smelt of sweet caramel, and coconut.

'Ever had your cock sucked, *habib*?'

Before he could answer I slipped his knob stickily into my mouth.

He jerked with shock, tangling his fingers in my hair, and I gripped the tops of his legs and kept the moist tip of his cock firmly in my mouth. His cock started jumping over my tongue, probing to get between my teeth. I stroked his legs, his stomach, his balls, and he arched, as if in pain, then relaxed. My hair trailed over him as I tipped myself forward and started to suck him, hard.

I heard the purr of an expensive car outside. The pause, and clunk of a heavy door. The murmur of voices, a low laugh. Were they glancing up at me? Could they see my white face, sucking on my chocolate lollipop?

He was huge now, swollen and pumping desperately. I wanted him inside me, but he was going to have to come back in the morning and beg me. Please, host mother, let me fuck you.

I smiled to myself at all that promise, tucked away in my little house, for my delight. I pushed his thick cock back a little with my tongue. But then he grabbed my head, a boy used to getting his own way, and his hands closed over my ears so that all I could hear was the rushing of my own breath. My *petit prince*. I sucked it back in to my mouth, towards my throat, so that he stiffened and swelled and started thrusting. His hands started to guide my head slowly but firmly while he groaned softly, and that relieved the pressure in my throat.

211

As my mouth slid up his cock, I nipped the hot, taut flesh. He pushed in more urgently, lacing his fingers behind my neck, jerking his hips to fuck my face.

I thought about the camera, my husband watching, too far away to stop me, maybe my neighbours watching, near enough to join in. Watching Mrs Caroline on all fours on her bed, her white bottom in the air, empty, but her red mouth filled with a thick young cock, sucked for the very first time.

Holding his cock with one hand, I let my other hand trail down to my pussy and push quickly inside. It welcomed my fingers, sucking at them while I sucked at his rigid dick, which was bouncing and straining in my mouth as my tongue licked the strong veins and rounded, leaking tip.

As I sucked, hot pleasure radiated through me. I felt my boy's body getting tight, his balls shrinking up with impossible pleasure, my own excitement bunching up ready to explode, and then his cock suddenly stiffened, swelled another couple of inches, and then pumped violently once, twice, straining down my throat and knocking my head back. My mouth sucked on him as hot spunk shot into my throat.

I rubbed at myself frantically, coming quickly and wetly round my own fingers as I held my boy's brown cock tightly inside my mouth and swallowed his creamy mess.

Two days later, and after a lot more tender licking, he was gone. Summoned, perhaps, by an all-knowing, scandalised family. Had they also posted web cams to spy on what he was doing with his host mother? Either way, I never got that velvety brown, virginal cock up inside me.

But the pale white quiet cocks kept on coming. The

web cam kept on rolling. And one morning, as I leaned in the doorway, in my slippery peacock dressing gown, waving my latest student off to school, a man walked up the cobbles towards my house. He wore a suit and carried a briefcase.

And as Graham stopped in front of me, tugging at his cuffs, we both glanced at the distinct bulge in his trousers.

Mr and Mrs Weinmeyer

'THIS IS THE EXACT style I've been looking for. Classic, but quirky. Where can I find Signor Tremelli?'

Chloe glanced up from her perch in the corner of the gallery where she was sketching the ironmongery of the newly re-opened High Line on the shadowy side of the street. She pushed her glasses up her nose. 'He's on a conference call in the back at the moment. Can I help you?'

The man kept his gaze on the central photograph. It was of Daniele posing in a deserted department store, taken after hours and from behind so no punter would recognise him. He was butt naked – God, that butt. Incredible in a man any age, but he was her *father's* age. It was high, and tight, kept fit she reckoned by incessant fucking. You could see those thick muscles flickering under the skin when he moved, or bent or stretched, or clenched them for thrusting. You could see, in the photograph, one muscle taut and tight as he posed for her, inclining slightly awkwardly on a plinth like Michelangelo's David, lit by a single spot, and being jostled by fully clothed mannequins.

'My wife collects things, you see.' The visitor turned now, looking at her properly. He had burning blue eyes and pale blond hair. An ageless face, but the kind of mature, suave good looks that would get him cast as a

Nazi officer. The threatening smile of a modern-day Dracula. 'Art. Photographs. Lalique vases. People.'

Chloe remembered her manners and stood up. He was very tall. His suit was expensive but his red silk tie was very slightly loosened. He saw her staring at his undone top button. The brief curl of gold on his chest.

'A tough day, and so hot.' He held out his hand. 'Ernst Weinmeyer.'

'Chloe, er. Just Chloe.' She shook it. Handshakes are so rare now. A real minefield between attractive strangers. His was a cold grasp, but very firm with none of the sweat-gathering linger of a letch. 'I'm Signor Tremelli's assistant.'

'Well, Just Chloe. No surname? All alone in the world?'

'Just my professional moniker. Pretentious maybe, but –'

'Aren't all the youngsters these days?' He waved his hand over his mouth to stifle a yawn.

She felt her cheeks burning red and turned back to the photograph, edging him round with her hand in the blatantly flirtatious way Daniele had taught her. 'So you're interested in this picture?'

'I guess you'd call it homoerotic, yes? Superb technique, lighting, and very classy. It could be a Hitchcock still. But I don't want to buy it, no.'

Chloe went very quiet, holding in her disappointment and with it her breath. 'You like the style, though? We hung it as a teaser, you see, to gauge reactions. The photographer is a *protégée* of Sophie Epsom.'

'Ah yes. That figures. My wife has an Epsom. She really is outrageously erotic, isn't she, but all class and elegance.' His eyelids lowered a little, making his eyes glitter in the spotlights. 'You know, we bid for that amazing image of one woman licking out another when Tremelli auctioned it at Christies, but it went for millions in the end.'

Chloe nodded. 'There's still a rush on the gallery's postcards of that image.'

'This one is, I don't know, there's something fresher.' Mr Weinmeyer took out a business card and waved it at Chloe's photograph. 'So I would like to know more about this photographer guy –'

'Yes,' Chloe said quickly, tucking her hands in the folds of her short floaty skirt. She still wasn't used to the sticky Manhattan heat. And until that second she'd forgotten she wasn't wearing any knickers. 'Well, she has an extensive portfolio, actually, mostly back in London, but she's in New York for the summer –'

'She? And she's in town right now? Even better. Tell Daniele I'd like her details. I want to commission a portrait.'

'Oh my God, that's fantastic! I don't believe it!'

He turned back to her, stroking his very smooth pale face. 'Very excitable selling technique you have there?'

'I can't help it!' Chloe practically drummed her teetering platform sandals. 'Because actually that's me! You don't need to speak to Daniele, because *I'm* the photographer!'

'There's a turn-up.' He took her hand but instead of another formal shake he lifted it up to his mouth and breathed in her skin as if it was a perfume or fine wine. 'Now I'm excited, too.'

The moment extended just that little bit too long. She wanted to pull away. Her palm was getting sweaty. Despite the air con she was getting hot and sticky. He would sense it, and be repulsed. But as he kissed her hand, watching her all the while, it was as if he was taming her. She stopped fidgeting and was still.

'My card, Just Chloe.' He let go of her hand. 'Give me a call when you've checked your diary and you can come to our apartment and meet Mrs Weinmeyer. I want this portrait as the centre piece for her birthday party next month. Will Signor Tremelli let you off the leash so we can have you all to ourselves for a day or so?'

'Oh, sure,' Chloe smiled, flicking the card between her fingers like a poker player as she walked him to the gallery door and let in a blast of hot summer air. 'He'll do anything I ask him.'

'So, Daniele, it's all arranged. My first commission. How about that!'

She watched him switch off the gallery lights and lock the door.

'Weinmeyer is rich, all right. And well connected. If he likes it your work will be seen by everyone who's anyone –'

Chloe perched on the edge of the gallery desk and wrapped one long bare leg over the other. 'So why are you marching about looking like thunder?'

He came up and took hold of her. She leaned into him, pushing her big breasts against his shirt and rubbing them across the cotton the way he liked it. The breasts she kept hidden under loose tops and had only ever unwrapped for him. His mouth opened slightly as her nipples pricked hard through the soft fabric.

'I just wish it wasn't him, of all people. He eats women for breakfast, Chloe.'

She jerked away from him. 'This is a commission, for God's sake, not a casting couch. My chance to earn some money, get myself on the map! I'm not a kid, Danny. He's posing for me, not the other way round. I'm in total control –'

Daniele slammed her down on the desk, his Italian eyes blazing. The blow buzzed through her bones, weakening her knees with dark excitement. His breath was hot on her face. 'You're a talented photographer, Chloe, and this is your big break, but you don't know the half of it! Christ, you've never even fucked another man!'

'What's fucking got to do with it? Stop making it out to be something sordid. This is a job, that's all. *My* job. *My* business.' She tried to shake him off, but his fingers dug into her skin through the thin shirt and he pushed his knee between her legs to open them up, so that her pussy was grinding against it.

'Fucking's got everything to do with it. You just wait and see.' Daniele laughed roughly. 'And it is my business, *cara*. Weinmeyer would never have seen your work if it wasn't for me.'

She was breathing hard now, but the fury was still shafting through her body, making it spark with a toxic, angry heat. 'So, you want me to thank you now?'

'That would be nice.' He whipped her glasses off and put them on the desk beside her. She couldn't move. He had her pinned down. He pushed her little skirt up her legs. Those she never kept hidden. They were sensationally long, like a dancer's, and made people look at her twice, but still she covered her breasts and even liked to keep her glasses on most of the time.

The chiffon stroked her thighs softly as she gave in, weakening as usual. He grabbed his cock out of his trousers and thrust it up inside her with no messing, fucking her across the hard desk so that her head banged on the aluminium surface and her long blonde hair trailed to the floor.

Outside, the city rushed as people came down off the

High Line and its flowers and attractions, and walked or drove or taxied home. The night gathered speed.

A few feet away from the street, Chloe's first ever lover fucked her as if it was the last time. She came explosively, digging her nails into him as she screamed his name, but although she loved him for breaking her in, she knew she was on the threshold of a whole lot more.

And as if he could read her mind, Daniele whispered, 'Just wait until you meet Mrs Weinmeyer.'

Daniele's words of warning hissed in Chloe's ears as she stood on the top step of the enormous mansion on the Upper East Side two days later, but they soon evaporated. Mrs Weinmeyer was a pussy cat. They both were. In fact Mr and Mrs Weinmeyer reminded her of Si and Am, the evil cats in *Lady and the Tramp* – cool, polished, slanted blue eyes, blond – but apparently totally charming.

She'd heard that princesses lived up this way, and this house was certainly fit for one. The front door swung silently open into a huge hallway as soon as she rang the bell. No butler or housekeeper. Just Mrs Weinmeyer, standing at the top of the stairs in a fuchsia pink, diaphanous halter-neck dress.

'Just Chloe, as my husband calls you. How lovely. Welcome!'

She was silhouetted by the light from the huge arched window behind her. The strong sun was like a back light, shafting straight through the voile fabric of her dress and rendering it see-through. Chloe could see that Mrs Weinmeyer's incredibly slim thighs were slightly parted and flickering with impatient muscles as she rotated her foot in its gold Laboutin sandal. As she lifted her leg to take a step down the stairs, the dress floated open at the top of her legs, briefly showing the corner, the curve, of one plump sex lip.

'Stop!'

Chloe dropped her equipment on the floor in front of her and hoisted her camera out of her bag.

'Why, honey, what's wrong?' Mrs Weinmeyer halted as instructed, one knee cocked in front of the other, her slim arms stretching to each banister. Her face was in shadow, but as she adjusted the exposure Chloe could see through the viewfinder her subject's fuchsia painted lips part slightly in surprise, showing perfect white teeth.

Her finger felt slippery on the shutter. 'Fuck. I'm sorry if that sounded rude – fuck, I shouldn't have said fuck – but Mrs Weinmeyer, please could you hold it there, because I think I've got my Grace Kelly shot!'

Mrs Weinmeyer shrugged one pale shoulder, looked over it, deep into Chloe's lens, twisted this way and that, then continued smoothly down the stairs.

'Darling, come with me. There will be many other shots, I can assure you. Just follow me round, and you can tell me where you want me.'

The house was all old European grandeur on the lower floors, but without the fuss.

Chloe followed her from room to room, watching the way Mrs Weinmeyer's buttocks twitched under the fuchsia silk as she walked ahead. The way her little bottom caught the material between her cheeks, then softly released it again. Every so often she would take a shot as she paused casually by a sofa, a fireplace, a mirror.

'So, Chloe, where do you want me?'

Mrs Weinmeyer watched as Chloe paced the huge wood-panelled drawing room and opened the French windows to let the natural, but shaded, north light flood in.

'Here. I'd like to try something fairly formal, classic, you know? Just your face and shoulders, Mrs Weinmeyer, looking out from these shadows into the garden.'

Mrs Weinmeyer did as she was told and leaned dreamily in the doorway, resting her head on one up-stretched arm. Chloe busied herself outside, setting up her tripod, making sure no direct sunlight fell on her subject. Then she looked up. The light was perfect, and she started to shoot. Mrs Weinmeyer kept her eyes focussed just past Chloe's ear as if she was staring out to sea, her pink lips parted, her pale limbs totally still.

There was only the rise and fall of her breasts as she breathed, making the silk shiver over her skin. And the sweat trickling down Chloe's back as she worked in the New York heat.

Mr Weinmeyer appeared through another doorway, speaking on a mobile phone.

'Christ, isn't she just gorgeous, Chloe?'

Without apologising for getting in the way, he clicked shut the phone and walked up behind his wife and slipped his hand through the slit in the dress where it fell open across her thigh.

'You should feel how soft her skin is. How warm. Just up here, you know? Just where it meets and gets all damp, and divides into that lovely pussy.'

'Want to feel it, Chloe?' Mrs Weinmeyer purred.

'Just hold it like that.'

Chloe grew hotter and stickier and jammed the camera against her nose to keep shooting. They were a pair of consummate performers. As his hand went into her dress, Mrs Weinmeyer's head fell back on his shoulder in its business suit, her eyes fluttering closed, her lips parting wider. He wrinkled open the dress with his other hand, gathering the folds on her hip so as to expose her pussy totally. Like all New Yorkers, she was perfectly Hollywood waxed.

Chloe's own pussy felt like it was going to cook inside the too-smart tailored shorts she'd put on for this commission. And she hated wearing knickers. The pussy bow blouse was already sticking to her armpits, but it wasn't just the summer sunshine making her hot. It was this debonair couple in front of her, he with his clean fingernails and snow-white cuffs looking cool as if he was about to address a board meeting, yet stroking his wife's gleaming white pussy, running one finger slowly up and down the red crack peeping between the lips, the inner fire blazing briefly pink as he tickled it open to show Chloe and her camera, before it closed softly shut again.

Mrs Weinmeyer's tongue mirrored his finger, flickering over her mouth.

'I think we should leave it there? I can see you both – this is a private moment.'

Chloe started to pack up her equipment.

'Why so coy, Chloe?' Mr Weinmeyer stepped out onto the terrace, leaving his wife to stroke herself. 'Your photograph back there in the gallery was one of the horniest things I've seen!'

'True.' Chloe remembered that this was a job. She was the professional. He was the client. 'But this commission was for portraits of Mrs Weinmeyer. I can do erotic ones for you separately, if you like.'

He smiled, but said nothing.

'It's just that I've never taken my subjects – er – interacting with each other so intimately before.'

'So cute, isn't she, with those stern secretary glasses and all that wild gypsy unbrushed hair. Just like your fraulein cousins. So innocent.' Mrs Weinmeyer joined her husband on the terrace and wound her arms round his

222

waist. Her dress was still open, the silk shifting across her thighs, catching in her pussy crack, attracted perhaps by the wetness there.

And then, in unison, they said, 'Come back tomorrow night, Chloe. Just one more session.'

'These proofs are sensational. Weren't they pleased?'

Daniele leaned over her shoulder as Chloe sat on the floor of his apartment above the gallery, working on her laptop. She'd kicked off her shorts and was cross-legged in just her knickers.

'Yes, but –'

'Christ, Chloe! What's he doing to her? They touched each other up in front of you?'

He took the mouse from her and zoomed in on the image of Mr Weinmeyer's hand slipping inside Mrs Weinmeyer's dress. He kept zooming until there were only his long, clean, white fingers, prizing his wife open like a shell, and the pinky red folds inside her snatch, glistening with excitement.

Chloe and Daniele stared in silence. Then Chloe turned the image to monochrome: monochrome fingers, monochrome pussy lips, then bleeding in just a wisp of fuchsia silk snapping at the edge, echoing the glints of living pink in Mrs Weinmeyer's invaded cunt.

'Like those Bailey photographs of all those vaginas – you could go a long way with these. God, it made me horny just walking round his exhibition in London and now, *signorina,* it's making me horny just looking at the way Mr Weinmeyer is touching Mrs Weinmeyer. See? He's doing this –'

Daniele snaked his hand between Chloe's legs, and she wriggled, tried to bat him off, but when he hooked his finger into her knickers and stroked her crack open, the desire that had been sizzling all day burst into life. She moaned and gave in, and leant back against him, opening her thighs and tipping herself upwards, an invitation for him to go further, more fingers, deeper, harder, scraping mercilessly against her clit, making her feel and sound all wet, until she couldn't bear it any longer and she sighed, 'Oh God, I've been keeping it in all day. Watching those two, all over each other. The way they move round each other like they're waltzing. Oh, fuck it, just do me, Daniele!'

So like the proverbial Italian Stallion her boss lay her down on the floor of his apartment – he liked unforgiving surfaces – and fucked her, good and hard.

'Watch out for Mrs Weinmeyer tomorrow night, *cara,* that's all I'm saying.'

The front door of the mansion swung open soundlessly again, but this time there was no Mrs Weinmeyer on the stairs. Just moonlight streaming in, and her disembodied voice purring from the entry phone. 'Take the lift, honey. Up, up, up to the penthouse.'

So she did, and when she got there the lift expelled her into a kind of a kind of plate glass box perched on the roof of the mansion, furnished inside with cool dark wood and white leather and outside with a plunge pool, lush tropical greenery and panoramic views over Central Park. Mellow saxophone music twined through the shadows.

'We thought we'd make the shots more edgy tonight. You know? More light and shade. What do they say? Chiaroscuro?'

Chloe turned from the window which had drawn her like a magnet, and saw Mr and Mrs Weinmeyer sitting side by side on a huge teak day bed strewn with soft white cushions. They sat there elegantly enough, champagne glasses in their hands, illuminated by accurately angled pin points of light, but he was naked except for a pair of white boxers and she was in a tiny white negligee.

Chloe held her camera up like a shield. 'Edgy,' she croaked. 'Right.'

'And we thought mainly monochrome? Just like Madonna's book?'

Chloe flapped about setting up her portable light boxes and umbrellas. As she bent to unzip the carry bags her little skirt flipped over her bottom and she regretted going commando again. But that's what the Manhattan heat did to her. She liked to feel it pounding off the sidewalks, off the skyscrapers, off the honking yellow taxis, and up her legs to a place that was even hotter.

'Madonna's book? You mean the English roses?' She turned, tugging her skirt down. But they weren't staring up it. Mrs Weinmeyer had hooked one leg over Mr Weinmeyer's muscular thigh, and they were kissing. Slowly, with their tongues visible poking in and out of each other's mouths, stiff and hard, like they were licking ice cream.

Chloe stared for a moment, then started shooting.

Mr Weinmeyer's hand slid up his wife's leg and under her negligee, peeling it back over her bottom, showing Chloe her beautiful thighs and buttock and the brief shadow of her pussy. Then he reclined against the huge pillows, lifting her easily on top of him.

Mrs Weinmeyer stopped kissing him for a moment and sat up to glance coquettishly over her shoulder at Chloe. Her lips were painted dark red today, but were wet with saliva. 'The photographic book Madonna did with Meisel, the one acting out her fantasies? It was called *Sex*. Oh God, maybe Chloe's too young to remember all that, Ernst?'

He didn't answer. Just smiled up at her. He fanned his hands over her bottom and started to rock her gently, lovingly, but very, very sexily. Chloe could see Mrs Weinmeyer's white bottom opening slightly as she let him move her over his groin, the dark dividing sliver of violet showing as her body opened and closed.

Chloe hands shook, and she lowered her camera for a moment.

'No, no, keep shooting, Chloe.' Mrs Weinmeyer was breathless. But she kept her blue eyes on Chloe. Her thighs softened, opening a little wider. 'You know, I wanted to audition to be in that book? For one of the girl-on-girl scenarios? That would have been *my* fantasy. Touching Madonna. Oh, yes, there were pictures of her being licked by girls, pictures of her licking girls, pictures of her crouched over a big mirror, watching her touch herself – you shocked at me, Chloe?'

Chloe swallowed, but couldn't speak. Mr Weinmeyer lifted his wife off him for a moment and in one clean movement she whipped his shorts off and landed lightly down again, sliding straight onto his cock.

'But maybe I was too white, you see, Chloe. Too blonde. Too like her, in fact. Because in the end, they used a beautiful black girl.'

Weird shocked laughter caught in Chloe's throat as her camera caught the white shorts flying through the air, Mrs Weinmeyer's long pale arm flinging them away as she arched herself at her husband's cock. Mrs Weinmeyer laughed, too. She was like one of those riders on a bucking bronco, waving her cowboy hat, but what the pair were doing was so quiet, so graceful, like a dance in slow motion, you still couldn't call it *dirty*.

Could you? She still thanked God for hiding behind her camera. Because what was going on through the lens was red hot. All the hotter for being framed. Her legs were buckling with lust as Mrs Weinmeyer lay on top of Mr Weinmeyer, her body sliding over his cock as it went up into her. Chloe stepped round them as quietly as she could, her camera seeing, catching, blinking, shooting, her body tightening at the sight of this elegant, white-limbed couple entwining in front of her, frozen for all those moments, then slowly starting to fuck each other on the white opium bed floating in its glass room above New York Burning out there with all those lights. All those eyes.

She realised they had stopped moving. They were posed, like a marble statue, Mrs Weinmeyer welded to Mr Weinmeyer's cock.

'Hey, Chloe,' cooed Mrs Weinmeyer, beckoning with her white fingers. 'Come over here. All this lovin' making you horny?'

'Honey,' growled Mr Weinmeyer, his eyes closed, 'you're coming on all southern belle –'

She laughed softly. 'And I prefer it when you come on all silent Aryan beefcake. And I like Chloe all shy and bespectacled. So, going to come round this side of the camera, Chloe?'

'Just for a break, maybe.'

Chloe perched awkwardly on the edge of the bed and took a glug of Krug but the cushions were so soft that she fell into it, spilling champagne on her blouse. Mr Weinmeyer rolled away, leaving Mrs Weinmeyer lying where he had been and Chloe falling on top of her.

Mrs Weinmeyer reached up and removed Chloe's spectacles, pulling her closer before she could wriggle away, and now she was on her hands and knees, crouching over her supine, sultry client, her hot, bare pussy clenching furiously, threatening to drip its sticky honey over Mrs Weinmeyer's flat, white stomach. Chloe hovered there for a moment, looking down at her. Mrs Weinmeyer was so beautiful and pale in the cool lighting, Manhattan piercing the skies all around.

'Oh, spilled some did you?' Then Mrs Weinmeyer yanked off Chloe's little blouse, pulled her down towards her and brushed her bare breasts across her closed eyelids.

'Mrs Weinmeyer, what are you – what do you want me to –?'

'Just relax, honey. Just indulge us. Indulge yourself. We do this all the time. Always looking for lovely young women to join us. You ever done this before, honey, with two people? A husband and wife?' She smiled, lips red and wet. 'Been *paid* for it?'

'No, not for this. You're not paying me for sex. You're paying me for my work –'

'Absolutely, and marvellous work it is, too, darling. We'll want all the shots. But right now? We want you.'

Chloe was losing. Mrs Weinmeyer caressed the rounded flesh of her soft young breasts with the merest touch of a butterfly, tickling with her fingertips, her eyelashes, even her hair. Chloe realised she was holding her breath. She was also arching her back, thrusting her tits towards Mrs Weinmeyer's mouth, and thrusting her bottom into the air where Mr Weinmeyer must be getting a good, silent eyeful.

Her nipples, exposed in the pinprick lighting, exposed for God's sake to anyone either side of the park who happened to be looking out of a penthouse level window, were sharp and burning as she waited for the other woman's lips, a *woman's lips,* to fold round them.

So this was the magic of Manhattan. She could never go back to London again.

Mrs Weinmeyer studied her for a while, all of her, like she was a tasty morsel, and then her red lips parted and her tongue flickered out, just touching one burning nipple before flickering in again. Chloe moaned out loud, embarrassed, frustrated. And so incredibly turned on.

From behind her, Mr Weinmeyer planted his hands on her bottom and stroked it, and now he was spreading open *her* cheeks. Chloe squealed, blushing red with humiliation, but she couldn't get away because now Mrs Weinmeyer was sucking her nipple into her lovely red mouth. Mr Weinmeyer parted her cheeks roughly with strong, eager fingers, making the dividing flesh sting, and then he paused, as if for permission.

Mrs Weinmeyer, her mouth full of Chloe's nipple, gave one sharp nod.

He prodded his knob into the warm, dark crevice inside Chloe's cheeks. He let it rest there for a moment. Chloe couldn't permit or refuse. She was already far away on a sea of ecstasy as Mrs Weinmeyer massaged her breasts and gently sucked first one aching nipple, then the other. Chloe hung on the intense moment of waiting between the two of them. She knew that each would take whichever part of her they wanted the most.

So Mr Weinmeyer felt his way further in. He shoved a finger roughly inside her tight hole, sliding it from side to side as it puckered and resisted until her arse went loose and let it in, opening softly and wetly and making her gasp with the embarrassment and novelty and filthiness of it. Then he obviously couldn't help himself, because he followed his finger with another, and then with the tip of his prick, knocking Chloe forwards with shock and with the force of it as her body tried to repel him but in he went, pressing her harder against Mrs Weinmeyer's mouth.

He grunted with triumph and started, very slowly, as with everything else he and his wife did, to fuck her bottom.

As he pushed himself inch by inch inside her, Mrs Weinmeyer now trailed her fingers down to Chloe's pussy, which was fighting the spasms of pleasure already overpowering her, and gently slid inside, opening up that part of her, too, and pushing her long fingers inside.

Chloe moaned loudly, rocking between the two Weinmeyers, and urgently she wanted to touch Mrs Weinmeyer, discover what another woman felt like. Bizarrely she imagined her to be cool and dry, like she was on the outside, but as soon as her fingertips brushed over the soft, wet crack of her nude pussy, it reacted like a second mouth, sucking greedily at her fingers.

'Yes, honey, yes,' Mrs Weinmeyer breathed, lifting herself slightly, still licking Chloe's nipples, so that Chloe's fingers slipped easily inside. Oh, yes. Far from being cool and dry she was hot and wet in there, fever-ready. Chloe felt the new, kinky power, so different, so subtle, of making another female want her.

As fingers and cocks went in and out of sighing, writhing bodies, Chloe was no longer torn between the Weinmeyers. They both wanted her, and she wanted both of them. She made them content just by climbing onto the bed with them, and they were both going to satisfy her, too. She plunged three fingers roughly inside Mrs Weinmeyer, letting her thumb trail behind until it caught the little nub of her clitoris, and then, as if she'd been doing this all her life, she rubbed brutally hard, making Mrs Weinmeyer fall back, biting her lips with pleasure and rubbing equally brutally at Chloe's clit, plunging her long fingers rapidly in and out of her photographer's cunt.

Mr Weinmeyer, strong and silent behind her, fucked

her arse, making it clench round his cock, gripping him in there as it hurt and yet felt fantastic and made sparks of evil pleasure dash through her.

She felt a demonic grin stretching her face as Mrs Weinmeyer started to writhe and buck frantically on her fingers, just as she was writhing and bucking on her fingers. They were like mirror images, the older woman on the girl, eat your heart out Madonna, and the girl still opening herself to Mr Weinmeyer's forcing, thrusting cock.

'Ah, Christ, I'm ready, honey,' Mrs Weinmeyer breathed suddenly into the jazz-sweetened air. 'Ah can't hold it, wanna come –'

'So do it,' Chloe gasped, shocked at the coarseness in her voice. 'Fucking *do* me!'

The wave was there, ready to crash inside her, and her moaning seemed to trigger the other two, so that all three rocked and writhed and pushed and groaned, until one by one they came, hands gripping, cock thrusting, pussies weeping, panting loudly, saying nothing, and then when they'd had more champagne they did it again, and again, until they were a sweating, panting heap on the tangled sheets as the first pink finger of dawn edged between the high buildings outside and stroked the glass walls.

And Chloe felt another layer of innocence falling away into the shadowy mansion below.

Skylar

ALL THE LIGHTS AND bridges and gables are starting to merge and blur. It's dusk. I haven't got my glasses. I can hardly breathe after hurrying over endless cobbles. I wouldn't normally dress like this, or wear these ridiculous shag-me shoes, but I have a rendezvous with my lover, and now I'm late.

When I came out of the Centraal station nearly two hours ago I was supposed to get a taxi or a tram but something made me hesitate. Within minutes I was allowing myself to be pushed with the human tide into a maze of enticing streets, some so narrow you could touch the sides. There were bright lights and the kind of heart-rate heavy music that beats in time with humping.

Somewhere in the city beyond was the Rijksmuseum. Van Gogh's working boots. The hotel. I had to get there. But right here in front of me were shops crammed with toys, books, videos and posters catering for every appetite. Dazzling, blinding lights and signs clamouring for me to come see a live show, watch the girls, sex sex sex, try, see, do, buy.

My eyes flickered, trying to avoid at first but then staring openly at the occasional flash of a pink cunt in a magazine, an over-sized cock arrowing into a pair of plump splayed buttocks. Soon I was stepping right inside one or two of the shops, picking things up and fondling them. The whips, handcuffs, great curved dildoes. They were stark and plastic, garishly artificial, brutally anatomical – and the more I looked the more I wanted to lift up my new, elegant, frilled skirt and push one of those false cocks, maybe the over-sized black one with the bulbous knob, up between my legs, maybe stand there in the shop, legs splayed, and show everyone how well it fitted, how high up it went, how wildly it made me shake.

Then I remembered the real cock that was, is, waiting for me at the hotel, zipped up for the moment behind the tailored pinstripes. He is on business, after all. It should have turned me on, standing in a sex shop and thinking about the moment when Ernst would acknowledge my arrival in his usual silent way, then walk ahead of me into the lift, silently. Silently unlock the bedroom door. And only when we were inside – he would have chosen the raspberry and elephant grey room with the curtained four-poster and the elegant canal sliding past outside – would he slam me against the wall for our first fuck of the weekend.

But thinking about that, the unzipping of his trousers, the glint of his wedding ring – Christ, *my* wedding ring – all the complications, only made me want these false toys even more, thick and hard, rubber, who cared, so long as they pleasured me. I wanted one pumping up me, hurting me, to clear my head.

But of course I didn't do any of it. Even in the middle of the red light district I behaved like the lady everyone thinks I am, my husband, my sons, I kept all that dark longing to myself. OK. I admit I did handle some of those dildos and vibrators far more enthusiastically than most uptight female customers might have done. And one or two people started to watch me. Men, mostly. Maybe they could smell the slut under the silk.

And they could see my hips moving very slightly, as I stood in front of the displays, to that deep, sexy, primeval, upmarket stripper music. There was a pulse beating inside me, responding to all that stimulation, pumping out my arousal, and God, I was so restless.

That's when I got lost. I told myself I was excited at the thought of our assignation, but I was distracted. There was a quiet parade down beside a pretty canal and I darted down there. Purple and orange migraine-inducing neon gave way to scented muted window boxes, autumnal flowers releasing their evening perfume, and then I was walking along another, wider canal, with barges parked up, full of tulips, my favourite flower.

Elegant buildings stretched skywards, all different pastel colours and gables, some with doors at roof level for loading something mysterious in or out of a barge below.

But the hotel wasn't here. These were all private town houses. Each painted door was bolted against strangers. They all had big square windows, though, mostly shuttered, very clean, some showing kitchens or ornate wooden living rooms, the domestic side of the city, politely shutting out visitors.

One window invited me to stop, though. Really stop, linger, and look. In the window was a riotous display of sumptuous underwear.

Creamy satin knickers, midnight-blue camisoles, uplifting wine-red bras with spaghetti-thin straps, mean black basques, sheer pink stockings and see-through negligees were all heaped abundantly in mounds or drifted artfully from slender chrome shelving, urging me to reach in and feel the expensive silk, satin, lace, slither between my stroking fingers.

Not an iota of brutal phallic painted plastic, or rubber.

No instrument of torture in sight.

In the centre of the window, lit by one spot, a voluptuous, pale mannequin reclined on a jade green velvet *chaise longue,* one shapely long leg raised like a ballerina's to show the sheen of its black silk stocking. Above a flat stomach and tiny waist, making me suck mine in, large breasts billowed out of a froth of black lace. One strap fell off one shoulder. I thought I saw it shrug suggestively.

I blinked. The movement drew my gaze up over the mannequin's pale throat to a pair of wide, pouting lips, glistening blood-red as if they'd just been licked. Green eyes, like mine but round not almond-shaped, glittered under the baby spotlight. Auburn hair, just like mine, was cut short in a kind of flapper's bob, and gleamed against the sharp cheekbones.

As I stared, the mannequin's luscious breasts started heaving as if she, it, was breathing. More enticingly, the nipples grew hard, poking through the lace work of her bra. The green eyes closed, and opened again. And one arm lifted. I swear the figure in the window was beckoning to me.

I glanced around, thinking this display was meant for someone else. My heart was pounding. But the only other people moving in the lamp-lit street were a group of rangy boys with blond surfer hair, free-wheeling their whirring bikes over the nearest bridge and into the shadows.

When I turned round, the mannequin's arm was no longer beckoning. The green eyes were surely made of glass. But my reflection in the polished window was wild-eyed. I could taste blood from my bitten lower lip. And the pulse in my pussy was still going.

So my feet are killing me, I'm seeing things, and also I'm

panicking. It's not like he's a monster or anything, but I'm two hours late.

My hip bumps the handlebar of a bicycle as I stumble up on to the bridge where the boys went, and for a moment I stop and look down into the canal. There's a boat, full of tourists and harsh striplight, cruising right under me.

Like royalty we've travelled separately. Well, we're meeting halfway. He's coming from Cairo, where he's left his wife to continue the holiday. I've dashed like a fugitive from London, where I've left Martin to, what, find another willing pussy to fuck probably. But Ernst will be pacing around the hotel room now, or more likely the plush lobby, still pale even though he's been down the Nile for the last ten days. Always tweaking his snow-white cuffs to check the time.

I should have known I would be useless at this infidelity lark. A quick shag from time to time with a delicious man is one thing, but this is dangerously close to a full-blown affair. It's gone on too long, got too complicated, and now I'm lost and late and that's my punishment.

I spin round, getting dizzy. Someone is hunched over the bike, chaining it up or unchaining it, I can't see, and I call out. 'Excuse me?'

The cruise boat slides under me, pale faces turned upwards, mouths open. I must have yelled louder than I meant. Screamed, even.

'Can you help me?' Christ, I'm not in London or New York now. This is Holland. 'I'm looking for the Keizersgracht. Or was it the Prinsengracht? Please! Do you speak English?'

The bike rattles against the stonework and he turns round. Tall, ruffled and blond and, oh my God,

236

ridiculously tall, like a basket ball player. They say the Dutch have the highest average height in the world but they're not freaks or giants. They match their height with broad shoulders, strong chins, such a chic way with clothes and amazing glossy fitness. My eyes travel skywards – and I'm pretty tall, you know – before they arrive at a handsome tanned face, young cheeks flushed with cycling or rushing through the stiff breeze, and wide, sea-green eyes.

'The Dylan Hotel?' I wail. 'Do you speak English?'

'Yeah. I speak English.'

I hold on to my map and wait as he takes a couple of loping steps to meet me on the brow of the bridge. Something about the way he walks – we keep staring at each other. He lifts his hand as it to point something out over my shoulder, but then stops dead and runs it through his hair instead, making it stand up in spikes.

'Mrs Epsom?'

I freeze, like a thief in the night. Is this how it happens? Is this how adultery is discovered?

'Sophie Epsom, yes, but –'

He runs his hand through his hair again, then holds it out, palm upwards, as if asking for something.

'I'm Skylar. Skylar Singer? I was at school and then uni' with Seb and Rickie – but my family's back here now.'

His voice is extraordinarily deep for someone so young, and has a lazy drawl, like he just woke up. I remember that voice, with the slight edge of his father's Dutch accent, and that loping walk, those long legs in tight shorts and wet wellies, lifting the boat off the river along with my gorgeous sons and the rest of the crew. God, he was strong. All the cute girls like a bunch of Pussy Cat Dolls wiggling their miniskirts like they needed to pee and adjusting their sunglasses on the boat house balcony to attract the boys' attention.

'Skylar! Sara's boy. Yes! How could I forget that heavenly name! You were all in the rowing club together –'

He leans against the bridge, crossing his arms over his pale blue sweater as if it isn't getting cold and dark and he has all the time in the world.

'And how could *I* forget?'

I clutch my hands together as if in prayer, shivering slightly. 'I'm a bit late, Skylar, and a bit lost –'

He steps nearer and runs his finger down my neck. I actually close my eyes because it tickles my skin. How's he to know how sensitive it is just there? He holds up a leaf that has got tangled in my hair. I ought to slap him. Instead I'm pinned there. That pulse in my pussy is throbbing rhythmically now, and beneath my coat and my cashmere cardigan my nipples go tight.

Skylar is so close I can see the gold prickles in his skin waiting to be shaved. I can see his tongue and his white teeth as he smiles easily at me. My tongue runs across my mouth. He runs his finger down my neck again, follows a trail across my cheek to my mouth, and pushes gently at my lips till they pout open. Then he puts his finger in his own mouth, and sucks it.

'Where did a good boy like you learn to be so dirty?' I whisper, shivering violently now. 'You, Skylar, were the polite one. The only boy who ever said thank you.'

He pulls at me roughly so that I bang against him and feel the long hard outline of his cock against my stomach. He puts his mouth in my hair to say something.

'And you, Mrs Epsom, were the only mother any of us wanted to fuck.'

My phone vibrates angrily and I jump and screech like

a naughty schoolgirl.

'Excuse me, Skylar – a text –'

Waited two hours. Gone to meeting. Have booked dinner at D'Vijff Vlieghen. All OK?

I reply with shaking fingers. *Yes. Sorry. Tell all later.*

'You look knackered. I could take you to the Dylan if you like,' says Skylar, walking away down the other side of the bridge as if nothing dirty was ever said, 'or you could come and take a beer at my place.'

I am too cold to think straight now. A wind cuts off the canal below us, lifting my skirt and freezing my knees.

'I don't know, Skylar, I really should be getting – is it far?'

'We're here already.'

He's disappeared along the tree-lined corniche by the canal, and then I look down and see him leaning one foot on the edge of a square jawed wooden houseboat. I start to follow him awkwardly down the bridge, then I wrench my shoes off. When he sees me running towards him, ripping my stockings on the stones, he nods slowly, looking me up and down in the lazy way of a hungry man about to enjoy a leisurely meal.

'Just one beer, Skylar, OK? Then you must take me to the Dylan Hotel.'

He hands me aboard and through a pair of little glass doors into a warm, wood-panelled interior done out like a Moroccan riad strewn with cushions and hung with lights. I cross the room and look out over his deck to the water, rippling with lights from the houses lining the canals, and from the neighbouring boats.

Behind me he lights candles in coloured glass pots and lanterns, and cracks open two beers. I glance about for any feminine touches, flowers, scent bottles, silk scarves, tasteful photographs, but this is a lad's pad all right. All quick comfort.

'Take your coat off, why don't you, Mrs Epsom? It gets hot in here,' he says softly, kicking off his biker boots and leaning on the galley counter. He pushes my feet in the sluttishly ripped stockings with his toe. 'You're half undressed already.'

I blush scarlet and then he's undoing the buttons on my coat. Before my arms are properly out of the sleeves I try to take a swig out of my beer can and spill it down my chin and onto my caramel cashmere.

'Not nervous, are you, Mrs Epsom?' He tuts his teeth and dabs at me with a towel. I freeze as the cloth swipes between my breasts, and so does he. He clears his throat. 'I mean, about your night at the Dylan? Very sexy hotel. You haven't told me what you're doing in Amsterdam.'

I wipe my mouth with the back of my hand and take another swig of beer. It feels good, flowing down my throat. I realise that despite my cold, anxious walk the nerves have made me thirsty. My head swims comfortably now.

'I'm meeting a friend, Sky. Actually, I'm meeting my lover. And it's all wrong. Here I am, with you, late for our rendezvous, and I've realised it's all wrong.'

He raises his eyebrows, then pulls his pale blue jumper off. The old white shirt he's wearing underneath rucks up his back as he tugs everything off, and I see the muscles flickering between his ribs and the inward curve of his brown stomach with its low down fuzz of golden hair.

'You don't fancy him any more?'

I laugh. 'Oh, sweetie, it's not as simple as that –'

He glares at me now, flopping down on the cushions. His shirt flies open over his stomach. 'Calling me too young to understand?'

I bite my lip. 'No, not at all. Look at you. You're all

240

grown-up. You're gorgeous.'

He laces his fingers behind his head, and waits. I come and sit beside him. My tight skirt makes it difficult to sit easily, so I kind of curl my legs primly under me and as I shift about trying to look and feel at ease, I feel a ladder run in my stocking from my ankle right up to my thigh.

'You always were.'

'So what's the problem with this guy?'

'It's all wrong, that's what. I'm not feeling the fun or the pleasure of it any more. And I think you may be right – maybe I don't fancy him any more.'

His shoulder is warm against mine. One of those tourist boats swishes past. It's all lit up, with dressed-up diners in there this time, not looking out or up or taking photographs, just gazing at the food they're forking into their mouths.

'Not good in bed, then?'

'Do we really need to talk about him?' But again, I start to laugh. 'He's incredible in bed, actually – I mean, he loves sex. He likes it really rough, sometimes. I've let him tie me up. I've – he's done things to me nobody else has, not even my husband, and Christ knows *he's* virtually a sex addict –'

'You're beautiful when you laugh, Mrs Epsom.'

Skylar strokes my mouth, all wet with beer, and then I find him kissing me. I try to purse my lips against him, this is the last thing I need, fumbling and groping with some kid, but when his tongue slides across my mouth it makes my lips tingle and they fall open, I can't help it, his tongue is so warm and firm, and eager, and young, and his hands come up to hold my face and it's so tender, as if in some way I'm fragile.

'Let's not talk about my lover,' I whisper.

'You know my name means "shield"?' he whispers

241

back.

And then I'm kissing him back, half crying as well, and we're falling against the cushions, kissing wetly and noisily like teenagers, and he's undoing my cashmere cardigan very carefully, popping open one pearl button at a time, making my breasts push eagerly at his hands, until I'm scrabbling at his shirt to feel his smooth warm skin underneath. His heart is thumping under my hand and then he pulls me on top of him, still kissing me, my cardi slipping off my shoulders, my skirt still on, his hands sliding up under it, feeling the tops of my ripped stockings –

'I should go.' I pull away and look down at him, shaking my head. 'We can't do this, Sky. I'm too old for you, and I'm too confused –'

He looks steadily back at me, his mouth bruised and wet. His hands rest easily on my thighs as if he already owns me.

'I want you, though, Mrs Epsom. Right now. I told you. I always have. And you want me.'

I laugh at the simplicity of it all, at the way he calls me Mrs Epsom, and that makes me feel beautiful. My stomach coils with excitement. We stare at each other for the moment in the flickering candlelight.

'And especially tonight,' he says, reaching behind me and unclipping my bra, 'you look as if you need a good fucking.'

My breasts tumble out, big and white in the darkened room, the nipples already taut and scarlet with longing. But a shadow falls over me. I think of the other bras he's undone, the girls he's seduced so coolly here in his Moroccan house boat. I think of the girlfriend he must have, who could be near, who could be about to burst in.

I try to cover myself.

242

'Skylar, this isn't right –'

'Don't stress, Sophie.' He pulls my hands away from my breasts and stares at them. 'It's totally right. And look what you've done to me.'

He plants one of my hands down to feel the hardness of his cock in his jeans, pushing between my thighs. I rub it, feeling it stir in response, and I start to arch my back, cup my breasts in my hands, squeeze them together, make them swell and push, pinch the nipples longer and harder until they're tingling with excitement.

'You look like one of those whores wriggling about in their windows. Who would have thought a lady like you could move like that?'

He pulls me down and pushes his face between my breasts, breathes on them, runs his tongue up between them and then over and round the jutting nipples, teasing and nibbling while his hands move under my skirt, feeling for my bottom.

I hang over him, watching his face, the light on his hair, feel the bristles on his chin scratching my skin. The world has shrunk to just this vulnerable little boat, unlocked, open to all comers, moored in the shadows of this lovely bridge, rocking inside this amazing city.

So I cup one breast and offer it to him. His tongue flicks across the nipple again, and I nearly scream out loud. His hands squeeze the breasts together until they sing with delicious pain. Then his soft lips nibble up the little nub of the nipple. His tongue laps round it. He draws the burning bud into his mouth, pulling hard on it, and begins to suck. It makes my whole body ripple with desire.

He turns from one bulging breast to the other, breathing more heavily now, biting and kneading harder and harder and the lovely pain empties my mind of everything else.

His mouth is getting rougher, more ferocious, and I'm pushing more roughly against him, daring him, searching for more pain to communicate more pleasure. I'm on top of him, my tits dangling down over him, their size and weight accentuated by hanging there, the soft globes pale in his brown fingers. I hitch my skirt right up and tilt my pussy desperately towards his groin and rub it briefly against the outline of his gorgeous cock

My knickers are getting wet, and his cock is getting harder, and we are really grinding against each other when I think I can hear footsteps on the pavement outside. Suddenly I remember the surfer boys I'd seen earlier, whirring silently with him on their bikes.

'Skylar – someone's coming!'

He pulls his head away, listens for a moment, then shakes his head.

'Just passing,' he says. 'And if they see in, how kinky is that? It won't be the first time.'

He lifts his hips, with me still on top of him, and slips his jeans down, and there's his cock, lying on his stomach, pulsing slightly, poking up big and warm and heavy between my legs.

'What do you mean, not the first time? For God's sake, Skylar, I'm sure I can hear – wasn't that someone on the deck? Christ, your girlfriend!'

I try to wriggle off him, but he's stronger than me. He fans his hands across my bottom, stroking it, and how weirdly soothing is that, because like my neck it's another very sensitive part of me, and the stroking makes my cunt clench with frustration.

'Don't have a girlfriend,' he laughs quietly, opening my legs wider and moving me so that my wet knickers slide up and down, catching on his resting, waiting cock.

'Who needs one when I get all the sex I need –'

I moan desperately. God, his cock's a work of art. Its surface is smooth like velvet, the mauve plum emerging from the soft foreskin which wrinkles back to show itself all gleaming. I weigh it in my hand and as I do it he bites my nipple so hard that I scream out with delight. I lean over him, kicking off the knickers I bought especially for Ernst to play with, and settle myself just above my living, breathing sex toy.

I want him to think he's died and gone to heaven. Any minute now I'm going to heaven, too. I'm just preparing the way.

Greedily I press him down, tilting myself over his still sucking mouth. I smile as I raise myself on my knees and aim the tip of his cock into my pussy. I let it rest there, at the opening, just nudging it past my wet sex lips. I wait. I smile again, lowering myself a little more, gasping as each inch goes in. I reach under him to cup his balls in one hand and he snaps his mouth away from my nipple with a loud groan of surprise.

This tension is ecstasy, but I can't hold on to it for much longer, and slowly, luxuriously, I let my boy's knob slide up inside me, further in, till I'm rubbing my open, wet pussy on his groin. It's so tempting to ram it, let our hips start jerking, but once it's right in I force myself to pull away again. He frowns, impatient for action, but I just ease myself down again, moaning and tossing my head back, and the next time I do that he's with me, pulling his own hips back, waiting when I wait.

I keep my eyes open the whole time. He's so beautiful. I try to see the cute but callow boy he used to be but all I see is this stud, who wants me and is fucking me in his little boat house and I'm riding him, pushing him back into the cushions, his lips on my tits and his cock moving slowly into me and I'm just thinking he's mine, all mine, he'll never forget this, when the candles gutter in their holders next to us and I see another shadow falling across his face. Someone, very close up behind me, so close I can smell cigarette smoke, says something unmistakably obscene, even though it's in Dutch.

'Oh, piss off, Pieter!' Skylar growls, but he's still looking at me, still hoisting me up with the strength of his hips, still fucking me. 'Go back to your poker game!'

'I wouldn't dream of it! I came back for more beer, but this looks like a hell of a lot more fun than poker!'

The new voice has a much stronger accent than Skylar's. It's speaking from just behind me. I go hot and cold but I can't move. Skylar's cock is locked inside me. I try to read his expression, but he's so goddamn mellow he keeps moving inside me, keeping me sweet, even though I'm drying up here with embarrassment.

Then there's the unzipping sound of another pair of jeans. 'Where you find this one, Sky? Down the railway station?'

Skylar frowns and shakes his head furiously, and then a filthy grin spreads across his face. He winks at me. I should be soothed, but I'm not. He looks bigger and suddenly he's a horny man on a mission, not a boy. Glancing past me at the newcomer, Skylar starts squeezing my breasts again.

The man behind me takes my hair, and bunches it up in a fist. Did I mention my hair is very sensitive? How I love to have it brushed, and stroked and, yes, pulled?

'She looks like Janni, from the knicker shop round the corner. Janni, is that you?'

He yanks my head round. He's one of those blond boys on the bikes, all right. Older-looking than Skylar, and with more of a beard, but very, very hunky. Brown, searching eyes, but what looks like a constant grin.

'This is no tart, P, this is Mrs Epsom, mother of some old mates from London, and she's red hot,' says Skylar, stroking my breasts possessively. 'We were just getting it on, so if you don't mind, fuck off.'

He pulls me forwards, jamming my tits into his mouth again, and now my backside is up in the air. I want to protest but I can't pull away from him. My butt is all exposed, bouncing in front of this Pieter guy, but so gorgeous is the feel of Skylar's newly confident, no, *aggressive* mouth sucking on my sore nipples that I can't stop him. As first one nipple then the other grinds into his mouth I automatically start rocking on his cock again. I'm acutely aware of my new audience. And it's unutterably sexy to be watched.

I slide up and down Skylar's cock, showing off now but also trying to ease the increasingly frantic urges to come. My body tightens each time to grab hold and keep him inside me, and his cock is hardening even more with each thrust.

I'm just poised to ram down onto him harder than ever when my butt cheeks are pulled apart and Pieter presses up against my back.

'I'd happily watch, but I can't let you have all the fun, Sky,' he says softly. 'The others can come back and watch. But I want to fuck her arse. Then I want to fuck her cunt.'

'You've got some catching up to do, mate. If she doesn't mind, of course.'

Sky pulls me harder down on top of him so that my breasts are squashed hard against his face and his cock is rammed right up inside.

'You don't mind, do you?' Pieter murmurs in my ear. 'Just say, Mrs Epsom. You don't mind, do you? Want to hear you say it.'

'No,' I gasp, barely able to speak. 'Don't mind. Want it. Want you to do it.'

I have no power left. No life. Nothing except my cunt and Skylar's cock.

I feel small and dirty and overpowered. They're treating me like a whore. I like all that. I like not having to think, or decide, or even be anything other than a female to be fucked. So I allow myself to fall, or rather be pulled, first forwards, my tits licked and sucked to burning point by my gorgeous new lover, and then to be tugged backwards by his older, stronger mate, who now has his own erection wedged up between my cheeks and he's sliding it rapidly up and down my warm crack, sliding right under to reach the tender spot where Skylar has me spliced open, parting my sex still further so that as well as having a big cock up my cunt, another cock and several fingers are tickling my exposed clitoris.

I'm dizzy now. I gyrate as if dancing on Skylar's pole, flinging myself wildly about as I lose control all together.

Both the boys take hold of me then and hold me still. Their fingers dig into my arms and thighs, and bottom and breasts. The pause is as titillating as the wild movement. My cunt keeps working, keeps gripping, my nipples tingle till they're sore. And I'm red raw with embarrassment and humiliation. Skylar holds me suspended above him, so that he can go on sucking my nipples. But he stops his thrusting for a moment and I let the hovering orgasm recede a little to relish the wait.

Pieter slides his stiff cock back up to my bottom and starts to push it towards the tightly closed hole of my anus. I stay rigid. I can feel the hole tightening like an angry little fist against the intrusion, but he's still wrenching my cheeks open till the flesh stings, and that starts up a deep, lustful throbbing inside.

I open my eyes. Just one glance at Skylar still engrossed between my tits increases the desire building like a fire inside me, and then the other little hole loosens to let Pieter's cock in, because I can feel his thick knob pushing inside, my own shy muscles trying to push it out at first, and then slackening to accommodate him and grabbing, gobbling, welcoming the new length of male hardness, so that inch by inch it grinds up my backside and I'm light headed with all this, how did I end up in a house boat, impaled on two stiff young cocks, both wedged inside me, and I'm welcoming them both in, straining and yearning to keep them there and to milk them for all the hot pleasure they're pumping into me.

Pieter is deep inside now. His thighs are propping up mine. He starts to rock back and forth, his breath hot on my neck, one big hand fanned out over my stomach to support us both in that position, and I let his rocking move me, carefully at first, the tender skin stretching for him, and I see my body as an amazing design, all conflicting zones of exquisite pleasure.

He's reading my mind, because he grunts like the animal he is, 'This is better than any of those live shows. Christ, you're dynamite, Mrs Epsom.'

They both laugh. From the outside looking in, from the pavement or the bridge, looking into this old wooden haven of sex, you'd see my white body, my bottom, my swinging breasts, all being touched, manhandled, used, sucked, fucked by these two gorgeous young studs.

You see? Tonight, I'm the sex toy.

I fall forwards first onto the rigid cock inside my cunt, then back onto the one in my backside, and then they're both ramming up me. As I move off one the other penetrates me so that the storm of orgasm is gathering at

249

both entrances, sluicing up both orifices. I can hear the gathering shouts of both the guys and my own moans rising somewhere in my throat and being snatched away in gasps, and then it's happening, we're all three rocking frantically, both boys going at me, ramming their cocks up in unison so that I'm spiralling down at the same time, welcoming the burning heat, my first boy smacking and pummelling my tits back and forth over his face until he can hold it back no longer and it comes spurting out of him, met by my own gripping, convulsive orgasm and then the hot spunk of Pieter bringing up the rear oh yes, as he goes at me like a dog and then comes like a rocket up inside me and he laughs and yells and at last I topple sideways, still gripping the first boy inside me and still with Pieter wedged up behind.

'You know what, Mrs Epsom,' Skylar says dreamily, pulling my skirt down for me much later when I've sucked Pieter's really huge cock and then let him fuck me, and promised Skylar another go. The candles have started one by one to burn out. 'I guess that makes us mother fuckers.'

They both laugh, but the aggression's gone.

'In a good way, honey.' I stand up, trying to button my cardigan. My legs are weak as a new colt's as I totter towards the door, knowing they are watching my every movement and still wanting me. My arse and my cunt ache and throb as if I'm still being fucked. 'In a good way.'

'And Mrs Epsom!' Pieter is holding up an over-sized black dildo with a bulbous knob. 'Come back tomorrow, and for a special treat you can ride this one.'

I saw you from the hotel window, Sophie. You were

standing on the bridge right here on the Keizersgracht. Dinner's fucked, too. Where are you now?

On my way, I text back, stepping off the house boat and scurrying back, on bare feet now and wearing no knickers, across the bridge towards the hotel which I can see burning brightly just across the water.

But I sure as hell know where I'll be tomorrow

First Love

REUNIONS ARE LIKE NEW shoes. Alluring in theory but agony in practice.

At least, that's how Mimi sums it up, stepping out of Nice station into the sizzling heat. She sucks in her flat stomach. Tugs tight her pelvic floor. Why couldn't Regina have organised this in London, or New York, better still Paris? No trains, or boats, or planes. Some cool hotel, nice city, easy to get to. Or escape from. But no, Regina has to be the hostess, the queen, as always, show off her fuck-off villa in Antibes or wherever the hell this chauffeur is taking her.

The limo sweeps her away from the Baie des Anges and all those comforting markets and restaurants and beaches, through the predictably ugly outskirts of the town, and up into the hills and the unknown behind Nice.

Fancy dress, darlings. I'll provide the costumes. Suzanne is doing the makeup.

Mimi squirms irritably on the white seat. Her bare thighs squeak on the clean leather as her satin summer dress rides up. She has spent the last two years tiptoeing round film sets, getting walk-on parts, acting the hysterical extra in a crowd or solemn extra in a restaurant scene, making tea and, yes, being fucked by directors on the casting couch. If she's honest, that's the part she's enjoyed the most so far. So much so that she's written a script about it. Anyway, the last thing she needs on a precious break is to dress up as someone else.

So what is Regina going to do to them? Why can't they just be themselves, as they are, photographers, lawyers, writers, whatever? She and Regina, sometimes Salome, they used to be the princesses. But you can bet your bottom dollar Regina will have reserved some amazing Marie Antoinette-style regalia for herself, and ordered the rest of them to eat cake and be trussed up as wenches.

She catches the eye of the chauffeur in the rear-view mirror. Don't know why, but he looks bland, like a tennis player. Direct black eyes. Smooth skin the colour of caramel. One lick of oiled black hair visible when he adjusted his cap to greet her.

She feels silly now. There is a definite gleam of amusement in the chauffeur's eyes, as if he can read her surly, childish thoughts. And he's right. What's the big deal? Mimi smiles at him, and lifts one leg to cross it over the other. The air conditioning whispers over her fanny. It's just a load of girls who were at school together, coming together for the weekend. She smoothes her skirt back down and retouches her red lipstick.

Somewhere over there is Elton John's villa.

The chauffeur frowns back at the road, which is beginning to curl and bend sickeningly up the hairpins carved into the mountains. Lorries thunder past, making the sleek car shake, dry stones scatter. Didn't Princess Grace drive off a cliff somewhere around here?

Suzanne has ringed Mimi's eyes, and everyone else's, with smoky shadow and kohl pencil, and stuck on spidery false eyelashes. In the mirror in her gauzy white bedroom overlooking the huge turquoise infinity pool and the misty Mediterranean far below, Mimi's eyes are now green and elongated like a cat's. Her mouth looks plumper. It's because she's pouting in fury, but it's also the peachy, glossy lipstick.

'I *never* wear gloss,' she glowers, as Suzanne starts yanking at her long red hair. 'I can't leave home without my Chanel matte red.'

'Barely there, is what Regina asked for. And you're not at home now. Don't worry, Mimi. Everyone looks the same.'

Suzanne dots some fake freckles over Mimi's nose. 'And you have to admit, it makes you look younger?'

Mimi smiles slightly. 'Except I never looked this raunchy at school.'

Her hair feels as if it's been twisted into a vice. And she also has to admit that the tight plaits have given her an instant face lift.

'That's because you princesses couldn't wait to grow up. You wouldn't have seen the irony in dressing like this.' Suzanne, already in her outfit, unhooks a coat hanger from the wardrobe. 'And after tonight you'll be begging me to make you over like this all the time so that you can be younger again. Why go under the knife? You'll only end up stretched and polished like a Stepford wife. Who needs Botox when I can give you a Croydon facelift any day of the week just by tying your hair back? Anyway, you've still got cheekbones to die for, Mimi.'

Suzanne's eyes glitter in the dressing table lights. She is the least changed of all of them. She always dresses like a schoolgirl, even though they're all pushing thirty, but with her round face and cute blonde hair she can still get away with it.

'I remember you now, Suzi. How you were at school.' Mimi stands up and lets Suzanne squeeze her into a tight white blouse with short puffed sleeves 'You had an almighty crush on Regina, didn't you? Didn't you kiss her once?'

Suzanne blushes, and starts to do up the buttons. The blouse is tiny, and the buttons strain to remain fastened over Mimi's big breasts. They both stare at Suzanne's hands as they hover there. Then they catch each other's eyes, and smile into the mirror.

'Yes, OK, I had a crush on her,' says Suzanne. 'But I never had a prayer of coming between you two. You couldn't keep your hands off each other.' She blushes, and fusses with Mimi's collar. 'We used to imagine what the two of you got up to in your special rooms upstairs.'

Mimi lets out a whistle of breath as the memories crowd back in. What did they get up to in those long, boring hours cloistered away from the world? They talked about boys, and cocks, and sex, but boys and cocks and sex were far away from their convent. There was only each other. Two ripening female bodies, side by side, and there for the taking.

She can feel Suzanne's sweet breath on her skin, puffing nervously, and her own skin prickles with excitement. The memories weaken her as Suzanne goes about transforming her, taking her back to a warped version of her teenage self. Mimi lifts each leg obediently as Suzanne rolls thick black stockings up her thighs, then zips up a tiny grey skirt.

Mimi can't wait to see Regina. The invitation, out of the blue, was like a horse kick in the stomach. They have met once, maybe twice since school, but always with a crowd of others. LA and Paris are a long way apart and so are their worlds. As Suzanne ties the finishing touch around Mimi's neck, Mimi sees it all again, feels those long nights closeted alone with Regina in their attic bedrooms at boarding school.

When you're young you think you have for ever. That she'll always be there, every morning, stumbling out of bed all warm and heavy-eyed, her brother's oversized tee shirt slipping off one shoulder. And every night she'll be there, tiptoeing into your room to smoke, gossip, giggle, spray perfume onto you then sniff it off your neck, creep closer on those narrow beds, pretending to be too cold, or too hot, or too tired, or too pissed, and then, at last, after wondering aloud how cucumbers and bananas and candles would feel shoved up you, too shy to try that, but fingers creeping nevertheless up each other's legs, pausing for permission, stroking the other's skin, so soft inside the slim thighs, both of you growing very still and silent when you reach the soft fur of each other's pussies, pushing your fingers in a little, waiting for rejection. No rejection – shock, maybe – but you pull back as if you'd been burnt when you brush the hot wetness there for the very first time and are desperate to touch it again – *let's find out how it feels when someone fucks you* – so, yes, brushing and stroking it again, going in further between the velvet folds, feeling the urgent twitches, no one said the person fucking you had to be a boy, that hot tight part of her trying to close in on your fingers, her whole body wincing with shock and shy pleasure, so you know this is a discovery for her, too, despite all that sophistication, all that jewellery, all those calls from polo players on her mobile.

You go in harder, push two fingers not just one, in harder, less gentle as the other girl's leg wraps round you – you're lying across her now – and her hidden cunt grips and sucks at your fingers and her head falls backwards on the pillow, all those black ringlets spread helplessly, her face hot and damp with sweat, she's pulling you down with her, your fingers still ramming,

256

ramming, loving that clutching heat, her legs opening and closing with shocked wanting, her bottom thrusting to keep up with you, the opening and wetness as she comes.

The wriggling frustration as you watch her shaking and whimpering, loving what you've done to her but impatient for your turn, trying to be sensitive and sexy like a boy might be, but you entice her, forcing her, by taking her hand and putting it up there under your nightdress, to do the same to you.

Nothing said the next day, in lessons, netball, choir. Nothing ever said until the next night, when they would slam their study books shut and do it all over again. And nothing said for the last five years.

'Come on, Mimi, wake up! You're the last one. They'll all be waiting.'

Mimi lets Suzanne drag her through the arched stone corridors of the villa and down the marble stairs. Her knees are shaking. Her clean white pants are damp now, remembering Regina's schoolgirl pussy.

'I can't go out there.' Mimi is breathless as they cross the huge Hollywood-style sitting room. 'Not dressed like this – we look ridiculous – Regina's a fashion designer for God's sake!'

Suzanne swivels her round and quickly knots her blouse over her navel, Britney Spears style, leaving her stomach bare.

'Hit me baby,' she hisses, 'one more time!'

Then she nudges her onto the starlit terrace where everyone is standing with long glasses in their hands. The pool shimmers in the moonlight, and the lush green garden beyond plunges away into the shadows.

It's not just girls. This isn't just a school reunion. There are men there, too, as well as the waiters, who include the chauffeur. Maybe the married girls have brought their husbands. Whoever they are, these men are dressed in cool cream suits and white shirts and look rich, successful and, as they turn to look at her, very aroused.

And the girls, Chloe, Annie, Salome, Olivia – she's obviously been let out of the convent for the occasion – they are all, like her, dressed in school uniform.

Suzanne trips away on her high heeled sandals, her blonde hair in Heidi whirls, her little skirt swinging from side to side over her bottom. Mimi stays right where she is, tugging at her gym skirt, kicking the floor with her shoe.

And then she sees Regina over by the pool, surrounded, no surprise there, by a group of men. They are fawning over her, and why not? Even though she's dressed as a nun, she is even more beautiful, even more like a stern queen than ever, arching her black eyebrows as she speaks, blowing cigarette smoke into the warm, still air.

Except that Mimi knows what her pussy feels like.

The chauffeur comes up to her with a silver tray and Mimi swallows the cold champagne down in one gulp. He hovers beside her. If she wanted, and she feels horny enough, she could have him right now. And he wants her. Who wouldn't, dressed like this? She smiles at him, but walks right past him, thrusting out her tits, through the chattering crowd, kissing her old classmates as she passes, but making a beeline for her hostess.

'I don't get it, Regina,' she says, pushing in front of the men, who seem only too happy to go off and explore the crowd of fake schoolgirls. 'You got us to fly halfway round the world, just to dress us up like little girls and humiliate us? And who elected you Mother Superior?'

'My darling Mim, it's so gorgeous to see you.' Regina

258

snakes an arm around Mimi's waist. The rough material of her sleeve scrapes across Mimi's hot, bare back. 'How else was I going to entice you here? You wouldn't have come if it was just you and me. Much too scared.'

'Scared? What do you mean? Of course I would have come! I wish it *was* just you and me. Christ, Reggie, I've missed you!' Mimi presses close to Regina.

Regina stiffens. 'Don't call me that.'

Mimi pulls away, stung. She points round at all the short skirts, the white knickers visible underneath, the socks and stockings pulled up over the still girlish, bare legs. 'So why these stupid uniforms?'

'Duh! It's a school reunion, princess! What else are you supposed to wear?' Annie is standing nearby, with two men on either side of her. One of them is clawing at her pert cleavage to pluck out an olive and eat it. She is swaying slightly on her vertiginous heels, trying to look taller. 'Come on, let's see that dazzling smile! It's meant to be fun!'

'Absolutely, Annie, darling. You're so right. Now lead into dinner, would you?' Regina laughs and kisses Mimi's cheek with a hard, dry peck. But still it burns. Mimi gasps and turns her face, and catches Regina's mouth before she pulls back. She may be dressed as a nun, but she can't resist the red whore's lipstick she's always favoured. Their mouths rest against each other for a moment as the other guests swarm round them like locusts, aiming for the long table laid out with candles and wine and food at the side of the villa under a vine.

Mimi can feel the red lipstick mingling with her own sticky gloss.

'Come on, Regina. It's me.' She slides her arm round Regina's waist as they walk together. 'We were so good together, you and me. Can't we just get away, be alone –

leave this tacky schoolgirl caper for this lot if that's what they want.'

'You calling me tasteless now?' Regina sweeps her arm about. 'Does anyone look like they're not enjoying it?'

They are all seated now, boy, girl, boy, girl, mouths talking, laughing, eating, sipping, swallowing, and hands are already beginning, between forking up food and swilling drink, to rove up bare necks, across flat stomachs, up skirts. Mimi has the dizzy sensation of stepping onto an alien film set where she's forgotten her lines.

'No, but – it's demeaning. We're grown women, not kids, and we look stupid –'

'Anyone here look demeaned? Come on, loosen up. Admit it. We all look fucking hot. Especially you, Mimi. A right little slut. Your breasts are positively oozing out of that little blouse!' Regina brushes her lips against Mimi's cheek again, making her shiver. 'I'm sure the men here will find them good enough to eat.'

The chauffeur leads Regina away to the top of the table before Mimi can reply. She stumbles across to the last spare seat and tries to catch her breath as her schoolmates' inhibitions fall away like blossom blown by spring breezes.

A small man sitting beside her, who looks like a kind of devilish Hercule Poirot, starts to ogle her cleavage. Regina's words echo softly in her head. *Good enough to eat.* Mimi shifts in her seat. Her knickers are damp.

'I am Jacques,' the man announces, in a thick French accent. 'I am a perfumier. Regina and I are designing a fragrance together. And you?'

Mimi bites back a giggle at his absurd accent. 'Mimi. I am an actress. But at school I was Regina's lover.'

Regina is watching her. Something flicks on inside Mimi. She leans towards her neighbour with her arm thrown over the back of his chair so that her breasts are thrust out for him and everyone else to admire. Across the table she sees Regina's big red mouth moving in flattering, seductive chatter. The man next to her is already salivating. Then Mimi sees Regina's brown fingers moving under the table. The man's teeth snap together as she obviously unzips his flies.

'Schoolgirl lovers?' Jacques licks his lips. 'Touching each other after lights out? What did the nuns say?'

'Oh, they had their own fish to fry!' Mimi runs her fingers up his arm. 'Regina and I and Salome over there had privileged rooms, because our daddies gave us permission to smoke, far away from the hideous dormitories and all those smelly girls, so it was just us, up in the attics, smoking and talking, and –'

Mimi catches Regina's eye across the candlelight. Mimi raises her voice.

'– and fingering each other, Jacques. Can you imagine it? Talking about boys, and cocks, but we were sex-starved, so we used to experiment on each other with our fingers, go right up into each other's sweet pussies –'

There's a gleam in Regina's eye as she turns away, but it could be anger just as much as lustful remembering. Another shiver goes through Mimi, and then she realises that her randy neighbour has started to stroke her thigh.

'Go on.' He leans hungrily closer so that his nose is level with her just-covered nipples. 'Did you suck each other's breasts, too? A schoolgirl's breasts, oh my God how delectable, did you lift up your nighties, and squeeze, like this, and suck, like this?'

One or two men hitch their chairs closer to see what's happening up her end of the table.

'Oh yes, Jacques, that's exactly what we did. We were both well developed, you know what I mean? I had the biggest breasts in the school. My daddy paid for expensive lingerie to hold me in, but Regina, oh God, she was good at undoing my underwear, finding her way in, feeling my breasts, comparing them with hers, touching, touching –'

Still watching Regina, Mimi fights to control herself. Some of it is wishful thinking. They never did kiss each other's breasts. Was that somehow too naughty, even for them?

She undoes the top button of her already gaping blouse. She's a grown woman now. Her breasts are for fondling and sucking, see, Regina? Yes. She sees a gleam of excitement in Regina's eyes. Regina, still staring back at Mimi, leans closer to her neighbour, runs her tongue across her mouth, and takes hold of his cock. Now Mimi is fired up. Poirot's fingers are trailing up her leg, sending shivers up towards her cunt, and she can't keep still. She opens her legs invitingly, and in go his fingers, inside her thighs, pressing at her thick white knickers, running along the hidden crack he finds there, sensing the warmth and dampness.

With his other hand he lifts his glass as if casually to drink, and tips it sideways, spilling cold white wine onto her chest. Mimi gasps as the liquid trickles down her throat and droplets seep between her breasts.

A couple of seats away, Annie and her two neighbours have given up any pretence of eating or socialising. The two men lift Annie up bodily and carry her across to a white sun bed, throwing her down there on all fours like a little doggie. As Poirot snuffles his nose into Mimi's blouse and starts to lick the wine off her breasts, she is torn between watching what the men are going to do to

262

Annie and seeing how far Regina is going with hers.

Annie wins her attention. Everyone's attention, in fact. Nearly everyone turns to watch, whispering and nudging, as one man sits at one end of the lounger and pulls his cock out of his smart cream trousers. He shoves Annie's head down and pushes his cock into her giggling, smiling mouth while the other man, unzipping his own trousers, grabs her upturned hips and pulls her backwards into his groin, where his cock is hard and ready.

The shock makes Mimi hotter and wetter. Poirot's tongue is warm and scratchy, like a cat's, as it laps up between her breasts and circles her nipples. She squirms with frustration. His fingers are probing at her knickers, his tongue is licking at her nipples. Despite everything, her embarrassment, her annoyance, her urge to be next to Regina, his eager groping is arousing her. She wants more. The pin-pricks of pleasure are prodding her into full-blown, uncontrollable desire.

Poirot hooks his fingers under the leg of her knickers and Mimi opens her legs wider under the table, staring across at Regina. It's Regina she wants. But she lets Poirot poke his fingers into her warm crack, her head swimming as he fingers her, his teeth clamping round one nipple now as he sucks at it and pokes his fingers faster in and out of her, pressing himself against her, rubbing his cock, still in his trousers, up and down her leg as she simply sits there, opening herself to him, not touching him, not helping him, just letting his teeth and tongue and fingers do the work while she watches her Regina across the table.

Regina's eyes are sparking like fire at the other end. Her tongue slides across her mouth. She even forks meringue and strawberries into it while the white tablecloth jerks up and down and her hand works on her

263

neighbour's cock, and he lies back in his chair, eyes closed in ecstasy, mouth tight shut to contain the yelps of noisy climax threatening to erupt. As Jacques rubs himself furiously against Mimi's leg, there is one final thrust under the tablecloth, Regina's man shudders and gets up hurriedly, zipping up his pants as he flees, and Regina tilts her nun-like head back to lick drips of creamy dessert off her spoon.

'Time for dancing!' calls Suzanne, clapping her hands and pulling Chloe to her feet. Jacques jerks against Mimi's leg and groans loudly under cover of the music, pulling his mouth away from her nipple and his fingers out of her pussy, leaving it to twitch in little spasms of wanting.

Suddenly dinner is over. Everyone starts to dance and writhe on the terrace, and the dark waiters glide once more in the shadows with champagne and liqueurs and even elegant white spliffs on silver trays.

Suzanne and Regina run over to the music system and Mimi's chest tightens with jealousy. There's the thrumming of dramatic Spanish guitar music. Regina starts clicking her fingers above her head and ridiculously, beautifully, she lifts the hem of her nun's black dress and starts swirling in a wild flamenco dance, whooping and stamping as the music becomes more frantic.

As Suzanne, Chloe and Olivia dance with her, Mimi's Frenchman runs over to join them. He tries to grab Regina but she pushes him away towards the schoolgirls who are gyrating round her, thrusting out their breasts, opening and closing their knees tantalisingly in a chorus line, flicking up their little skirts.

Jacques dances round behind them and picks Suzanne, planting his small hands on her gyrating hips and guiding her. He is just the right height to press his groin right in between her buttocks. Suzanne gives a little start and glances over her shoulder, then she tilts her bottom invitingly against him before grinding her crotch playfully forwards against Chloe. They are all lost in the game.

Olivia dances alone, touching herself, perhaps missing Sister Benedicta. Behind Mimi, Annie is moaning as the two men fuck her mouth and her cunt.

Mimi idly touches herself, too, as she watches Suzanne flinging herself first against Chloe, rubbing her fanny up against her, and then back against Jacques, offering her bottom.

Regina is joined by another man. The flamenco music has slowed and they are circling each other slowly like combatants, a few inches apart. Regina has pulled her dress right up her legs and now they can all see that she, like Mimi, is wearing unholy black stockings. The man is licking his lips, his hands itching to touch her. Regina keeps twitching herself out of his reach until he grabs her roughly, his big hands digging into the soft flesh of her upper thighs, and lifts her so that she is wrapped round him. Maybe he's her husband, or lover. Mimi hasn't a clue what Regina has been up to in the last few years. She's lost her.

He is big and strong, and carries her round like a feather, but then Mimi can see, in the dazzling illumination of fairy lights and torches, that Regina is resisting him. She starts to struggle, and looks round, and she is surely searching for Mimi because their eyes lock, and Mimi holds her breath.

Regina stops struggling then, and lets herself go weak. The man lowers her to her feet. She rewards him by putting her hands on his shoulders. He obviously thinks she's going to kiss him, because he closes his eyes. But it is Mimi she is looking at. She gives a sly wink and runs her red tongue slowly over her lower lip in a gesture so sensual that Mimi can almost feel her warm, wet lips fastening on to hers.

Then Regina pushes the man down until he is on his knees. She hitches her dress up to show him the scarlet thong dividing the tanned lips of her pussy. She pokes her finger in, pulls it sideways and there it is, waxed Hollywood style, glistening with arousal, or wine, or honey, who knows, inviting him to lick it, then she straddles his head, and pushes herself into his face. Mimi's fanny clenches in response. Everyone, other than Annie, is transfixed. Regina tenses her fine legs to angle her crack against the man's mouth, and they all see his tongue come out, long and red, and start lapping at her, his fingers scrabbling to open her sex lips and get to the fruit inside them.

The chauffeur is beside Mimi, offering more champagne. Mimi takes it, aware of his warm body next to hers. She watches Regina. She wants to feel a wet tongue lapping at her. This guy would do it if she asked him. She's that close to asking him. She reckons everyone has permission. But she wants Regina's tongue. Why did they never do that when they had all the time in the world? Her fanny is hot and prickling with frustration.

The waiter points. On the other side of the room Suzanne is now tossing herself wildly back and forth between Chloe and Jacques, rubbing herself up and down their groins, letting the movement lower her white knickers, her tiny skirt giving easy access to her bare, ready cunt. Everyone is sweating. Jacques' cock is huge in his trousers. One of his little hands is bringing it to life while Suzanne parts her legs and wraps one round Chloe and sweeps up and down her friend. Her buttocks clench

266

and her head falls back as she starts to thrash wildly against Chloe, who is grinding against her, too, frisking herself.

Suzanne's throat is bulging as she moans out loud, 'Somebody screw me, while I'm hot!'

There is an electric silence in the room. All at once Suzanne arches herself away from Chloe and collapses as her climax overwhelms her. Jacques just stares. Salome creeps up behind him to get a closer look at the writhing, jerking Suzanne, and then grabs Jacques' still hard cock out of his trousers. He rocks on his neat heels as Salome yanks it out to his full length, enticing the rounded end of his cock from its foreskin until it stretches for more. She pulls and strokes for a moment or two, then starts to pull him backwards. Some of the other guests form a circle and close round the pair of them, clapping and cheering as if they were at a bullfight.

Mimi steps closer to see. The little man has lost no time. He clambers between Salome's long, open legs, pushes her back onto the hard terrace stones, and pushes his cock up into her.

Over in the corner Regina has the man's hair tangled in her fingers as she keeps his head clamped between her strong brown thighs. Her pelvis tips and twists and her long throat stretches with pleasure as he laps and sucks at her pussy. His big hands have pulled her buttocks apart and his fingers are probing and prodding inside the dark crack. He locates his target all right because Regina's veil falls off and her long black hair swings free across her back as she bucks and thrashes against his face. Mimi touches herself frantically as she watches the man's wet mouth tonguing and nibbling Regina's cunt remorselessly and finger-fucks the hidden hole of her arse at the same time.

The perfumier, his jacket still buttoned up, is fucking Salome with vigorous thrusts of his neat bottom, his eyes and mouth closed and silent while her arms and legs wave like tentacles around him and her long plaits curl happily across the floor, on and on until they are coming with little shrieks and everyone around starts to applaud. The little man jumps up, leaving Salome sprawled there, and bows.

But the applause is cut short by the music being turned off sharply.

'Enough!' cries Regina, her skirts flying, cheeks flushed as she pushes everyone aside. '*Mi casa e tu casa* and all that, but you're all behaving like cats on heat!'

Everyone shrugs and titters. Regina whisks out, from behind her back, a small black switch.

'Time to bring everyone down to earth, I think. Isn't that what we do, when we've sinned? A little penance or two, I think? A little punishment?' She looks round. 'Olivia? What about you, our little fledgling nunlet? I'm sure Mother Superior has gone at you with a whip for all that wickedness between you and Sister Benedicta. Gonna show us how it's done?'

Annie pokes her head round behind Jacques. He glances at her, his eyes alight with recognition. At last! Someone his own size –

'She's gone!' Annie cries, glancing sideways at Jacques. 'I just saw her in the limo with the chauffeur, screeching off down the drive.'

'Off to shag the chauffeur? Or running back to Sister Benedicta?' Suzanne titters weakly.

'In that case, Annie, since you were the first to sin this evening, you can be the first to be punished. On your knees.'

Annie's eyes go round and she shakes her head.

268

Regina points at the space in front of her and so Annie obediently crawls along the floor. Regina doesn't look down at her feet but straight over her head to Mimi. 'Jacques, perhaps you'd like a go at this? I can see you've got the hots for her. Ever whipped a girl before?'

'No, *madame,* but –'

'Look at her. You can have her later. All cute and sweet. But first she needs punishing, because she's a little whore!' Regina hands him the switch. 'She's done it with two men already this evening. Sucked one off. Got fucked. Then the other one went up her arse. Don't you think that's filthy behaviour?'

Jacques licks his lips and nods. 'Delicious.'

Regina flicks up Annie's skirt and yanks down her white knickers to show her pale little buttocks thrust up in the moonlight.

'Now, punish her!'

Jacques hesitates.

'Or I'll thrash you!'

The other men cheer and punch the air.

Jacques smiles, then positions himself sideways, holding the switch like a golf club. One of the other girls steps forward and zips up his still-open fly. The gesture seems to wake him up because then the switch is flicking through the air with a quick hiss and cuts down on Annie's bottom with a hot, wet, swipe. Annie jerks and whimpers, her back arching, her buttocks quivering. Her knickers are stretched tight, cutting across her thighs. Mimi flinches in sympathy, wonders whether she should step in and stop this, but then she sees the way Annie wriggles excitedly, bites her lower lip, thrusts her bottom up higher, inviting more punishment.

Jacques runs his hand tenderly over the bright pink stripe slicing across Annie's buttock. Mimi can almost

269

feel that soft stroke across her own bottom.

'Three more!' barks Regina, pushing her hair off her hot face. 'Punish the little slut!'

Mimi watches Annie's reddening bottom as Jacques whips it again, hears Annie's whimpers of pretend distress and the way her tongue flicks cat-like across her mouth and she mouths the word *yes* as the whip lashes down. Her squeals turn into moans of wicked and unmistakable pleasure. Doesn't the voice of a woman being whipped or fucked, the man's grunts of lust, just turn you on?

Mimi glances at Regina and her body goes tight with wanting, because Regina's red lips are parted, and she's panting, dancing from foot to foot. She's bristling with triumph. And she's very horny.

'Your turn, Mimi.' Regina spins round and heat floods through Mimi. 'You deserve punishing for being so up your own arse, so above it all this evening.'

Mimi flushes, feels sweat springing in the tight arm holes of her blouse. Now she has Regina's attention, humiliating as this is. It's either this, or she slinks away after Olivia, and disappears out of Regina's life for good.

'So punish me, Regina.' She keeps her eyes, and her voice, lowered. Even that tiny, fake gesture of submission excites her. 'I've been naughty. Very naughty. I haven't contacted you for years. I haven't been polite this evening. I haven't joined in –'

'Not contacting me for years is the worst of it.' Regina says, very quietly, her Latina accent suddenly strangling her voice. Mimi knows what that means. That Regina is letting go. 'So it's time to say sorry.'

Mimi bends over slowly, praying that Regina will relent. But nobody rescues her. Acute embarrassment shears through her as she grips the back of a chair. No way is she going down on all fours.

Jacques tosses the whip over to Regina. Annie's bottom is striped with red. Her bottom opens and closes as she wriggles and squirms and protests and giggles. Jacques settles himself behind her, opens up her bottom so they can all see the secret flash of darkness. When he shoves her head down further so that her cheek is resting on her arms, they can all see the seam of moisture seeping between her pussy lips.

And so can he, because out thumps his permanent erection again and he's up and at her, humping rapidly and vigorously like a dog.

At last, everyone's eyes turn to Mimi.

'When I got my first spanking, I was made to lick out another girl while he was doing it,' murmurs Suzanne, nudging Chloe, who is twiddling her *fraulein* plaits. 'I dare you, Chloe. Go and spread yourself in front of little smart-ass Annie–'

'Not right now. This is going to make such a series for my next exhibition,' says Chloe, grabbing her camera off the table. 'And I've waited years to see this! One princess chastising another!'

'Lift up your skirt, Mimi.'

Mimi lifts it up, exposed inch by inch. She's facing out across the swimming pool, over the shadowy countryside dipping towards the sea. And she's facing her old schoolmates, girls she used to tease and taunt for being uncool, now sexy young women with long tanned legs and very much the upper hand.

There is a pause. She scrapes her fingernails across the flagstones and remembers what Olivia told her once, that hot summer after they'd all left school, when Mimi had made a surprise return visit in her sports car to collect something and found Livvie digging the rose garden with

Sister Benedicta sleeping in the shade. Olivia had told her all about the flagellation she'd got when they found out about her and Sister Benedicta, how she'd prostrated herself on the cold floor of the chapel beside her beloved. Imitated the grunt of the Mother Superior as she brought the whip down on them, and the quiet panting and pleasured moans of the other sisters as they watched.

'I'll get a good thrashing tonight for talking to you,' Olivia had whispered, wiping the sweat off her face as Sister Benedicta woke up, hitching up her skirts to scratch herself. 'Can't wait!'

Someone pulls Mimi's knickers down and now the warm night air ruffles over her bare bottom, creaking and hissing with the cicadas in the shadows.

'Lift your bottom up higher, Mimi, where we can all see it. I want you to feel every inch of this fucker.'

The air shivers with anticipation and muted laughter from her audience.

Mimi straightens abruptly, tries to cover herself. 'Come on, Regina. It's me. Mimi. I can't do this –'

'You'll do it, bitch, for not getting into the spirit. Bend over!'

Someone pushes her down again, wrapping her fingers round the arms of the chair. Suzanne is there, tying her wrists and hands to the heavy wrought iron with her school tie.

'For that, an extra strike!'

Then there's a vicious swishing through the air like the swift winged dart of a wasp, and the switch smacks down on Mimi's bottom, painting a red hot line of fire and pain across her tender exposed skin. She bites down on her lips – fucked if she'll give them the satisfaction of hearing her scream – as the harsh sting extends through her, radiating an excruciating, singing pain. She hates everyone.

But then she feels a hand stroking on that red hot line, soothing her, and the pain recedes into a raw kind of warmth, then a softer throbbing. She relaxes as the throbbing jabs persistently at her cunt and she feels its quick bite of response. Regina's hand grazes over her soreness for a moment.

And right there on the same spot, the switch stings down again, and this time she can't control the spasms which ripple through, making her jerk like a marionette. She opens her mouth and screams, really means to scream but her voice breaks up into a series of orgasmic moans instead because that's what she really means, and the looks of evil delight she catches from her audience excite her all the more, all swaying and jostling in their circle round her, some moving away into the shadows to stroke or smack or screw each other, who cares? All Mimi knows is that she is one sore patch of bare bottom and Regina is punishing her for being a very bad friend. A very bad girl.

'Please, Regina,' Mimi moans, as the switch comes down a third time, shaking her with its viciousness, but this time the hot pleasure pokes straight at her cunt as the pain radiates through her like a returning lover.

And as Regina whips her again, she gets it. As she struggles against the restraints she sees how dark this pleasure is. Being helpless is kinky and liberating. She loves that everyone's watching. She loves the stinging pain that strikes, then spreads, then stabs at her cunt. The nastier and cheaper the thrill, the better. And the excitement isn't in her memory any more. It's all right here, between her legs, and it's her beloved Regina doing this to her.

When the whipping stops as abruptly as it started

273

there's an emptiness, and a silence. Everyone moves away. There's only the whisper of the breeze in the trees.

Then fingers are stroking her bottom, exploring each bright red smarting stripe. Her skin is so tender that she flinches even under that soft touch, spasms of real and remembered pain.

'All over. For now.' Two hands on her shoulders, a warm mouth whispering into her hair. 'So, wanna see how you've turned me on, *cherie?*'

The ties slither off her wrists as Mimi nods and tries to stand up. She kicks off the white pants and steps towards Regina in her black stockings.

Regina leads her to the steps leading into the pool where some of the others are splashing, some clothed, some naked. As Mimi tries to stop shivering, Regina lifts her arms as if they are wings and Suzanne and Chloe, like acolytes, remove her habit. Mimi can see now that it was a stripper's costume all along, with Velcro instead of the genuine hooks and eyes and buttons Olivia described wrestling with to get at Sister Benedicta.

And underneath is Regina's gorgeous, voluptuous coffee-coloured body, the waist tinier, the breasts and hips bigger than Mimi remembers from school days, breasts and snatch kissed by wisps of scarlet underwear.

'Remember how you used to touch me at school?' Regina's voice is husky as she takes Mimi's hand and pushes it between her thighs, up into her crotch, trapping it there against the wisp of red silk for a moment so that, yes, the wetness there tells Mimi how scolding her, whipping her, seeing her bare bottom, humiliating her, has turned Regina on. 'Still feels good, doesn't it?'

'If you wanted me to touch you, I would have done, Reggie. I didn't have you down as a bully –'

'Dominatrix, stupid. Not bully. She does it for her

own, and your, and our pleasure.' Suzanne comes up to her, with Chloe, and starts manhandling her. 'Just knocking you into shape, I guess, for being so stuck up.'

Mimi is too dazed to argue, and lets the girls whisk off her little skirt and the tight blouse, pull off her bra, too, and Regina's tongue runs across her lips as she steps backwards, still in her underwear, to tug Mimi with her into the pool and under the water.

The coolness embraces them as they float up and Mimi is met by the soft bounce of feminine flesh against her hands, and there are Regina's big round breasts, bobbing on the surface of the blue water. Regina lies back on the side of the pool, arms stretched out along the edge, breasts rolling in the water. Steam rises. Mimi's limbs feel feathery as the water shifts and the knot of excitement tightens in her stomach as Regina parts her lips, licking the corner of her mouth as if finishing a sugary doughnut. She always had a sweet tooth. She lifts her shoulders right out of the water so that her breasts are in full view. Mimi's nipples harden like nuts. Her breasts brush against Regina as she puts her arms on either side of Regina, trapping her against the side.

She can feel no bone, only soft, yielding flesh, and as her hands close round Regina's breasts, her own nipples startle into stiffness. She pinches Regina's nipples and feels them sharpen into points. As Mimi starts to tease each tip, Regina smiles and moans and arches her back, wrapping her legs around Mimi's and tilting back her throat. The desire in Mimi burns. She opens her legs a little so that her parted pussy lips can rub against Regina's and now under the water they're grinding against each other and Mimi is greedy for it, greedy really to be alone with Regina on some big white bed somewhere upstairs.

The dominatrix has gone quiet. The audience has lost

interest. Mimi rubs her nipples against Regina's and when she hears that sexy sucking gasp in response oh God, she wants to come. She leans forwards and tickles Regina's red lips open with the tip of her tongue.

It's the first time, because they never did this at school.

And there's Regina's lovely wet mouth, opening to curl her tongue around Mimi's, and as they start to kiss there's the tang of surprise as their sharp nipples scrape and their hips push and grind, legs hooking and tangling, pussies opening like flowers under the steaming water.

There's the whirr of a shutter above their heads. Chloe's creeping round the edge of the pool, snapping from every angle, as the two women make out in the moonlight.

Under the cover of the water Mimi edges her hand towards Regina's snatch, parting the soft lips with her fingers, and gasping with surprise Regina falls back, her body rising to the surface again so that her breasts lie invitingly on offer and Mimi can't help it, she licks her way up Regina's stomach and nibbles one taut nipple, sucking it into her mouth, her mind blown by the explosive excitement, and she feels an answering pull on her fingers as they are sucked up into Regina's greedy pussy.

Mimi licks and sucks. Regina's cunt tightens and loosens as she starts to jerk and writhe in the water. Mimi sucks harder on the tight nipples, ramming her fingers further up into Regina, just like she did at school, only harder now, faster, further, deeper, she's the dominatrix now, and then her darling Regina is coming, moaning loudly, her head splashing back in the water, and everyone on the edge of the pool starts clapping.

Regina smiles lazily, pulling Mimi out of the water with

her, accepting the slinky robe that Salome, frowning, wraps round her. She catches the jealousy in Salome's eyes. Remembers other evenings at school, when sometimes it was the three of them … and it was Salome who brought the big bowl up from the refectory that time, tanned, pissed and reckless after a weekend exeat, and dared them to fuck themselves with fruit.

'We're not done here,' she hears herself say to Regina, mopping hopelessly at her naked wet body with her discarded blouse. 'Your turn to pleasure me now, Regina. I want you to take me to your bed.'

Regina tries to protest, but then a filthy smile overtakes her. She puts her hand on her hip. 'And?'

Mimi picks up a couple of bananas and a candle, still burning, and waits in the doorway. 'I want you to fondle me. I want to play with fruity sex toys. I want you to roll with my body, fit it with all your curves, I want your big lips kissing me again, going down on me, nibbling my clit, tonguing me –'

'Christ Mimi! When did you get so dirty?

'At school, honey. With you. I've just been waiting all this time to get you back in my arms.'

Upstairs, a little later, Mimi goes limp at last as Regina licks her to ecstasy and Salome awaits her turn.

Sex in the City Range

Four fabulous city collections
edited by Maxim Jakubowski

Sex in the City – London
ISBN 9781907106226 £7.99

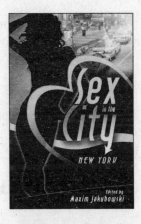

Sex in the City – New York
ISBN 9781907106240 £7.99

Sex in the City – Paris
ISBN 9781907106257 £7.99

Sex in the City – Dublin
ISBN 9781907106233 £7.99

Xcite Dating – turning fiction into reality!

Xcite Books offer fabulous fantasy-filled fiction. Our unique dating service helps you find that special person who'll turn your fantasies into reality!

You can register for FREE and search the site completely anonymously right away – and it's completely safe, secure and confidential.

Interested in spanking?

Spanking is our most popular theme so we have set up a unique spanking site where you can meet new friends and partners who share your interest.

The Education of Victoria
A novel by Angela Meadows

Lessons in love and a whole lot more are in store in this saucy romp set in a European finishing school for young ladies.

Packed off to a continental finishing school, 16-year-old Victoria thinks she will be taught how to be a dutiful wife for a gentleman. But she soon discovers that she has a lot to learn in the arts of pleasure at the Venus School for Young Ladies.

There she encounters the strictness of Principal Madame Thackeray and her team of tutors. Under their guidance she learns the finer arts of sexual pleasure and discovers that there are plenty of fellow students and staff willing to share carnal knowledge with this sweet young English rose.

On returning to England, she finds her father in financial difficulty and must turn her newfound education to good use to survive.

£7.99 ISBN 9781906373696

The True Confessions of a London Spank Daddy

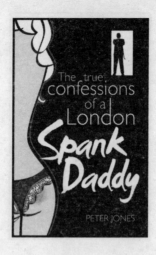

Discover an underworld of sex, spanking and submission. A world where high-powered executives and cuddly mums go to be spanked, caned and disciplined.

In this powerful and compelling book Peter Jones reveals how his fetish was kindled by corporal punishment while still at school and how he struggled to contain it. Eventually, he discovered he was far from alone in London's vibrant, active sex scene.

Chapter by chapter he reveals his clients' stories as he turns their fantasies into reality. The writing is powerful, the stories graphic and compelling. Discover an unknown world...

£7.99 ISBN 9781906373320